The Mural

The Mural

—

A Novel

Jeffry R. Halverson

Grand Strand Press
Myrtle Beach, SC

Text copyright © 2014 by Jeffry R. Halverson

Printed in the United States of America

ISBN 13: 978-0-692-22586-8
ISBN 10: 0692225862
Library of Congress Control Number: 2014910355
LCCN Imprint Name: Grand Strand Press, Myrtle Beach, SC

FOR THE PALE BLUE DOT

I

The front side of the white SUV was thoroughly smashed. It had spun over 180 degrees and now sat still, pointed due east. The driver had tried to make an ill-advised—and illegal—turn over the light-rail tracks, swerving around the crossing barrier. Now shards of glass and crumpled aluminum were scattered across the hot pavement. The distinct scent of burnt rubber lingered in the air. Bright orange cones were aligned in a row. Phoenix police had closed the northbound left-hand lane, directing slow-going traffic to merge and move along. Paralyzed on the tracks, the train had been emptied and its passengers loaded onto a shuttle to the next bus stop. The driver of the SUV, a man in his forties now sitting on the curb, was explaining what happened to a stern-faced officer writing in a note pad.

Standing a safe distance from the SUV, Tyler Anderson surveyed the scene along with a small crowd of onlookers. He held his hand above his eyes, shielding them from the sun.

"What are you doing here?" a veteran female reporter asked as she took the open spot beside him.

"Just looking. I'm covering the track expansion."

"Can you believe this guy? The barrier's down, lights flashing, and he tries to save himself maybe *two* minutes by going around it. Idiot."

"You think the train was in a blind spot?" Tyler said.

"The goddamned barrier was down. Red lights blinking. Bell ringing. Hello? He doesn't have to see it to know the train is coming."

"I just don't understand some people. They know better."

"Look at all the traffic backed up. For Christ's sake. I hope they take this guy's license. Throw him in tent city."

"Here come the hand cuffs," Tyler said. The man on the curb rose to his feet and turned around with his hands behind his back. The officer had put the note pad away and taken a pair of handcuffs from his belt. Another officer stood beside him reciting something to the man. He wore dark sunglasses and looked the man in the face as he spoke. The man nodded and looked down at the ground. The handcuffs went on around his wrists. "Well, I got to go," Tyler said, looking down at his watch.

"Go get out of this heat," the veteran reporter said as she fanned herself with her hand. "God, I've been here fifteen years and I still can't stand it."

———

The next day Tyler was barely awake as he trudged toward the newsroom—a prison without bars. Passing door after door, his leather shoes slapped against the blue floor tiles, the hallway amplifying the rhythmic sound. As he walked, his mind wandered. The routine made it easy. He listened to the musings of the monologue in his head, fueled by old short stories he'd revisited at home the night before. He gravitated toward an open door, as if preprogrammed to go there. He stopped. "Here we are," he thought. Back to work. He looked down and found that the tiles beneath his feet had turned inexplicably green. He immediately wondered what circumstances had occurred to put those green tiles there. There must have been a reason.

"I love how you burn me when I touch your concrete skin," he'd once written of the city. That was back when Tyler had first started at Phoenix's *Valley Observer*, a local news site. The city was exciting and new once. Now he stepped reluctantly through the open door into a dull and familiar office space. The room looked embalmed, appearing the same as it had the day before and the weeks before that. Squinting, he walked inside. A blinding light from the afternoon sun poured in. It was the final weeks of summer in the valley, and daytime temperatures were still well into the triple digits. Summers in Phoenix constitute three months of hell.

The office was warm and slightly uncomfortable, the air conditioners working hard but failing. Six identical cubicles occupied the room, each with an identical brown desk. Beneath the desks sat rows of electrical plugs and computer cables coiled like sinister nests of snakes. Two other journalists were already at their cubicles. These two men—many years older than Tyler—were typing very fast on well-traveled laptops. One of them smelled of cigarettes. And possibly a hint of gin.

"Good morning," Tyler said to no one in particular.

"It's the middle of the afternoon, Anderson," one of the men, called Harry, said sternly, continuing to type at a furious pace.

"Right! Sorry. I was up late." That was true. Tyler went to the cubicle farthest from the others. He'd chosen it on his first day at the *Observer*. It sat next to a window overlooking a sunny stretch of downtown Phoenix. Recently he'd spent considerably more time looking out of it. Once settled into his chair, Tyler leaned back and sighed, knowing that the other two men would hear him.

"What are you working on?" said Bruce, less irritated than Harry.

"The light-rail expansion."

"How's it going?"

"Terribly," Tyler said quietly.

"Sorry?" asked Bruce, leaning toward Tyler.

"Fine," he said louder, professionally.

Outside of Tyler's window, beyond dusty panes of tinted glass, a solid ocean of concrete spread out below him, rippling with heat. Caravans of cars and trucks streamed through avenues wedged between big squares of brown and gray toward the far-off horizon. The sky overhead was perfect and blue, but empty of the playful white clouds he'd watched as a child growing up back east. It became a color field when he squinted in the sunlight.

"I want to get out of the city," Tyler said abruptly. "There's got to be a story out there."

"No one cares about the boonies," Harry said, still typing.

Tyler stared blankly at him. Had the city robbed this man of all curiosity and life?

"I'd talk to Rebecca. She might have something," Bruce said.

Across the hall Tyler stood outside a door and gave it three quick taps. No response. He looked down at the scuffs on his brown leather shoes. His father had given him a tin of polish years ago, but Tyler never used it. Instead, he watched the subtle shift in shades of brown appear. That tin of polish was now sitting in a shoebox in his closet beneath the one navy blue business suit he owned. It only came out for special occasions. It had never been dry-cleaned. Tyler had never dry-cleaned anything. How much did it cost to do that? One day he would polish those shoes. Maybe even dry-clean that suit too. He felt no urgency yet.

"Come," a woman finally shouted, muffled by the closed door.

He found Rebecca—the *Observer*'s managing editor—sitting at her desk. Professional. Pretty. She was only five or six years older than Tyler. A consummate overachiever. Inside her cluttered office, he smiled politely without opening his mouth. Then he quietly shut the door behind him, as if he had just entered a church. He disliked this office too.

Small, it felt crowded and uninviting. Stacks of papers and books and odd trinkets collected dust on shelves. An unused monitor sat against a wall, still in the original factory box. One entire corner served as a makeshift storage space. On the wall there were several certificates and shiny metal award plaques. Tyler didn't recognize them. How long had it been since he was last in this office? In the air there was the distinct but faint scent of day-old pizza, probably from Sal's, across the street. He'd eaten there many times. Alone. Sal's was always great for a quick slice on the go.

"How are things going?" she asked.

"Fine," he found himself saying. "I'll have that train business done tonight."

She didn't look up, fixated on the computer at her desk. "I want it online first thing tomorrow morning." She finally glanced over and paused for his reaction.

"Sure," he said with a nod. "No problem."

"Great," she said, managing a smile. "Was there something you wanted?"

"Yes. It's about my next assignment. I was wondering if I could do a story outside of the city."

"*Outside* the city?" she said. "That's not your beat."

"I know—nothing permanent. Just a story."

Rebecca looked down at her screen. Then back over at him. She sighed quietly and lowered her fashionable black-rimmed glasses onto the end of her nose. Tyler shifted in his seat. Rebecca studied him.

Tyler's eyes darted down to the floor and back. He had seen that look on Rebecca's face before—over those glasses. Prison. He immediately regretted even bothering to ask. She would never let him out of the city. Tyler put his hands on the arms of the chair and slid forward.

"How long have you been in Arizona? You went to State, right?" she said.

"Six years," he said, stopping in his seat.

"Looking for some variety?"

"I guess so."

"Well, let me see what I can find." Then her tone changed slightly. "I can't promise anything though."

"Thanks, Rebecca." Tyler stood and turned back toward the door, shoulders slumped. His leather shoes shuffled back out into the hallway, where the mysterious green tiles waited. The warden wasn't letting him out of the prison. "Maybe I should quit," he thought. Move to some faraway place. A place with a name that no one had heard of and write. *Just* write. Good writers did that. JD Salinger did that. But he was already famous. No one read much anymore, though. "Jesus Christ," he thought. "I don't even read much." These days, people read stories about boy wizards. Or Scandinavian murder mysteries—after they'd seen the movie. Part of Tyler longed deeply for the Paris of Picasso and Gertrude Stein. Or the Istanbul of Orhan Pamuk.

"Any luck?"

"She said she'd get back to me," Tyler explained as he returned to his cubicle and sat down.

"Worth a shot," Bruce said. "You can always write what you want on your own time."

"I don't have the time."

"You have to *make* time."

Tyler paused. "I guess I could try throwing my TV out the window."

II

Sitting in his one-bedroom apartment, Tyler Anderson shared bits of his dinner with his cat. The handwritten notes for the light-rail story were spread out in front of him. A drawing of two trains crashing into a ball of fire ran along one margin. A digital recorder with ten minutes of interview sat off to the side. Despite the deadline, Tyler hardly looked at his notes. He preferred to roll bits of chicken up between his fingers for the cat.

The chicken gone, Tyler watched the small television he'd brought to Phoenix six years ago. A can of tomato soup cooked on the stove in the kitchenette—the leftover chicken hadn't satisfied. Waiting, Tyler sat in the same chair he'd sat in for three hours the night before and two hours the night before that. The show on the television seemed so unoriginal that Tyler swore he had seen it once or twice before. Around him, the sparse white walls of the apartment were adorned with only a few select items. A framed photograph of his father was hanging by his desk. On another wall, giving the room a hint of style, a cheap print of Picasso's *Guernica* was tacked.

Tyler's father was a writer once. He wrote a pair of unpublished novellas seldom talked about. Tyler still had the manuscripts. One was a noir mystery, the other a sweet romance set in New York. Tyler and his mother had read them, but almost no one else. His father stopped writing when still a young man. He took an office job at a local factory and raised his son to write instead.

Tyler's diploma from the state university once hung on the wall too, but it fell down months ago. He left it where it lay. It seemed strangely cool to let such an expensive piece of paper sit on the floor. He even turned his desk lamp ever so slightly to illuminate it there. He'd earned his degree in journalism, making it his major after sophomore year. He'd initially been an English major, and drifted periodically toward art history. But journalism was clearly the most practical choice.

His roommate in those days was an engineering major named Guiren—the son of Taiwanese immigrants. Everyone called him *Rennie*—presumably because he liked it. Tyler and Rennie hit it off well after the first few weeks of school. Neither one was very popular. Tyler felt lucky about the pairing though. When Tyler slept in, Rennie woke him for class. When Tyler left things out on the floor, Rennie picked them up and said nothing. A perfect relationship. After graduation, Rennie took an internship in Chicago and later went to graduate school back east. Last time Tyler spoke to him, Rennie talked about a job with a corporation in Taiwan. Maybe settling down. Buying a house. Tyler was skeptical he'd find happiness there, but said nothing.

When the can of store-brand soup began to boil, Tyler poured it into a bowl. He sat down at a little painted countertop where he could still see the small television. He ate, and he drank purified water from a big plastic bottle. When finished, Tyler left his dishes unwashed in the sink. He sat back in the chair, cat nestled comfortably on his lap, and gave no thought to his job. Tyler drifted away to thoughts of a new life in a faraway place. He would smile there. He'd just need to send an occasional postcard to his mother. "All is well, Mom. Love, Tyler."

Tyler's mother had recently started dating again—an ex-Mormon divorcé she met at work. She'd settled into a full-time position as a bank teller three years ago. Things were going well there, according to the most recent report. She struggled with alcoholism after Tyler's father died, but had been sober for close to four years. Tyler was happy that she'd found someone but preferred not to know the details. And lately, Tyler and his mother increasingly communicated solely by voice mail and text messages, always missing one another. More recently, there was talk of a big weekend visit. Perhaps, his mother mentioned, he could meet the man she'd been seeing. Tyler hadn't responded to the suggestion yet.

———

The next morning, Tyler walked down the same ninth-floor hallway in the same leather shoes. He listened to the familiar slapping sound. The tiles turned green. The sun, however, still low on the horizon at that hour, was hiding behind tall shining buildings. The office was only aglow with the artificial light of computer screens. He paused before entering the room, as though summoning strength to take that one extra step. He glanced back down the empty hallway, where the tiles were still blue. No one was there to save him. It was just him and the room. Tyler inhaled.

"Tyler," a voice called out from across the hall. "Can I see you for a minute?"

"My savior," he thought. "Unless she's going to fire me." (He didn't actually want to lose his job.) "Then she's the devil."

The door to Rebecca's office was open. She sat at her desk, just like the day before, save for the different color shirt she now wore. Tyler wondered for a moment if she had ever gone home. She was a prisoner too. A strong scent of freshly brewed coffee hung in the air. The stainless steel travel mug on her desk was enormous, resembling a small bucket with a plastic handle affixed to the side. He imagined the amount of caffeine that must course through her veins. Perhaps she needed it to survive.

"Yes?" he said.

"Great job on the track expansion story."

"Thanks," he said, relieved. His shoulders loosened. His chin picked up.

"Really nice work," she said. "I—" But the phone on her desk interrupted, ringing loudly. "Hold on," she said, and she answered it.

Tyler stood waiting at the door. He glanced at the plaques on the wall, which he recognized now. What else did she want? She hadn't waved him away. She had said, "Hold on," hadn't she? His body remained halfway through the door. A momentary step into the office was followed by a step back out onto the tiles. The green ones. He fidgeted awkwardly until she waved him inside, whipping her free hand back and forth, and over to the chair in front of her desk.

Tyler sat down. He sat in the same chair the day Rebecca hired him. Fresh from the university, he was still filled with ambition and dreams of great things. He had dressed in his navy blue business suit. He smiled widely. Rebecca praised his résumé. She "loved" his work and enthusiasm for "the craft" of writing. Tyler was gracious and agreeable and comple-mented the work that the other writers at the *Observer* had done, even though he'd read little of it. But most of all, it was a job. And he was so happy just to find a job. How things could change.

"Thanks," Rebecca said as she hung up the phone. "Sorry about that. So, Tyler, I wanted to talk to you about that assign-ment you asked about."

Oxygenated blood surged through his veins. "Yes?"

"A friend of mine just got back from a road trip. There's this little town she drove through. Apparently an artist out there has people really excited. Would that work for you?"

"What?"

"To write about this artist. You know something about art, right?"

"Yes," he said without hesitation. "That's perfect."

"Good. It'll go on the arts page. I'd like to revamp it. Do some bios of Arizona artists. Give a sense of the art scene here in the state. Anyway, the town—I'd actually never heard of it. So, let me see. I wrote it down." She shuffled through scraps and stacks of papers on her desk. Pencils and pens rolled back and off the desk and bounced chaotically onto the floor below. "Ketchum," she said after finding a yellow sticky note. "Ever heard of it?"

"No," he said. "Only the one in Idaho." Tyler sat up straight, his body barely still on the edge of his seat.

"It's about three hours east-southeast of here."

"What's it like?"

"Typical old copper mining town, I guess."

"Sounds great," he said, almost in a daze.

"Well, you can go tomorrow and check it out. Promise me, though—even if the artist story doesn't pan out, find a haunted mine or a quirky museum or *something*."

"Absolutely," he said. "I won't leave without a story."

"We can't afford more than a couple of days," she said. "So, stay longer if it's really necessary, but it'll be on your dime. Deal?"

"Yes," he said. Tyler was smiling.

"Okay, go." Rebecca smirked and gave a quick wave of her hand.

"Thank you, Rebecca," he said as he left her office with shoulders back. He pumped a fist in the air as he passed over the green tiles.

Back at his cubicle across the hall, he sat at his computer and accessed a news archive. "Ketchum" he thought. "Let's learn about Ketchum." He typed the name of the town into a search engine, but hardly any stories came up. Old news. A sad story about a girl's murder on Halloween night. A few articles about a mining company closing down operations. Its demise had left Ketchum's economy in serious trouble. And there was something else about a golf resort and the town's mayor too.

III

The sun set behind him, but the air was still hot. Every inch of concrete and metal radiated heat. Tyler wiped the sweat from his brow and knocked on an orange door adorned with stickers. He waited, and a gust of warm dusty air blew past him. Two clicks of locks rattled the orange door and it opened. A man standing five foot ten, tattooed down his arms and neck, leaned forward. A respirator mask with twin filter cartridges was pulled up over his forehead.

"Hey—hope I'm not interrupting," Tyler said, apologetically.

"Nah, you're good. What's up?"

"I'm going out of town. Tomorrow. I need someone to feed my cat."

"Big Redd? No worries."

"I'll reimburse you—"

"Forget it. No trouble," Rivera said, swatting at the air.

"I've got a key," he said, taking one from his pocket. "You painting?"

"Yeah, all day. Want to take a look?" he said, taking Tyler's key and opening the door further. "I got a show coming up downtown."

"I got to get packed. Where's your show downtown?"

"Place on Central called the Haunt. You know it?"

"No," Tyler said, slightly embarrassed. "Is that the place near the San Carlos?"

"No, it's way south."

"Oh," he said, and then he paused. "Hey—you heard anything about an artist out in Ketchum?"

"Where's that?"

"Just a few hours east, I think."

"Oh—no, don't think so. Why?"

"That's where I'm headed," Tyler explained. "Going to do an article on it."

"That's great, man. I told you something would come along."

———

That evening Tyler packed his bag. Inane noise and commercial jingles played in the background on his small television. The sound of monotonous commercial entertainment was better than silence. He knew that somewhere, someone was listening to the same monotony. And when that didn't work, there was always his neighbor Rivera. Sometimes Tyler would go next door, have a beer, and watch him paint, or look at his recent work. He even shared a short story with Rivera once—something he wrote back in school. It was his way of trying to relate.

On the stove, a pot of water began to boil furiously. A generic white box of spaghetti sat beside it. Redd the cat bathed himself on a windowsill nearby. When Tyler finished folding his shirts and counting his socks and putting his toothpaste into a small zip lock bag to keep it from leaking onto those shirts, he zipped up the bag and returned to the stove. He opened the spaghetti box, tearing the cardboard in such a way that it would never close properly again without tape or some type of clamp. He dropped all of the stiff, dry sticks into the boiling water, and they jutted out like tall brown grass. The boiling subsided just in time. Tyler waited patiently until the submerged ends softened enough to slide the rest below the surface. A few feet away, his cell phone sat quietly on the countertop next to his car keys—the battery slowly draining away.

After dinner, Tyler studied a map on his laptop. He checked roads and found the proper dot for Ketchum once he'd zoomed in twice. Redd walked in front of the screen—tail up—several times. Then came the sudden sounds of an argument outside—a man and a woman. Then a door downstairs slammed shut. Tyler continued looking at the map, ducking and leaning when necessary to see around a leg, paw, or tail. When Tyler moved into his apartment, he hoped the colorful environment there—his own "moveable feast" perhaps—might inspire him to write. It hadn't. It had only made him tired and his pen heavy.

IV

In Phoenix, the early morning hours are the finest. When the summer months come—and the ground is literally burning beneath your feet—those short hours make the valley livable, offering a brief respite for those longing to breathe or step out from their air-conditioned bunkers. Grateful for the respite, Tyler said good-bye to Redd, locked his apartment door, and carried his bag down to his 1997 sedan in the parking lot to find a forgotten place called Ketchum in the eastern Arizona desert.

Tyler found the steering wheel still cool to the touch at that hour. He had come to appreciate those little day-to-day comforts. The engine sputtered uneasily for a few seconds, but then settled into a metallic hum. Tyler switched on the radio to the inane silliness of a morning disc jockey, filling airtime between the latest heavy rotation pop songs. He sneered at the excessive energy of the disc jockey's artificial voice. "Too early," he thought.

In his shirt pocket, Tyler kept the folded piece of paper with his handwritten driving directions on it. He'd worked out the best route the night before. He would use those notes if lost, but his only real concern was getting out of the city. The only direction he really needed was east. He required no map for that.

Concrete gave way to brown and red rocks and sand and coarse clusters of green bushes and gnarled trees as the car rolled through the outskirts of metropolitan Phoenix. He passed the final outposts of human civilization. The radio signal in the car scrambled and popped with static among the majestic saguaros standing on long outstretched carpets of brown and green. When he turned the radio off, Tyler listened to the growing hum of the engine and whispered a quiet prayer to the gods that it would survive the journey.

Out there along Route 60 past Globe, among towns and census districts with names like Star Valley and Peridot, the desert pushed upward into obscure national forests and depressed Indian reservations. The state highway, almost as isolated as an ancient trade route, snaked through the occasional pocket of life, like the obligatory gas station with an oversized sign and some kitsch souvenirs in the window. Down along the old mule trails and abandoned infantry camps from the westward expansion, a motel was built to look like a cluster of grand plastic tepees. They seemed strangely space age in their sparse rocky surroundings with otherworldly red mountains encroaching from every direction.

Tyler swerved the car slightly to avoid a dead rattlesnake. It had been baking in the sun for days. Things in Arizona don't just die; they bake and fry in the heat until there is nothing left. The desert would do the same to a human being if given the opportunity, with a fair chance that no one would ever know. Plenty of migrants traveling north from Mexico perished that way. It was so common now that journalists in Arizona seldom wrote those stories anymore.

Seeing the orange arrow dipping down toward *E*, Tyler turned off the highway at the first opportunity. The car rolled down to a gas station. There was a shuttered fast-food stand there selling something called a kachina burger. A bell jingled as the car came to a stop by a single pair of pumps. They were red with a corporate star logo. The vintage metal exteriors were covered in a fine layer of brown and chalky white dust. Manning the pumps was an old man with a name tag reading Gus. Clean-shaven with a mahogany complexion, Gus wore a sun-bleached state university baseball cap and oil-stained overalls. Despite his age, he reached the pumps before Tyler could put two feet on the ground.

"What'll it be, sir?" Gus said.

Tyler bristled for a moment at being called *sir*. He glanced down at his own clothing, assessed how old he looked, and back up at Gus.

"Fill it up, please," Tyler said.

The man's face was prematurely aged by the Arizona sun. There were tiny scars from small cancers that had been cut out. His eyes had settled into a permanent squint over time but still had the sparkle of life, and he had a polite, old-fashioned charm about him that immediately put Tyler at ease.

Tyler yawned and stretched his hands high above his head. Gus whistled quietly and went about his work. He squeezed the nozzle with a coarse bronze hand while he watched the dial spin and the numbers increase.

"Where you headed?" asked Gus when the silence went on too long.

"A town called Ketchum."

"Ketchum?" he said, suddenly having more than a polite interest. "Going to see the mural?"

"The what?" Tyler asked.

"*Mural*. People say it's something else. I haven't been out there yet."

"I guess so. I heard there's an artist out there."

"Oh, no one knows who painted it. It just showed up one day, if you can believe that."

"How do you mean?"

"Well, it appeared overnight. Strangest damned thing."

"That's in Ketchum?"

"Right in the middle of town, from what I've heard," Gus said. "You can't miss it."

Tyler paid Gus for the gas and tipped him before returning to the road. Rebecca had said nothing about a mural. Maybe Tyler hadn't been listening. He shook his head. He was going to write a biographical sketch of a local artist. Something poetic about living life for art rather than the dollar. "How could I write an entire story about a painting on a wall?" he thought.

As the minutes passed, Tyler couldn't help but notice the presence of white crosses popping up along the shoulder of the highway—the lone evidence of civilization, aside from the highway itself and the occasional billboard. They were small and wooden and always close to the road in seemingly random fashion. One had flowers. Another one had a color photograph stapled to its head. Names were scrawled across them too, although Tyler failed to read them as he raced by on his way. He knew what they were, but preferred to see them as markers for pilgrims traveling east. Places to petition the holy courts and saints to secure a safe trip. The distant city in the desert had an archetypal mystique.

As a student, Tyler took a class on the myths of different cultures. Many of those stories stayed with him over the years, especially one about a holy city in the desert. It was told in Arabia at a time when stories weren't yet found in books, and it was still told by Sufis. It started with an ant, the type you step on without thinking twice. This ant had only three legs but set out on a journey to the holy city. The road to the city through the desert was very long, and it was a difficult journey, but the ant's thoughts of the far-off city gave him the strength to keep going. After traveling on the road for a long time, he came across another ant. Unlike him, the other ant had six legs and traveled the pilgrims' road very easily. The six-legged ant looked at the three-legged ant and inquired about where he was going. The three-legged ant replied that he was traveling to the holy city. To this, the six-legged ant said that the three-legged ant would never make it, because it was a long and difficult journey, even for a six-legged ant. "You will die on the journey," the six-legged ant said. The three-legged ant thought for a moment and then smiled at the six-legged ant and said: "At least I'll die on the road to the holy city." Indeed, it's often been said that the journey—the willingness to take those steps—is more important than the destination.

Ketchum was close now, or so it said on the green metal sign marking its distance. The excitement grew. Tyler watched carefully for evidence of a town ahead. His foot grew heavier, pressing against the accelerator. He was speeding down the road before he knew it, oblivious to any danger. Soon, an unnatural square shape appeared in the distance—distinct from the rock formations—and then another. A large wooden sign rose up on his left with finely painted letters and a few modest ornamental carvings on top: a mine shaft and pickaxe: Welcome to Ketchum. Incorporated 1899.

The quiet simplicity and antique charm of the town made Tyler relax in the driver's seat. His foot grew lighter. He brought the car to a slow cruising speed and went down Main Street with his windows down. He took in the air, the scents, the sounds, and whatever else he could. The sun had risen to its zenith, and it cast short stubby shadows within which very few things could hide. Tyler could see the Western-style stores and narrow brick refurbished buildings. He smiled at the sight of benches made of whole tree trunks instead of concrete or metal. And his eyes widened at the absence of graffiti or nightclub posters on the undersized light posts. The traffic in Ketchum was a calm current too, drifting through the streets. It allowed him to swim rather than race for his destination for fear of being submerged.

When the car reached the end of Main Street—which was not long—Tyler had the option to turn or continue straight ahead. The car stopped at the intersection. Then Tyler heard voices. To his left, Tyler found a crowd gathered next to a tall and narrow brick warehouse. Noting the size of the building, Tyler looked down Main Street again. Yes, it was the tallest building in Ketchum.

Tyler's first thought was that someone was hurt. He didn't see an ambulance though. And those people weren't looking down at someone either. Their heads tilted back. They were gazing up at something on the warehouse wall. Some of them pointed. A few were taking pictures. Most of all, Tyler noticed the strange looks on their faces.

Curious, Tyler parked his car on the street alongside the tree trunk benches. He stretched for a moment, then he set out across the street toward the crowd. He hadn't even bothered to retrieve his note pad from the car.

As he approached the warehouse wall, his head tilted back. He gasped. His feet ground to a halt like anchors stuck in the concrete. His hands rose and clung to his chest, as if he was checking to make sure that his heart was still beating. For a moment, it seemed that the world had vanished, and there was no one else in Ketchum. There was no question that this was the mural that Gus had mentioned. Tyler Anderson was now looking up at the most wondrous thing he had ever seen.

V

The warehouse stood at the end of Main Street, before an intersection with Copper Avenue. It was a conventional rectangle with a few windows on the front, over and around a double door entrance. Some fifty feet tall, it was 150 feet wide on the adjacent side. It was the perfect place for a Saturday game of handball. No one would dare throw a ball at that wall now though. Indeed, the wall with the mural was only days away from becoming a veritable shrine.

No one had ever seen such a concentration of color, so vibrant that it seemed to make the delicate lines and shadows shift as one's eyes moved from one corner to another. The splashes of azure and cerulean blue seemed to cool the air around everyone who looked at it, allowing them to stay a bit longer and endure the Arizona sun. The subtle hues of gold and yellow and the fresh greens and the pepper red seemed to spiral into a kaleidoscope of shapes and forms that made the tips of a person's toes tingle, so that some were inclined to remove their shoes in its presence. And at its heart stood the most delicate and graceful figure, with arms outstretched to the sky.

Tyler almost stumbled into a woman holding a camera to her eye, still taking pictures by the dozen, as if the painting were constantly changing. As he braced himself and apologized, Tyler never looked down or away from the mural. He leaned his shoulder against the person next to him without regard for personal space. "Have you ever seen anything like this?" he said.

"No," a woman said. "I came all the way from Albuquerque to see this."

Tyler stared. His head was tilted back with the rest of the crowd. He took a deep breath, locking eyes with the mural in an almost mystic trance. Closer now than before, new details about the painting revealed themselves. Tyler failed to find a stray brush stroke or a sloppy line or unintentional drop of paint anywhere. It was truly immaculate.

"Who did this?" he said. "Who did this?"

"No one knows," said a man in the crowd.

"Incredible," another added.

The symmetry of the mural, which encompassed the entirety of that massive wall of the warehouse, was impeccable and so balanced that the world itself seemed crooked in comparison. And yet, each section and corner could have been a self-contained work of fantastic beauty. But together, all the elements created a garden for the human soul, enticing the eyes, heart, and mind, and leaving no one untouched by its majesty.

VI

Sunset dispersed the crowd at the corner of Copper and Main, since no streetlights sufficiently illuminated the wall for further viewing. The mural's many admirers had to wait—biding their time until the next day—to return to the warehouse with their morning coffee or leashed family dogs. But the homes and hallways of Ketchum were still abuzz with conversations about the mural's beauty and origins. When the sun rose, they would return to sit at the street corner. They would talk and read their newspapers, taking breaks between the countless tragic stories of the world to gaze up at the beauty before them. And later, when the night returned, they would look forward to the sunrise all over again, and they would rest soundly from their labors.

Tyler took refuge at the Saguaro Motel a couple of blocks away, a small, one-story concrete building with white walls and maroon trim around tall rectangular windows. In the small parking lot—its concrete slabs cracked and bleached by the sun—there was a sign shaped like a tall saguaro cactus. It had clearly been painted by hand. It was done in a bold and almost unnatural green color. Quick dashes of black and white were added to suggest sharp cactus spines. In almost any other setting, it would have been tacky. Out there in Ketchum, it had its charm.

The Saguaro Motel was an easy choice—the only choice. It seemed clean. It was close to the mural. Very convenient for Tyler's short-term needs. If nothing was available in the town, he probably would have slept in his car—he'd done it before. He would have been happy to do it too, free from the blue tiles and his cubicle-shaped cell.

The woman at the motel's front desk—stationed on the far end of a sparse no-frills lobby—was called Doris O'Brien. It said so on the plastic nameplate. It sat beside a bell and handwritten note instructing visitors to ring it. Doris was shorter than the average American woman. She had thick white hair kept short. She wore the sleeves of her light plaid shirt rolled up high. She was not the type to waste time on makeup or hairspray anymore (if she ever had been). She spoke with confidence between frequent awkward pauses and seemed to know everything about Ketchum. And she was more than happy to share that knowledge with anyone interested in renting a room at the Saguaro Motel.

"Tripled, I'd say. Maybe even quadrupled, over the past few days," Doris said, discussing the growing number of visitors in town.

"Where are they all coming from?" Tyler asked.

"Everywhere. New Mexico, Colorado, California—all over Arizona, of course."

"Sounds like you've been busy."

"Heavens, yes," she said. "And here *you* are. So you're going to write a story about it?"

"That's right," he said, signing a rental form. "I want to talk to the artist."

"Don't we all," Doris said. She stared at Tyler for a moment, giving no indication of what she would do or say next. Over her shoulder was a large framed photograph of a bald man in his fifties. He wore a plaid cowboy shirt with a bolo tie. The man looked forward blankly at the camera. He had just the slightest hint of a smile.

Tyler looked at Doris across the desk and back toward the picture and back at her again. He didn't know whether to speak or keep waiting. He wondered if *he* was being awkward or it was her. "Do you—"

"I think it must have been someone passing through."

"Like who?"

"Maybe a movie star," she said. Her eyes lit up with excitement.

"A movie star?" he asked, puzzled.

"Well, they always do strange things," she said, defensively. "I see those shows."

"What shows?"

"The dinnertime tabloid ones."

"I don't watch them," Tyler said, dismissively.

"We like *Entertainment Tonight*," she said, gesturing slightly at the picture of the bald man. "Who's a famous artist these days?" She looked up as if the answer might appear on the ceiling. "All the ones I know—Picasso, Van Gogh, Michelangelo—Georgia O'Keefe, of course." She was counting on her fingers. "They're all dead."

"Well, there's David Choe. And Banksy," Tyler said, struggling to make a list himself.

"No, I don't think so," she said dismissively. "No, I have a feeling about this."

Tyler was unsure what she meant. He waited for some further explanation. It never came. "Who's the handsome guy in the photograph?" he finally asked, eager to move off the subject of contemporary art.

"Oh," she said, glancing over at the photograph. "That's Bob." Doris paused again and stared ahead, her eyes drifting upward, as if thinking for a moment. Then she turned and looked at the wall beside the front desk. There was a clock there.

"Who's Bob?" Tyler asked.

"My husband," she said, turning back and smiling.

"Handsome guy," he said politely.

"Not really. Heck of a sweetheart, though. Have you eaten anything?" she asked.

"No," Tyler said. "Do you have room service here?"

"Just a glass bottle Coke machine." She smiled again. "There's a diner though. Up the street. Guy from out of town—has an odd name—bought it some years ago. Wasn't sure about him at first. I go there all the time now though," she said with a laugh. "Usually stays open until eight or so."

"That sounds good. I'll—"

"You know, those crowds around the mural? Warehouse owner can't stand it. Welch—that's his name—doesn't give a hoot about artsy stuff. Bob and I think it's damn hysterical."

Tyler glanced up at Bob's picture again and then back at Doris.

"How long you in town for?" she asked.

"Not too long."

"There's a house worth seeing, you know. Gorgeous, really. Like architecture? Old place—*big*."

"I probably won't have time."

When Doris began to slip into another awkward pause, Tyler thanked her and snatched up his room key off the front desk. His stomach churned and gurgled as he walked. Good sign. Tyler forgot to eat when he was excited about a new project. His basic survival instincts—hunger, thirst, sleep— were suppressed. He was running on creativity.

VII

The diner was open and closer to the motel than Tyler had imagined. He wondered how he'd missed it when driving into town. Something else must have distracted him. Everything was close in Ketchum. Almost all accessible by foot. The population of the town was about a thousand people. A person could easily dispense with a car in Ketchum, even without recourse to public transportation. No buses needed. Using a bicycle might even create the mistaken impression that someone was in two places at once. And the convenience of it all meant that a map was never really necessary, because if someone took a wrong turn it was no trouble to turn around and try the other direction.

The large illuminated window of the diner shown bright against the orange glow of the undersized streetlights that began and ended on Main Street. Inside, dark wooden booths ran along a wall. There were white vinyl topped tables with paper placemats and napkins. Neatly arranged salt and pepper shakers and red ketchup bottles and yellow mustard bottles were on every table. There was an old-fashioned lunch counter too. It had six round, red, padded stools on shiny metal poles. It all seemed straight out of a Norman Rockwell painting. A dusty upright piano sat unused in the back near the one restroom, designated for use by both men and women. Framed photographs of mine shafts and pioneers covered the walls. Each one told a story of the town's history.

Tyler sat down at the counter and swiveled playfully on his stool. In front of him stood a man with a broad back dressed in a white T-shirt and apron. There was a cloud of steam and smoke wafting up around the man and rushing through a metal vent positioned above a hot grill. Tyler swiveled a bit more and waited patiently.

The large, strongly built man—standing like a golem at the grill—did not acknowledge his arrival. His back faced the counter. Tyler cleared his throat, but the sound was lost beneath the hissing of cooking meat. He waited a few seconds more. Just as he prepared to try again, he realized that someone else was there too. Tyler turned to see the lone waitress standing there. She was waiting for him to notice her.

A young woman in her twenties, the waitress had pretty blue eyes that seemed older. She wore her dirty blond hair up in a pragmatic ponytail and kept a sharp pencil behind her right ear. She wore no name tag. Her uniform consisted simply of a white T-shirt and tight fitting jeans. It was the pencil and the order pad that gave her away.

"Can I get you something to drink?" she said. Her voice was sweet, friendly and youthful.

"I'll take a glass of water, please."

"Glass of water—anything to eat tonight?"

"Do you have a menu?"

The waitress nodded. "We have lots," she said. She pulled a one-page laminated menu from an adjacent table and presented it to Tyler. It had worn edges and some traces of maple syrup on one corner.

Tyler looked the menu over and found the usual diner fare. As he pondered his limited choices—hamburger, BLT, chicken tenders—he felt someone looking at him from behind the counter. He glanced up to find the golem at the grill watching. He was wiping his meaty hands on the end of his sullied white apron. Tyler looked back down at the menu and quickly made his selection. "I'll take a cheeseburger and fries," he said. It was a safe choice. And he would watch the golem prepare it.

The waitress nodded and scribbled down the order in her pad. The cook had heard the order, but she followed her familiar routine. She tore out the paper, clipped it to a rotating metal stand and spun it quickly before disappearing into the back. A minute later, she returned with a glass of ice water and a straw. She smiled at Tyler as she set it down on the counter in front of him. "Your water," she said. Then she slipped away again to attend to the other customers in the diner, all of whom Tyler took as locals. The waitress addressed the people by their first names—Sue, Frank, and Luis.

"You just get here?" said the golem.

Tyler looked over at the cook, unsure if he was in fact talking to him. He turned his head slightly toward Tyler, awaiting a reply. His blond hair was meticulously cut and sculpted into a short fade. "In town, you mean?" Tyler asked.

The cook nodded.

"Yeah, I just arrived. Great town you've got here," he said, earnestly.

"How do you want your burger, man?"

Tyler said simply, "Medium." The cook nodded and said nothing more. Tyler inched closer on his stool. The diner was a major social hub, he guessed. It was the perfect place to collect stories. He hoped the cook might have an idea how the locals felt about the mural. Maybe the cook even knew something about the identity of the mysterious artist.

"Can I ask you a question?" Tyler was leaning up and over the counter now.

"Depends," the cook said, raising his voice over the hiss of recently flipped meat.

Tyler explained to the cook why he was visiting Ketchum. He was writing a story about the mural, he said. The cook seemed to ease after hearing this. Now he faced Tyler and introduced himself. The cook's name was Abdullah Park.

"Where are you from originally?" Tyler expected Abdullah to name a hardened city neighborhood. Somewhere in Los Angeles or Chicago. There were several thick scars across his hands and forearms—difficult not to notice.

"Everywhere," Abdullah said.

"What did you do there, before coming here?"

"Everything," he replied. Abdullah looked at Tyler and smiled as if they were playing a game and he was winning.

"Interesting," Tyler said. "Your name's unusual; is that a family name?"

"No, man, it's mine," he said.

"Right," Tyler said.

Abdullah smiled. "It's from another time in my life," he said.

"What time was that?"

"I'm not really much for the past, you know?"

"Sure," he said. "So, how long have you been here?"

"Maybe six years. Seven. I don't know, really."

"Came out here for a new start?"

"I like the sunshine," Abdullah said. He turned back and flipped the meat cooking on the grill. "I can't get enough."

"What are you two talking about?" the young waitress asked. She was carrying a tray of used dishes from a now empty table. Two locals had left the diner while Tyler spoke to Abdullah. After the waitress put her tray down behind the counter, she stood there, wiping her hands with a small dish towel.

"He's a journalist. Came out here from Phoenix to write a story," Abdullah explained.

"Really? A story about what?"

"The wall over there," Abdullah said.

"The artist, I hope," Tyler added.

Abdullah introduced the waitress to Tyler as Audrey Betz. She too was averse to saying much about herself, but less mysterious than her apron-clad boss with the scars on his arms. She smiled and shook Tyler's hand politely.

"What do you think of it?" Tyler asked.

"It's so beautiful," Audrey said.

"It's pretty good," said Abdullah.

"Just pretty good?" Tyler said.

"It's good. What else can I say?"

"He talks about it all the time," Audrey said.

"Do I?"

"Yes."

"Well, I don't believe in much, but I can believe in *that*," Abdullah said.

"How often do you go to see it?"

"Every day," Abdullah said.

"Really?"

"Yeah, something wrong?"

"Nope," Tyler said. "What about you?"

"I don't know. I went by it yesterday." She paused for a moment. "I know this sounds strange, but it felt like I was seeing it again for the first time. That's weird, right?"

"That's because it's so big," Abdullah said, raising his arms for emphasis. "It's like your eyes can't take it all in or something." He assembled a cheeseburger and a side of French fries on a clean plate as he explained. Then he slid it across the counter in front of Tyler.

The smell of the cooked beef and fried potatoes was enticing, but it failed to overpower Tyler's interest in the mural. "Thanks," Tyler said quickly. "It *is* big. I heard the mural showed up overnight too. Is that true?"

"That's true," Abdullah said.

"True," said Audrey.

"How does someone do that in *one night*—in the dark—without anyone even noticing?" Tyler asked, incredulously.

"You've seen it right?" Abdullah asked. "How does anyone paint that thing, period?"

Tyler had no explanation, or at least offered nothing in response. He looked instead to Audrey.

"Aliens," she said, and she burst out laughing. It was the first time Tyler saw Audrey Betz's real smile. Not just the polite one she wore for customers.

Abdullah smiled and shook his head dismissively. "There were some people in here the other day. Talkin' about how aliens must have done it. Crazy, man. They paid for their lunch though. So what do I care?"

"We thought we should put a sign up," Audrey said.

"Believers welcome, or something," Abdullah said, laughing.

"Any guesses about the artist?" Tyler asked, not indulging in the tangent.

"Nah, I don't know."

"There must be someone here in town," Tyler said. "A painter?"

"There are some artists, but not like that. Not that I know about," Abdullah said.

Tyler turned to Audrey for another reaction or at least something entertaining. Anything worth writing down would do. Maybe just another smile.

"Sorry, I've only lived here for a year."

"Oh—a transplant?" Tyler said. "Where you from?"

Audrey's shoulders tightened immediately. Her smile went away. "Phoenix," she finally said.

"Did you get sick of the concrete?"

"What?"

"The concrete. It's everywhere—baking in the sun. It radiates heat all night so it never gets cool."

"Oh. Kind of. It was just time to go."

"We're like nomads, man," Abdullah explained. "How's that burger?"

"It's good," Tyler said. He took another bite to be polite. As he chewed, Audrey escaped to the back of the diner. Tyler heard the sound of water beginning to pour into a metal sink and dishes going in under the water. "Did I say something wrong?" he asked between large bites.

"Her? No, she just has work to do. We don't have much staff here. I can't afford it. You know how it is."

"Has business picked up since the mural appeared?"

"Yeah," he said with a nod. "It's a good thing too. I wasn't sure we'd make it much longer. Honestly, this town was struggling. If I knew who painted that warehouse, I'd give 'em a jumbo cheeseburger on the house."

"Well, if my story goes well, I think you'll get a few more customers."

"Make sure you write something good about my cooking," Abdullah said, pointing at Tyler in somewhat intimidating fashion.

———

After finishing his meal—feeling the wonderful sensation of fullness in his stomach—Tyler explored the diner. He walked down along the walls and looked at each of the framed photographs. Most of them had been there for years—even decades. They contained faces of men from another age, miners standing beside dark shafts with pickaxes and shovels at their sides. The faces carried strong and distinguished features smeared by dirt and soot. Moustaches were in vogue at the time. And there were labor union banners hanging over their heads—symbols of solidarity among workers struggling to support themselves and their families.

"Did you want some dessert?" Audrey said. She had resumed waiting tables. Her pencil was again nestled comfortably behind her ear.

Tyler noticed that a lock of her blond hair had come loose from her ponytail. The hair was hanging down along the side of her cheek and curling underneath her chin. She'd also freshly applied pink lip gloss.

"No, I'm fine," he said. "I could use some advice, though."

"Advice? About what?"

"You've been here a year. Who do you think I should interview?"

Audrey thought for a moment and bit her bottom lip. "George," she said. "He's the mayor. He comes by for coffee. Chitchat. Sometimes pie. We have *really* good pie."

"I assume he has an office?" Tyler asked, dismissing her pitch to try the pie.

"Town Hall, just down the street," she said. "There's a miner statue out front."

"What's George's last name?" Tyler opened a note pad of his own and held a pen at the ready.

"Correa—George Correa. He's hard to miss."

"Correa," he confirmed as he wrote. "Thanks. Well, I guess I'll head back to the motel."

"Are you at the Saguaro?"

"Yes. You know it?"

"Only motel in town," she said. "Doris comes in a lot."

"Yes, Doris," he said. "We've met."

"A little weird, I know. She's sweet, though."

"She's been helpful so far," he said. "She told me about this diner."

Tyler left encouraged by the new lead. Despite his remark earlier, he was in no actual hurry to return to the motel. Instead, he walked slowly and looked up at the stars in the sky overhead—he could see them clearly. He basked in the stillness. He breathed deeply, as if savoring the flavor of the cool night breeze.

Stopping for a moment, he looked at a window display for the local hardware store. Then he stopped again at a movie rental shop with posters for the latest releases in the window. The stores on Main Street were all closed by that hour, but Tyler imagined who shopped and worked there. He imagined patrons in pairs walking hand-in-hand down the sidewalks. Colorful shopping bags on fingertip hooks. Then, walking in seemingly random fashion, the pairs he pictured in his mind broke out into a synchronized waltz, gliding over the sidewalks hand in hand. There was a graceful flurry of feet, extending out over the street into the night.

A blue bicycle was displayed in one window. Its chrome wheels glistened. Tyler thought about the boy or girl who would ride it. That child would discover so much on that bike—find secret places and build forts in the hills to fight dragons and giants. Tyler remembered the adventurous simplicity of his own youth too. It was very different than his daily reality as a man. He felt like a painter forced to draw corporate product logos—not an Andy Warhol, but an anonymous ad agency draftsman. The types of sterile logos found on scented body scrubs. Or the latest bottled water brand. As a journalist, part of Tyler remained wholly unsatisfied and frustrated. Revelatory earthshaking stories and exposés were elusive, no matter how hard he tried to find them. Instead, there were train stories. Or car accidents after football games. Creative suicide, he thought. He hoped that if he was patient—gratefully earning his modest but steady paycheck—a better opportunity would come along. He knew it could take years. Or, worse, it could never come at all. There was no guarantee after all. No, he was a good writer, he reasoned. He would find something. He could go to a bigger city—larger than Phoenix. A new city would have more—new problems—to write about. Something would move him—but what?

Tyler knew he was privileged to get paid to write. He hadn't forgotten that. That privilege was particularly apparent in the context of Ketchum, where so many men had made a living in the brutal conditions of the mines. The humble old cemeteries in Ketchum were full of such men. Indeed, he knew so many still struggled in similar working conditions today. He was one of the lucky, he reminded himself.

As Tyler reached the end of Main Street, he looked at the warehouse. It was dark there now. There was no crowd. The mural was hidden by the night, except for the sudden flash of color that appeared when a random car drove past with its headlights on. There was no moon out either. Only the stars were watching overhead.

Tyler stood on the sidewalk looking over at the warehouse. It seemed strange that something as stunning as the mural could be silenced by the passivity of the night without even a whimper of protest. Tyler found himself staring into the darkness, as if waiting for the mural to awake. It never stirred or groaned though. It was entirely quiet in Ketchum. There were no car horns or police sirens or angry drunks stumbling home from the local bar after last call. The mural slept quietly that night, and Tyler agreed to visit again in the morning.

VIII

A few miles from the corner of Copper and Main, there was a vast area of barren land where a local seer and politician once envisioned a land of milk and honey with eighteen holes. George Correa—Ketchum's mayor—saw the Promised Land. He assured the trusting people of Ketchum with a wink and a nod that he would bring a grand golf resort to town and an economic boom along with it. For a time, it seemed like he would succeed. People were abuzz with optimism for the future.

The big business deal fell through in the end. Investments were lost. Many in Ketchum never forgave or forgot. And even as the passage of time helped to dull the pain, people still slipped out there from time to time. They parked their cars in front of that plot of land, staring into the distance, thinking about what could have been and cursing the winds of fate.

The way George Correa and his wife behaved, no one would guess that dreams had died in that town. George seemed to forget the whole thing. It was a gift he had. He would wave to everyone he saw, even people who hated him. He knew their names and the names of their children. He had a friendly question ready for anyone within earshot. "How's that truck running?" he'd say to Mr. McNeil at the post office.

"I sure enjoyed that book you lent me; do you have another?" he'd ask Mrs. Perry by the freezer at the grocery store. He smiled so often that it seemed like he was a perpetually happy man. Tall and husky with unnaturally dark brown hair and twinkling eyes, George treated the town of Ketchum like a stage. He was always performing for the crowds.

The mysterious appearance of the mural meant new possibilities for Ketchum. A veritable spotlight had turned toward the little town. It was getting brighter by the day. George saw a big opportunity, and he was on a mission to capitalize. He and his wife, Daisy—a quiet woman and George's opposite in nearly every way—were on the telephone, making calls across the state. Caravans were coming to see the "miracle on Main Street," as George called it. He even invited street vendors to set up shop in front. He wanted to keep people there in a crowd as long as possible. It was a circus in the making and everyone was welcome to participate. The bigger, the better, George believed. It had to be an event.

———

When Tyler awoke the next morning at the Saguaro Motel and stepped out of his room, he immediately noticed the change. Cars filled every spot in the motel parking lot. Two had license plates from New Mexico. A man dressed in a maroon polo shirt and khakis was carrying luggage into a room three doors down. And the traffic had grown to a mighty stream; cars and vans and trucks were lining the side streets and congesting the thoroughfares. It seemed as though the quaint little town— the one Tyler had reached only one day before—had disappeared overnight.

Curious, and perturbed about the sudden influx of activity, Tyler went to find Doris O'Brien. A little bell jingled when he opened the lobby door. The sound annoyed him at that early hour. Doris was inside but busy with another visitor. "Prescott," he heard the man say. Doris was going on about Ketchum, its history, and pausing awkwardly between questions and answers.

Tyler waited with his arms crossed. Then he paced back and forth in a four-foot space between a plastic plant and a broken gumball machine from 1983. Periodically he glanced over, hoping to catch her attention. But she acted like he wasn't there. Doris's pauses seemed like an eternity. Tyler started to mumble to himself bitterly. Finally she was finished. The visitor thanked her and left the lobby, a key in his hand. The bell jingled again as the man went out the door.

"Good morning," Doris said. She spoke to Tyler without any sense that he was waiting. "How'd you sleep?"

"Where did all these people come from?" Tyler asked, bluntly. He didn't bother to hide his frustration. His mood was sour. An addict's need for caffeine needn't help.

"Same as you," she said. "They're here to see the mural."

"Why today, all of a sudden?"

"George! The man is a salesman," she said, before pausing for some sort of response.

"George Correa?"

"That's the one."

"I was planning to see him. Today, probably."

"Bet you he's down there right now." Doris slapped the surface of the front desk and reached for a phone. "I can call his office if you like?"

"No, don't do that," Tyler said. "I'm headed there now. Thank you." He turned, shoulders tensed, and walked out. Doris simply gave a nod and watched him go.

The short walk from the motel to the mural was no longer simple. The quiet town was gone. Now he navigated amorphous pockets of pedestrians on the sidewalks. People came in and out of the stores. They stopped abruptly to take pictures. People stared at cell phone screens. Tyler walked awkwardly through it all, shifting and winding around. It felt like he was back in the city. The public trash bins were full too. People were filling them up too quickly. They were ruining the otherwise picturesque scene. Flies were buzzing around the worst of them. There was a rancid stink too. Garbage festered in the heat. On the ground, bits of paper and dirt swirled around his feet. Every time the breeze picked up, it gathered more trash in every open nook and crevice.

These visitors would be disappointed, Tyler imagined. There was no Starbucks, no McDonalds. They wouldn't find anything like an Arizona resort with its accoutrements. But he knew that it wasn't the town they came to see, despite its rich history and little charms. The mural was the sole attraction. And it more than compensated for the shortcomings of Ketchum. Its splendor would carry their thoughts away to heights unknown. He felt almost jealous that so many others now had access to it.

Swelling by the hour, the crowd outside of the warehouse was three times the size it was the day before. There were vendor carts and kiosks now too. These were stationed in front, only a few feet from the mural. Money was changing hands. One cart was selling bright yellow popcorn. Another one had every color of snow cone and some other sweet treats. A short wooden platform was constructed between them. This let patrons climb up and pose for pictures beside the "miracle on Main Street." Tyler twirled in a circle, taking it all in. So many cameras. They took photographs of the mural from every angle—filling up digital memory and rolls of film—as if no single angle was sufficient to capture the brilliance before them. There were professional cameras too. They bobbed around with enormous long lenses. Their owners carried bulky shoulder bags with every possible accessory inside. A television camera rested on the shoulder of a man in the crowd as well.

Tyler was dismayed at the sight of the media covering *his* story. He had lost his exclusive. He squared his shoulders; he was determined to outdo them. He would start with an interview. It was easy to pick George out of the crowd. He was dressed in a clean, pressed suit, and was the only one not thoroughly entranced by the mural. Instead, he was personally greeting everyone he saw. He introduced himself by name, smiling and laughing raucously. He was larger than life, and anyone who even glanced in his direction was ensnared by his charisma and his firm handshake.

"Excuse me, Mayor?" Tyler said.

"Yes. Hello," George said. "Welcome to Ketchum!" He took hold of Tyler's hand, and Tyler's shoulder began to bounce from the force of George's handshake.

"Thank you, sir. I arrived yesterday from Phoenix. I work for the *Observer*. I'm doing a story on the mural."

"Terrific! We're so happy to see some journalists out here. Incredible, isn't it?" George turned and took a long look at the wall. "Amazing!"

"Do you have time for an interview?"

Just as George was about to answer, he was suddenly distracted. His head turned. The man with the television camera caught his eye. He was locked in. Beside the cameraman was a pretty brunette holding a microphone. They were working their way through the crowd and pointing at a place to set up for the best shot.

"Excuse me for a minute," George said, lured away like a fish after a worm.

It was a small setback, but Tyler was patient and willing to bide his time. He mingled and kept an eye on George. There were plenty of people to meet. Those that arrived snapping pictures were now stopping. They stood, gazing. Some were silent, but others were eager to express their overwhelming feelings to anyone who would listen. In fact, words and phrases were spilling out all around Tyler, addressed to no one in particular. Tyler could almost pluck them out of the air like fruit falling from a tree.

The crowd outside of the warehouse included people of every age and color and economic caste. There were white-haired professor types, studying the mural and discussing it in hushed tones, as though they were visiting an exhibit at a museum. And there were sad-eyed mothers with quivering lips, wiping tears away from their eyes with big wads of tissue. Even a skinny, angst-ridden teenager—clearly dragged along on the trip by his worried parents—was staring at the wall with wonder.

Only steps away from Tyler stood a middle-aged woman with wild frizzy hair and long, dangling earrings. She was answering questions from people in the crowd. Tyler gave the strange woman a look out of curiosity, but she spoke so loudly, he couldn't help but overhear her conversation. That was when Tyler heard her make an incredible claim.

"The mural is the work of one of my students, I tell you," she said.

Kathleen Morales was an art teacher in the local unified school district for over twenty years.

"I recognize the style and the brush technique. I'm sure of it. Positive."

"Excuse me." Tyler slipped in front of her audience. "Did you say one of your students painted this?"

"That's right."

"What's your name?"

"Kathleen Morales," she said proudly.

Seeing her up close, Tyler noticed that Kathleen wore an odd shade of dark red, almost purple, lipstick. Her lips stuck together at the corners of her mouth when she spoke. Along with a flowered blouse, she wore a long flowing skirt. It fluttered like a sail in the wind. The fabric featured colorful Native American patterns that formed thick horizontal stripes. Tyler concluded that it was actually something a tourist might buy at an Indian reservation in the area. Something cheap.

"You recognize the work? You know the student?" Tyler said, looking her in the eyes.

"Well, I've had so many students. Many very talented," she said with swelling pride.

"I'd love to talk to the artist if you can give me a name."

She looked away.

"Maybe the artist wants to remain a mystery," a woman said. "After all, the art exists as a pure and independent entity now. Doesn't it?"

"That's a lovely way to put it," Kathleen said to her. "Just lovely."

"My job is to tell the story. No one knows the story here better than the artist. Right?"

The woman merely shrugged and drifted away as quickly as she had come into the conversation. Her place in the crowd was quickly filled up by other visitors gazing at the wall.

"If I were the artist, I'd want to take credit for this," Tyler explained to Kathleen. "It's genius."

"It is a masterpiece, isn't it?" Kathleen was visibly moved as she gazed up at the mural. "I come here every day. I can spend hours here, really."

"You must be very proud."

"Oh yes, I am. You know, I had a student about ten years ago who became a wonderful sculptor in Santa Fe. Have you been?"

"No," Tyler said, dismissively. "The student who painted this mural. Can I meet him or her this afternoon?"

"I don't know," she said. Her tone was odd.

"What's the name?"

There was a puzzled look on Kathleen's face. "I really don't recall a name, just the technique and the color. I'm sure I've seen it before."

Tyler's heart sank. His excitement instantly evaporated. She knew nothing. Kathleen had no idea who painted the mural. She *believed* that she did—that much was certain. But it was nothing more than belief. Tyler sighed. He had no further interest in her bizarre whimsical observations.

IX

George Correa finished his interview with the television reporter. He smiled. Then he shook hands with her, more gently than before. George was pleased with his performance. When the questions stopped, he told charming small-town jokes. Those continued until the camera went off completely and the cameraman lowered it from his shoulder. Then George scanned the crowd for his next target. It took only a few seconds. Marching over to a cluster of tourists, George gave a grand hello and started shaking hands like he was running for office again.

Tyler saw his chance. Pushing his way through a group of senior citizens in oversized hats, he set out to chase the mayor down. But before he could reach him, a sudden stir in the crowd interrupted his pursuit. There was angry shouting. Multiple voices. It came from the front of the crowd. Like frightened cattle, people started stepping and stumbling backward and colliding into each another.

Tyler managed to hold his ground against the tide. But several senior citizens and their hats were swept away. He pushed and stretched to look over the sea of heads. He looked toward the mural. Everyone else turned too. Hundreds of sweaty necks were stretching and arching to see what was going on next to the wall.

Exacerbated by the summer heat, two vendors had fallen into a loud argument. They were bickering over shrinking space by the wall, encroachment into each other's territory, and the growing disorganization of the lines. Crude personal insults followed. There was a physical altercation and then the crash of metal. A collective gasp swept through the crowd. People froze in their places. Hands covered open mouths in horror.

Amid their shock, Tyler politely made his way to the front, chanting the great mantra, "Excuse me," again and again. There he found a metal vendor cart lying on its side. It was surrounded by scattered bits of hotdog buns and bright yellow popcorn. The cart, overturned by the angry snow cone vendor, had struck the surface of the mural. A large scrape now ran through the paint. It was about five and a half feet long.

Fingers from the crowd pointed at the snow cone vendor. Others at the popcorn man. Wide eyes stared down at the damage to the mural. As word spread, a stunned expression spread out over the hundreds of faces like an Arizona wildfire.

"Everyone move back!" George shouted. The sea parted as George pushed his large body through the crowd. "Get these carts out of here," he said. The order came out again in loud angry bursts. "Right now."

The two vendors and the closest onlookers—some still holding melting snow cones in their hands—hurriedly picked up the cart and carried it away out of view. A few pictures were taken, but people threw dirty looks. Cameras were quickly put away out of respect for the gravity of the situation. The circus at the corner of Copper and Main had come to an abrupt end.

George knelt in front of the mural. He looked closely at the damage and sighed with dismay. He held his fingers over the chunks of scraped paint. He traced over the surface in the air. His arm moved up and down the length of the wound. No one dared move.

Tyler stood to the side of George and watched intently. Then he got down on his knees to observe George's ongoing performance. The mayor was showing the full range of his abilities now. This was a new emotion. Tyler had not seen it before. George was performing sorrow.

"Is Kathleen here? Kathleen Morales?" George said, loudly. He stood up and turned quickly to the crowd. When he didn't see her, he stretched upward on his toes and made a face to convey his impatience to the audience. "Kathleen?" he yelled.

There was a sudden surge of whispers and turning heads. Soon Kathleen—the woman with the frizzy hair and purple lips—came forward to join George at the front of the crowd. Together they turned to face the wall and kneeled down, as if preparing for mass. George whispered something that no one else could hear. But Tyler saw a terrible look of concern on Kathleen's face. She sat for a moment and made a long and serious evaluation of the damage inflicted on the masterpiece. Again there were whispers between the two. Finally, a somber nod of agreement.

Kathleen stood and pointed to several other sections of the mural. She started to explain something quietly to George in some detail. He listened attentively. They looked at each area as her finger moved. Then they looked down at the damage again. George seemed to consider Kathleen an authority on the matter. Teaching art to local school kids had turned her into a curator.

Yellow police tape and metal fencing was placed around the site by the sheriff, Dale Weaver, under orders from the mayor. Everyone had to keep a safe distance away from the wall now; any further damage to the mural had to be prevented. George seemed to forget that he was the one who had put the vendors there in the first place. Later that afternoon, George announced that a town meeting was being held to discuss the matter further.

"Only residents of Ketchum are allowed to attend," he added.

When Tyler heard George say that only residents could attend, his hand shot up in the air. "Excuse me, Mayor. What about the press? You believe in a free press, don't you?"

"A few journalists can come," he conceded.

That was too easy, Tyler thought. Now he just had to get there. Secure a seat before anyone could shut him out on the street.

X

The meeting at Town Hall started with a lively discussion between the residents of Ketchum. People exchanged all manner of ideas about how to repair and restore the mural to its original condition. George Correa, meanwhile, took the opportunity to make a desperate plea. He stood up and asked for the artist to come forward. Only he or she could truly restore the work, he said. Daisy Correa spoke too and reminded everyone of their civic duty. Kathleen Morales—who had claimed that the artist was one of her students—supported the Correas emphatically, arguing that any attempt to repair it by someone other than the artist might lead to further damage.

Once everyone who wished to speak had spoken, silence fell across the room. People turned and looked at each other, one by one, hoping that someone would stand up. Everyone hoped to see someone rise from his or her seat and say what they all wanted so desperately to hear.

Finally, amid the silence, a man rose from his chair. He was sitting in the back of the room, where few could see him. A sudden rush of optimism fluttered through the crowd, along with an audible murmur of questions. Recognizing the man, however, their optimism evaporated like a raindrop in the desert. Hope gave way to despair. The man in the back of the room was Samuel Welch. He owned the warehouse. He was most certainly not the artist. In fact, it was widely rumored that Samuel Welch was incapable of expressing anything other than anger.

Samuel was a fiercely independent man, always wary of intrusions into his personal affairs. The few times he dared open his heart to the world, he was sorely disappointed. And because of that, he had long since decided not to subject himself to those aspects of life again. Instead, he devoted himself to his work, which he did constantly and tirelessly. Now in his advanced years—two years older than Daisy Correa—Samuel was largely content to maintain his properties and monitor his stock holdings. The big old warehouse at the corner of Copper and Main was one such property.

"I've sat and listened to all of you tonight," he said. "And it seems that everyone is forgetting one very important point. None of you actually has any say in this matter."

There was a rumbling in the crowd.

"That painting, as far as I'm concerned, is an act of vandalism on my private property," he said. "And no one can say otherwise. That includes you, Correa."

The room erupted.

Tyler was intrigued by the sudden confrontation. He quickly opened his note pad and wrote as fast as he could. He transcribed Samuel's defiant words verbatim and recorded the impassioned reactions of his neighbors.

George jumped to his feet. He waved his arms, pleading for everyone to calm down. He begged to be allowed to speak again. For a second, it seemed as if he might tackle someone to the ground. Daisy implored those seated next to her to remain composed. Those out of reach were summoned from afar with hand gestures. "Is Samuel insane?" a woman in a T-shirt asked.

Amid the chaos, Tyler cast his gaze around the room, noting who was yelling at whom. Most of the people were shouting at Samuel. Then he noticed Audrey Betz. She stood quietly across the room against a wall. She was watching Samuel and seemed not to notice Tyler at all. He was pleasantly surprised to see her. She had let her hair down that night.

"Please, everyone!" George said for the sixth time. "Samuel, you have every right over your property. Every right. But you have to consider the town."

"No, that's your job, Mayor," Samuel said. "I don't work for anyone."

"Do you have eyes?" Kathleen suddenly exclaimed, her voice cracking.

"I've seen graffiti before," he said, deliberately prodding her. "And I treat it all the same. I'll whitewash it and save everyone the trouble of wasting time on this nonsense."

There was a second eruption. Kathleen was so angry that she seemed to be having a seizure. She jumped from her chair, arms whirling and whipping around her head, and she started ranting as though she were speaking in tongues.

Tyler discerned only a few words as the commotion in the room swelled. He distinctly heard the word *fascist* and the phrase *how dare you* and something about a dead body. It sounded like she'd said, "Over my dead body."

George was shouting too. There were two small hands with slender fingers grabbing onto his sleeve. Daisy was trying desperately to calm him. She was failing.

"Do you have any idea what this could do for the town?" George shouted, his big body shaking.

"The town? Or your reelection campaign?" said Samuel.

"How dare you!"

"I'll have it whitewashed in days," Samuel said. "Better get your cameras." Samuel stormed out alone through the doors of Town Hall.

Those who remained in the meeting room sat in stunned silence. Bodies slumped over in metal folding chairs. Some people rested their faces in the palms of their hands. Kathleen was shaking. She took a seat after she seemed to lose her balance for a moment. Others consoled one another with arms around shoulders. Someone was coughing badly in a back corner. Everyone else turned to George, seeking some comfort in his eternal optimism, even though they all knew he had failed them before.

"We have to do something," a woman said.

"She's right. We need to organize," an older man said in the back.

"I promise you—all of you—that I will do everything in my power to protect that mural, even if I have to chain myself to the damn wall," George said. He tried to smile, but it was forced and awkward. Rarely had George ever failed to pull off a good smile.

Few were convinced by George's assurances.

XI

A t the Saguaro Motel, Tyler fell backward onto his bed with arms outstretched, palms upward. He lay there completely still and stared at the white popcorn ceiling tiles. Probably asbestos. These seemingly uneventful moments were an integral part of Tyler's writing process. He called them sitting-quietly, staring-at-things moments. It was the time when words and sentences were pulled from the mysterious place where creativity originated and words assembled in his head before being put down onto paper or typed out. Admittedly, he didn't always have the chance to write this way. Sometimes he had to force it out. Those were the times when sentences and words were scooped and pulled and written down because there was no time to debate them in his head.

Sometimes, during these treasured moments of contemplation, Tyler would fictionalize or dramatize real events. In some cases, a bit of dramatizing had purpose. But mostly these creative tangents were for fun, a release, the inner novelist teasing the serious journalist irreverently. He imagined the Town Hall meeting was overrun by vagabond poets who forced everyone to listen to haikus for hours amid copious screaming. Or Audrey took him by the hand and they danced down the aisle, while no one else could see them. Or a secret society, the Order of the Cactus, was watching and awaiting the proper phase of the moon to reveal the esoteric meaning of the mural to the world. After his imagination was satisfied, the real business of writing began. The task was to separate the meat from the bones. It was usually a messy process.

Tyler reviewed the strange events of the evening. Images ran through his head like a slide show. He cut away the insignificant and incidental. Those bits were tossed away from the juicy core pieces. He slid the excess tissue and tendons away and reorganized the good bits on his plate. Those pieces were translated into words and catchy phrases and assembled like a new life. When he struggled to recall some bit of detail, he would pass over it. Later, he would turn to his notes. This was good to recall an exact wording. Samuel Welch's threats. George Correa's promise. And when he was ready, Tyler started writing and did so quickly—traversing the abyss—so that he wouldn't forget or lose a single word.

That was the moment when a curious smell first crept into Tyler's motel room. It was pungent, unnatural, and bothersome, but still faint. "Smoke," Tyler thought. There was a distinct sweetness to the aroma too. There was no fire that he could see. He heard no crackling wood or curtains bursting. No one was cooking either. It was something else. There was no need to call for help. Not yet. Tyler returned to his writing. He tried to restore the flow of words to his fingertips. But the smell of the smoke grew stronger, and Tyler could not ignore it. He sighed with frustration. What the hell? He left the laptop, cursor blinking, and pushed open the window curtains. He looked out the dusty glass into the parking lot, but saw nothing. It was dark outside at that hour. No one was standing within his view. But then a small rock came bouncing across the sidewalk. It came to rest just below his window. Someone had kicked it.

"Come on," Tyler said. "I'm trying to write."

Tyler marched over to the door, turned the deadbolt, and flung it open to the desert air. A sudden cloud of the sweet smoke came rushing into the room. The smoke filled his nose so quickly that he stepped back for a moment to catch his breath. He could see more of it hovering in a faint trail outside. He poked his head out, trying to find the source of the mysterious cloud.

"Is it bothering you?" a man said in a grizzled voice. He spoke from somewhere inside the cloud. Tyler stepped outside, squinted into the smoke, and found him. It was the man from the room next door. He was seated comfortably on a plastic chair with his legs crossed. In his right hand, up and away from his chin and pinched between two fingers, was a half-smoked crackling cigarette.

"What are you smoking?" Tyler asked.

"Indonesian cigarettes. They taste like cloves," the man said. "You want one?"

"No," Tyler said. He hadn't smoked since college. His roommate Rennie couldn't stand the stink. Tyler wanted the man to drop his Indonesian cigarette, stomp on it, and go back inside his room. Lock the door behind him. Say nothing and sit quietly inside. There was writing to be done. "You've been to Indonesia?"

"Oh—once or twice. I tell my friends these are less addictive than American ones," he said with a mischievous smile.

"They believe you?" Tyler said, reaching back to close the door to his room to prevent more smoke from floating inside. He leaned against the wall, arms crossed.

"So far," he said, looking at his hand. "I should really quit. They're all too damned expensive now. I used to get a carton of Drinas for what one pack costs now." He mumbled some kind of curse word under his breath.

"Drina? Is that what those are called?"

"No, not these. No, Drina is a Bosnian brand. Former Yugoslavia."

"Have you been there too?"

"Once or twice," he said, smiling. He took another drag from his cigarette and sat quietly.

"Are you here to see the mural?" Tyler asked.

"No. Just traveling through. How about you?"

"I'm a journalist. Doing a story on it."

"Really? From Los Angeles?"

"No, Phoenix."

"Oh," he said. "I've never been there—good American city. Pretty hot, right?"

"Dry heat."

"That's what I hear," the man said. "In DC, we have humidity."

"Oh, do you work for the government?"

"Sure do. Yeah, I'm really more of an academic though."

"You're at a school?"

"A type of think tank."

"Lots of those in DC," Tyler said, glancing down at the man's hand to see if his cigarette was nearly done. It wasn't. "Do you like it?"

"Not really," the man said, scowling. He flicked the long tip of ashes from his cigarette onto the ground between his feet. "I serve my country though." There was an awkward silence.

"Are you traveling for work?"

"I'm using up my vacation days."

"How many do you have left?"

"Twenty-six," he said. His exactness suggested he might know the number of hours too. The Indonesian cigarette crackled and popped again as he held it to his lips and inhaled deeply. "So, you're writing a story about this painting?" he asked, his words coming out in a cloud of smoke.

"That's right."

"Well, it's your lucky day."

"Really?"

"I think you'll be interested in something I found," he said. "If you care."

"Sure."

"Well, all the hubbub over this painting made me curious. Naturally. I did a little digging. I have access to things. My line of work and all."

Research was part of the analyst's job. He was paid well for doing it. In this case, he'd delved deep into some archives—expansive ones that government analysts could access. The mural took the analyst on a quest of sorts. He wanted to know if something like it had happened before—was it part of a pattern? The analyst theorized it was some sort of tribute, maybe copycat art done in reference to something else, maybe from a previous era. Street art was all the rage worldwide, after all. But maybe there was no precedent at all. It took time. A lot of digging through gigabytes of useless data. Then he found something. He had found something he said was *very* interesting.

Tyler stood there listening, arms still crossed, amid a faint cloud of aromatic smoke. He tapped his foot anxiously on the pavement, but stopped when he noticed he was doing it.

Finally the analyst extinguished the butt of his Indonesian cigarette under his heel. Then he started talking about Germany
and the war and Hitler. He said he'd found an obscure and
otherwise insignificant record in the preserved Nazi archives
obtained by the US military after the war.

On July 18, 1937, Adolf Hitler gave a speech in Munich
to inaugurate the *Grosse Deutsche Kunstausstellung*, or the
Great German Art Exhibition, the analyst explained. The
Nazis wanted to purge German culture of "degenerate,"
"Bolshevik," and "Semitic" corruption in the arts. They
championed "pure" art. Art that conveyed true Aryan ideals
to society. It was the start of a grand propaganda effort to
promote the mythic nobility of the Germanic spirit that the
Third Reich sought to bring to global dominance. The day
after the inauguration, the Nazis opened a second and very
different exhibition in Munich. It was called *Entartete Kunst*,
or Degenerate Art. The work in this exhibit was declared the
antithesis of Aryan ideals. Consisting of over six hundred
works by over a hundred artists, including Marc Chagall and
Max Beckmann, the Degenerate Art exhibit was a showcase
that revealed how flawed, corrupt, and dangerous modern
society had become. The Nazis saw these works as having
been made by mentally deranged artists. The art itself was
thought to be incoherent and full of insults that demeaned
the German people. These works of degenerate art were
haphazardly displayed in small crowded rooms with slogans
painted across the walls to inform visitors about the true sinister nature of the work.

Many of the best known degenerate artists managed to escape the Nazis into new lives in exile. Max Ernst fled to America with the help of the Guggenheims. Paul Klee escaped to Switzerland. But the remaining unfortunates were subjected to surveillance and periodic raids from the infamous Gestapo. Banned from producing art or even possessing materials for creating art, violators were arrested and sent away to a special labor camp. Their crime was making art. The Nazis believed they had to keep the degenerate artists separate from other prisoners for fear that they would contaminate them with their deviant minds. Strangely, the name of that special camp, the analyst explained, was blotted out of the archival records with black ink. No one he consulted knew why. He could not find the name anywhere.

One of the artists taken to the camp was a thirty-two year old painter named Otto Fischer, arrested in 1939. His crime was keeping a small studio hidden in the cellar of his cottage outside of Mainz. During a surprise raid, just as the Gestapo was preparing to leave the Fischer cottage empty-handed, the commanding officer detected the faint scent of oil paints in the air. The Gestapo tore the room apart and found a hatch to the cellar beneath two carpets strategically placed across the floorboards. Fischer was beaten and hauled away immediately. Aside from his identification number and some scant information about his prison barracks, the archival records are entirely silent about Fischer's life in the camp. He was a faceless, starving slave, like countless other prisoners, but he survived.

The records thereafter jumped forward to the winter of 1941, when Fischer caused an enormous scandal that reached all the way to the office of the minister of public enlightenment and propaganda, Joseph Goebbels. Fischer had miraculously managed to escape the camp without a trace. But not before he had inexplicably obtained painting materials and produced a large elaborate mural on the wall of the largest barracks in the camp, presumably under the cover of night. The guards on duty that cold winter night, the records stated, were imprisoned for their unprecedented failure. The officers in charge of the camp were demoted and reassigned. Fischer's mural, it added, provoked great disorder and disobedience among the prisoners. There were crowds around the wall, and the guards had to use extensive force to disperse them, despite their fragile physical conditions. The Nazis feared that Fischer may have left secret instructions encoded in the mural explaining how to escape the camp and that only degenerate minds could decipher the message. Enormous tarps were quickly brought into the camp to cover the mural until intelligence officers could inspect it. A fierce manhunt began for Fischer in order to capture and thoroughly interrogate him.

"Here's where things get really strange," the analyst said. He had Tyler's full attention. "Fischer was never found. That entire camp? Abandoned. The Nazis razed the damned thing."

"What happened to everyone else?" Tyler asked.

"Transported to Sachsenhausen."

"Why would they destroy the camp?"

"I don't know, but the order came down from Goebbels himself," the analyst said quietly, as if sharing a secret. "*Goebbels.*"

"No sign of Fischer?"

"Gone. Presumed dead. He probably froze to death."

Tyler contemplated what the analyst had found. Was someone trying to reenact Otto Fischer's defiant act in the prison camp? Why in Ketchum, Arizona? There was no obvious connection between the two, but the parallels were intriguing. Tyler was about to ask more questions when someone approached along the walkway. It was Doris O'Brien.

"Did you lock yourselves out?" she asked.

"No," the analyst said. "How are you tonight?"

"I got a noise complaint," she said. Doris stopped and stood there staring.

"We didn't call," Tyler finally said.

"I know that. You're the noise," she said, looking at the analyst's cigarette on the ground. She pointed. "That's not marijuana, is it?"

"That?" the analyst said, looking down. "No, it's just a cigarette."

"Marijuana isn't legal in Arizona," she continued. "Have to go to Colorado for that."

"It's just a cigarette," the analyst repeated.

Doris paused awkwardly, looking at the analyst with her hands on her hips. "Finish your story yet?" Doris said, turning to Tyler.

"Still working on it," Tyler said. He was tired of that question. "In fact, I should get back to it."

"Yes, I'll say good night too. I'm off tomorrow," the analyst said.

"Headed for Colorado?" asked Doris.

"No, the Grand Canyon, I think."

"Well, good night then," Doris said. "Bob and I have a show to watch." She started down the walkway toward her office. Neither Tyler nor the analyst returned to their rooms when she was out of sight.

"She is odd," said the analyst.

"Somewhat. Did you find anything else about Otto Fischer?"

"I'm afraid that's it," he said, raising his hands like he'd just made a dove disappear.

"There's nothing?"

"Everything else predates the war."

"Well, thanks for sharing it. It's useful. I didn't catch your name?"

"Wood," the analyst said. "Jerome Wood."

"I'm Tyler Anderson." The two shook hands. "Is it *Doctor* Wood?"

"Yes," he said. "But I think it sounds pretentious."

"You earned it. Might as well use it."

"I suppose."

"Are you really going to the Grand Canyon?"

"I'm headed that way," he said.

After saying good night, Tyler returned to his room. His laptop was waiting for him on the shoddy old desk. Much to his chagrin, he could still smell the smoke of Wood's cigarette in the air. He sniffed the sleeve of his shirt. The smell had locked into his clothes. Annoyed, he confronted the greatest of his frustrations: the flow of words to his fingertips had stopped. It would take some work to get them running again. Tyler reviewed his notes from the town meeting. He flipped pages and studied his messy handwriting. He double-checked the way he'd worded a few things in the material that he'd typed up before his discussion with the analyst. It didn't take long. He glanced over at the bed and considered flopping down on his back again to stare at the ceiling. There was a TV in his room too. He hadn't even touched it since arriving. It was bigger than his TV at home. Maybe he could relax and watch a show for an hour. That might help. He would even take off his shoes.

Tyler turned on the TV and sat down on the edge of the bed. There was a network cop drama on the first channel. It was one of the shows with countless spin-offs. Tyler didn't know the name of it, nor did he think he'd seen it before. Somehow he recognized it though. A murder had occurred. Two attractive detectives were interrogating a witness or suspect (he couldn't tell which) with aggressive, straight-to-the-point questions. It was formulaic and dull. Tyler pondered taking a second look at his notes. He kicked his shoes against the wall with two thuds.

Hearing the ongoing discussion of the murder on the TV, Tyler thought about the possibility that the artist had died. Maybe he or she was murdered. In Ketchum though? Perhaps a suicide—someone in financial ruin. If that were true, there could be a connection to Otto Fischer. Maybe it was all about making art as a final good-bye statement. Fischer had presumably died, after all. One would think such a painting would look panicked and anxious, not beautiful and awe-inspiring. It was all a stretch, he decided. Tyler turned off the TV and lay back on the bed to stare at the ceiling.

XII

As Tyler wrote, the disturbing look of pleasure on Samuel Welch's face flooded his mind. Tyler stirred, rubbed his eyes, thought. There was something in Samuel's eyes and the tone of his voice back there. The enmity between him and George Correa was deep, Tyler was sure. It went far beyond some disagreement over a painting on a warehouse wall. It must have festered for years. This bizarre incident was just the latest in a long history of bitter quarrels. Tyler was interested in knowing the stories of that long history. His obsessive curiosity would demand answers. As would his editor Rebecca.

The next morning, Tyler walked down Main Street. He worked the crowd by the mural, asking everyone about the two men. He conversed with impatient dog walkers near the motel. He talked to an old woman by the hardware store. Some people edged away quickly. A few who took the time suggested it was all political. Indeed, politics was an ugly business, even in small towns like Ketchum. But most people agreed that the enmity stemmed from one man's broken heart. Back at the motel, Tyler went to see Doris to hear her thoughts.

"Samuel Welch had a thing, you could say, for Daisy—Mrs. Correa. *Years* ago though, mind you. He wasn't such a sourpuss back then."

"She turned him down?" Tyler asked.

"Sort of. She strung him along, I guess—spent time with him. He took her out. Dinners and such. I suppose she liked him. He was a gentleman."

"Just not her type," he said, familiar with such situations.

"*George* was her type. The man has charisma. Some men just have it—like my Bob," she said, smiling at the last part. "Anyway, Sam never got over it. Like an old festering wound—pardon the analogy. He probably doesn't even remember why he hates George so much. It's been so long now."

"This is great—I mean, very helpful," Tyler said.

"Oh, you're not going to print all that—are you?"

"No," Tyler assured her. Writing about gossip was beneath him. He would treat it with the utmost care and sensitivity. Tyler had no interest in exposing the personal grievances of small-town folks for the amusement of the city dwellers. There was no point in that. But he couldn't ignore the bitter rivalry that might decide the fate of the mural either. The idea that one man's heartbreak might destroy an artistic master-piece was shocking, yet tragically poetic. It was a most delicate matter indeed.

Tyler left the motel in search of solace and salty food at Abdullah Park's diner. Having the chance to see Audrey Betz again was also enticing. Indeed, Tyler couldn't recall the last time he felt this way—there was excitement in his chest. In the past, such feelings usually led to bad decisions and irrational behavior. Nevertheless, he found some joy in it.

XIII

Down along Main Street, Tyler Anderson ambled toward the diner. There were people everywhere. A young man was sitting alone on one of the tree-trunk benches Tyler so admired. He was noticcably different than the other tourists in Ketchum—the ones bustling around with cameras and shopping bags. The young man held a smoldering American cigarette between his lips. He stared down at the sidewalk with tired eyes through crooked eyeglasses with dirty lenses. On his forearm—exposed by a faded short-sleeved shirt (ideal for the Arizona heat)—Tyler noticed a tattoo, and his short brown hair was cut haphazardly, as though he'd done it himself.

"Look at all those people," Tyler thought. He was hesitant to immerse himself in the crowd just yet. The sun was shining and cooking the concrete beneath his feet. Sweat had gathered on his brow and a salty drop of it had managed to invade his right eye. He blinked uncomfortably. The damp bodies bunched before the diner looked like a fence. The bench, meanwhile, was situated under a storefront awning that created a good stretch of shade. The pedestrian traffic in front of it was light too.

Tyler decided to join the young man and sit on the end of the bench. Working hard all morning, he sighed to indicate that he was just taking a rest. He wouldn't stay long. He leaned back and watched the people on the street, listening to snippets of their conversations. Most of it was about the amazing mural.

"Are you from Ketchum?" Tyler finally asked the young man.

"No," he said, pulling the cigarette from his mouth. He turned his head to blow the smoke out.

"Where are you from?"

"New York."

"Manhattan?"

"No, New York State," he said, a hint of irritation in his voice. "I'm moving to Phoenix though."

"I live in Phoenix." Tyler said. He paused, waiting for any questions the young man might have. None came. "Are you here to see the mural?" Tyler said.

"I guess so. Sort of hard to miss, right?"

"Yes. Pretty incredible, isn't it?"

"Yeah," he said with a nod. He took a long drag from his cigarette. Then he exhaled slowly through his nose.

"It's an impressive work," Tyler said. "So strange to find it out here though."

"Yeah, the world is a weird place."

"I'm writing a story about it."

"Really? What kind of story?"

"It's an article for a news site. We're based in Phoenix."

"You get paid for that?"

"I sure do."

"That's pretty cool. You're not going to quote me, are you?"

"No, I'm off the clock."

The young man smirked, nodded and smoked. He looked at the crowds and the people snapping pictures at the warehouse. "I was thinking I might just stay."

"Stay in Ketchum? Really?"

The young man shrugged.

"It's a nice town," Tyler said.

The young man took another drag from his cigarette. "I like it here," he said, looking over at Tyler to see if he agreed or not. "How hot does it get in Phoenix?" he said, changing the subject.

"It's a dry heat," Tyler said.

The young man nodded. "I've heard that. Are the people there nice?"

"Nice? Same as anywhere, I guess," Tyler said, pondering the meaning of "nice."

"People share so much in common, you know? Too many people focus on the differences. I can't even watch the news on TV. It just depresses me too much."

Tyler understood, but he had no time for a deep conversation. He wished the young man good luck in Phoenix and left him to his thoughts on the bench.

Getting closer to the diner, Tyler watched a flurry of activity. Customers were coming and going like ants from the entrance at an almost constant rate. A pair of little boys spilled out, licking towering ice cream cones. A bit further over, a man was waiting for someone and anxiously looked at his watch. Then a woman in a sundress arrived and walked inside with the man. Meanwhile, a family of four piled out the door and nearly knocked the couple over.

Inside of the diner, Tyler found all the little white tables occupied. Mostly by unfamiliar people. Tourists. Audrey and a second waitress raced around the room, carrying trays of food and cold drinks. The air was buzzing with the indecipherable hum of conversation—a striking contrast to the quiet of last night. Tyler felt an immediate sense of anxiety tighten his chest. But in his head, a little voice encouraged him to stay.

Tyler took one of the only available seats, a stool at the counter.

Abdullah, tending the grill, tossed him a smile and a nod. The air was teaming with rich succulent smells from the grill and the deep fryer bubbling beside it. Abdullah was busy, but happy to have the business. He turned his big body toward the counter. "Another burger?"

"I'd love one," Tyler said.

"Good man." Abdullah smiled and dropped a red meat patty onto the hot grill. It hissed as it started to cook beside a row of brown meat and bacon. "How's the story coming?"

"It's complicated," Tyler said. "I thought small-town life was supposed to be simple."

"People are complicated everywhere you go. Trust me on that."

"I suppose you're right. How come you weren't at the meeting last night?"

"Had to work, man."

"Yeah, looks like you're staying busy."

"Almost nonstop," Abdullah said. "That mural's definitely good for business. Might even run out of fries."

Tyler smiled. He could hear the excitement in the golem's voice. The people in the diner seemed excited too. There was laughter and storytelling. People were enjoying their food, even if it didn't meet the standards of fine cuisine for the health conscious. Tyler looked over his shoulder to find Audrey. A quick glance would do. To his surprise, he found her heading for him. His heart fluttered.

Audrey held an order pad in her hand and pulled a pencil down from her ear. A hint of perspiration made her face glisten ever so slightly under the ceiling lights. She brushed a strand of hair away from her eye and smiled. She took a deep breath.

"Hey there, did you order yet?" she said.

"Yeah, I'm all set. How are you?" he quickly added to keep her from leaving.

"Busy! Can you believe all these people?"

"They heard about my cooking," Abdullah said loudly, as he stood over the hot grill.

"Anyway, how's your story going?" Audrey said.

"Good, really good." Tyler tried to sound positive and interesting. "I saw you over at the town meeting last night."

"Yeah? You couldn't say hello?"

"I didn't have the chance. Working."

There was a customer waving his hand from a table in the rear of the room, urgently trying to get Audrey's attention. Meanwhile, a young couple came in the front door and sat down at a newly open table. Sweaty, they headed right for the drinks section of the menu.

"I better get back to these tables." She sounded deflated.

"Could we talk later?" Tyler said.

"Sure. About what?"

"I need more advice."

XIV

Tyler and Audrey met that evening after her shift was over. She lived a short distance from the Saguaro Motel. It was a small, refurbished apartment. It once served as a type of guest residence for the disgraced family of Argus Gord. The unit was reportedly the most affordable rental in Ketchum. Associated with a troubling past—the sort of things that feed small-town gossip and urban legend for decades—the Gord house had become the apogee of local lore.

The large, charming, and well-built house, despite the reputable conduct of its current residents (retirees with dogs), was forever linked to tragedies of the past. In fact, the people of Ketchum seldom spoke the name of Gord without some sneering hint of disdain. It had become a part of the local dialect. A girl named Karen McKee had died there—murdered. It was many years ago now, but those sorts of dark events were few and far between in Ketchum and not easily forgotten by the community.

Tyler arrived at the house in his 1997 sedan with the A/C on full. The trip was just far enough to warrant driving rather than walking, especially in the heat. Much to his surprise, Tyler managed to arrive without any wrong turns. His father used to call them "scenic tours." It had helped that there were so few wrong turns to make. He reached Audrey's address quicker than he expected as a result, so he sat for some time and looked out the window at the Gord house. He admired its style and craftsmanship. It was well-maintained with unusual gothic elements, like pointed arches and a steeply pitched, cross-gabled roof with ornate bargeboards.

The seclusion of the house—no neighbor within sight—struck Tyler as he sat waiting. It sent a curious chill up his spine. Why would someone as lovely as Audrey hide out here? He imagined several fictional scenarios to resolve the mystery. Meth lab. Or maybe a recluse who hoards garage-sale trinkets. Or maybe an eccentric outdoors enthusiast who values easy access to the uninhabited desert for communing with nature in the nude.

Tyler watched the digital clock in his car tick—slowly. He put his fingertips against an air vent on the dash. Tyler wondered if the A/C was about to break. He checked the clock again. One minute had passed. "I could be writing right now," he thought.

When Tyler saw that sufficient time had passed and he was no longer too early, he went around the back and knocked on the door as instructed. Quiet. He waited until he saw her face peak out from behind the curtain of a small window overlooking the driveway. The mere sight of her made Tyler smile. The sound of footsteps coming down wooden stairs followed—a series of thuds that grew louder. Then he heard the firm click of the door being unlocked.

"Did you find it okay?" she said as she opened the door.

"Yeah, no problem. Thanks."

"Well, come on in," she said with a laugh, and she ushered him up the stairs. "Can I get you a soda or some water?"

They reached the top of the stairs and entered her small, warm apartment.

"Some water would be great," he said. "This is an interesting place. How did you find it?"

"Word of mouth." She took a small glass from a cupboard and filled it at the sink. Audrey placed the glass on the table and sat down in a chair that creaked loudly under her modest weight. "I like it. Plenty of privacy. So, what did you want to talk about?"

"Right, the advice. So, let me see. What can you tell me about Daisy Correa?" Tyler said, picking up the glass of water.

"George's wife?" Audrey said. She tucked her feet up onto the chair. "Why? You think *she* painted it?"

"No. That argument earlier—between Sam Welch and George," he said. "People tell me those two were rivals once. That would add a whole new dimension to this."

"How so?"

"Well, what if Welch destroyed the mural to get back at George?"

"Ew—I don't know. Men do crazy things over women," she said.

"I know I have."

"Really? Like what?"

"I plead the fifth," Tyler said.

"Oh, spill it. I gave you water."

"Sam Welch," Tyler said, quickly steering the conversation back on course.

"You should go talk to him. Don't you think?"

"You're much easier to talk to," Tyler said.

"Part of the job. It's all about the tips." She rubbed her thumb and index finger together and smiled.

Tyler adored that smile. It made him feel positively stupid. It had even started to rival the mural. Being in her apartment and laughing over the bickering Samuel Welch was so wonderfully different than what he had known as so horribly routine back in Phoenix. Nevertheless, her modest home reminded him a lot of his own apartment—the sparseness and simplicity. He tried to ignore the familiarity of it and focus on her smile instead.

"Can I ask *you* a question?" she said. "Is that allowed?"

He chuckled. "I think that's only fair."

"Great! So, why did you become a writer? Is that what you've always wanted to do or—?" She broke off, eyebrows raised.

"Sort of; I was raised to be a writer," Tyler said. "Novels, though, I guess. Not the news."

"Are your parents writers?"

"No. My Dad wrote, but not professionally."

"Why the push then?" Audrey said.

"Well, when I was growing up, we revered writers like saints. We didn't talk sports; we talked Hemingway, Faulkner, and Fitzgerald. Dad insisted on reading everything I wrote for English class. He'd even take out a red pen and give me his edits." Tyler drew invisible corrections in the air.

"That doesn't sound like fun."

"No, it wasn't," Tyler said. "I couldn't write a sentence without worrying about what he was going to say about it. And that's no way to write."

"How did you get into journalism?"

"That's a long story."

"I asked you, didn't I?"

"It's boring. I'll bore you," Tyler said.

"I'm not bored."

"But you could be."

"Just tell me," she said.

"Okay, I'll try to make it short. So, there was this big legal case. This is when I was a freshman. It involved a drug company. It was all about this drug called Vexor. It made tons of money. But it turned out that the company hid these studies showing that the drug had all these dangerous side-effects. People even died from taking Vexor. And they'd funded counterstudies to show the drug was safe."

"I think I remember that."

"Yeah, it was a big story. Well, the people that blew the lid off the whole thing were these two journalists. They forced the drug off the market—saved lives."

"That's amazing."

"Yeah. It really made me stop and think, 'Hey, I want to do that. I want to change things, hold people accountable. Do it by writing instead of fighting or something.' Art can be socially transformative."

"Totally," Audrey said, supportively.

"Although, I have to admit, I do struggle with it sometimes. You know, journalistic writing—it puts these limits on creativity. The stuff I do is rarely what I would really call 'art'."

"Well, that's still cool," she said. "Have you had any big stories? Like the drug company one?"

"No," Tyler said, looking down at his water. "Now I'm just trying to make ends meet."

"I think the mural's a good story," she said. "I'd like to write about it."

"Yeah. It's new, at least. I'll give it that," Tyler said. "So— think George can save it?"

"No," she said bluntly. "But he'll try."

Sitting at the table for the next two hours, Audrey shared stories of impatient and eccentric customers from the diner and Tyler laughed like he hadn't in a long time. Then she told him about how a snake once slithered up into the engine of her car. Tyler countered with a story about how he'd once caught Harry Gleason asleep at his desk. Tyler woke him by playing the state university fight song as loud as he could over his computer speakers. Harry was not amused, he said. Audrey laughed. The sound of Audrey's voice was a nice change. And she put her smile to good use that night. Neither Tyler nor Audrey took notice of the time. It was only Tyler's buzzing cell phone, tucked away in his pocket, which finally broke the spell.

He knew it was Rebecca before he even saw the number on the screen. A blue light was blinking. She had left a voice mail message. Tyler turned the phone off and tried to return to the conversation as if he'd never left it. It was like trying to return to a dream by going back to sleep. It didn't work.

"Is that important?" Audrey asked, acknowledging the call.

"No."

But Tyler's thoughts had been diverted to the story. He had lots to write. He glanced at the clock in Audrey's apartment for the first time. Did he have more questions to ask her? "I have a few more questions before I go," he said.

"Okay," she said.

"The mining business is largely finished here, so economic opportunities are few and far between. Why did you choose Ketchum of all places?"

Audrey's smile was replaced by something else; an unconvincing expression of ease. Disappointment seeped into her eyes. She turned and glanced at the clock in the corner. There was a brief pause, and it seemed like an eternity. He desperately wished he could take back his question. It wasn't even important.

"I just got tired of the city," Audrey said, and she left the table. "This seemed like a faraway place. I figured I'd find some sort of work." She put the two glasses, long since emptied, into the kitchen sink. "Sometimes you just need to get away."

"I understand completely," he said, trying to reassure her. "That's the reason I wanted to cover this story about the mural."

Audrey glanced over at the clock a second time. She hesitated. "It's starting to get late. I have to work in the morning. Is it okay if we call it a night?"

"Yeah, sure," Tyler said. He collected his notes and stood up from the table. "Sorry, I got caught up in your stories. I didn't mean to take up so much time."

"It's fine. I just need to stay on my schedule, or I'll be a wreck tomorrow."

"Lots of customers these days," Tyler said.

"Yeah. Abdullah will never shut up if he sees me dragging my feet all day."

"Sure," Tyler said, smiling.

"Thanks," Audrey said, and she ushered him over to the door.

"Hey, by the way, do you know if Abdullah is a Muslim?"

"A Muslim? No, I don't think so," she said. "He's kind of private, but I think he's an atheist or an agnostic. Whichever."

"Interesting," Tyler said. "I thought with the name—anyway, thanks again."

Tyler left that night with the feeling that he might have ruined something before it started. "Great job," he muttered in the car. He should have gone to George's office. He should have tracked down Samuel Welch for an interview. That's what he needed to do. He was letting himself get in the way. It had to stop. It was "a dereliction of duty," he imagined his father saying, although he couldn't recall his father ever actually using that phrase or saying anything remotely like that.

Tyler looked at the clock in the dashboard of his car. He'd been inside Audrey's apartment for over two hours. He remained unsure whether or not it was time well spent. His brain said no, but his heart said something else.

The illuminated cactus sign of the Saguaro Motel was a welcome sight when it appeared on the road ahead. Tyler's car rolled into the parking lot and came to a stop. He turned off the engine, paused to clear his head, and stepped outside. There were cars in nearly every spot. The presence of more cars, the outside world coming into Ketchum, was an unwelcome reminder that time really was ticking away. The city would pull him back soon.

Inside his motel room, Tyler placed his laptop beside him on the bed. After staring at it for several seconds, he began an e-mail to Rebecca. He didn't want to call her. He preferred not to talk on the phone. His message to Rebecca was short and professional. Tyler assured her that everything was going well. He would have his story finished and over to her "very soon."

After Tyler sent the message, he returned to the story. His old friend—the cursor—was waiting and winking back at him. He could see the narrative taking shape on the electronic page. Coming into being. It had its form and its characters and its conflicts, and his story's villain was Samuel Welch.

XV

Samuel Welch—the man, not the villain—first noticed Daisy Monroe at school when they were teenagers. She was two years his junior. When it was time for the senior dance, Samuel knew instantly whom he wanted to invite. He summoned up the courage to ask her, despite all impulses to the contrary in his head. His hands were sweaty. She smiled and blushed. Daisy was terribly flattered by the invitation. She had never been invited to a dance by a boy before, much less an older boy from the senior class. Samuel was the first.

The night of the dance, Daisy wore an aqua-blue dress with ruffles around the collar. She adorned her sky blue eyes with a hint of black mascara. Her hair was up. Around her exposed neck, she wore a silver necklace. Samuel had never seen her wear makeup before. He thought she looked so glamorous. He was speechless when she met him at the door. That memory would endure in his mind like a photograph. He would never forget the way she looked that night.

The young couple danced to nearly every song. They spoke about small things, and when she was thirsty, Samuel brought her a glass of fruit punch with ice. When the last song played and the gymnasium emptied, he brought Daisy home in his father's truck, which he'd borrowed special that night. Samuel wanted to kiss her, and he watched carefully for any hint or sign that she felt the same way. In the end, though, he asked only to hug her, and she gave him a brief embrace before disappearing into the house. Perhaps next time.

Samuel came to visit Daisy from time to time after that. He hoped his attention and a few tokens of his affection might win her over. He brought her flowers some days, chocolates when it was cool outside. On pleasant evenings, he and Daisy would sit together on the front porch and talk until it was dark and her mother called her inside. In time, Samuel grew fond of telling Daisy how she was the most beautiful girl he had ever met. Daisy's reaction was never quite what he hoped for. She would smile and laugh, or change the subject, or thank him and compliment something about him in return, usually his manners.

Mr. Welch, Samuel's father, was a stern but successful businessman. He made a good living as a small shareholder in the local copper mines. It was always understood that Samuel would follow in his father's footsteps and take up the family business. In fact, Samuel started working for his father that same year, every day after school. The conversations around the dinner table at the Welch house were always the same, sounding very much like business meetings. That was what life was about there. Samuel had little choice in the matter.

Sometimes, the pressure of Samuel's inheritance proved to be too much, the family's expectations suffocating. He would get into fistfights at school just to breathe. No one in the school or the community seemed to recognize the responsibility he'd been given, nor did they properly respect it, in his view. He deeply resented being lumped in with the children of laborers and cooks and cashiers in Ketchum. He deserved a life in the city, he thought.

After high school graduation, Samuel went away to study in Phoenix for a time, much to the chagrin of his father. He returned home during the summers. When home, Samuel visited Daisy often. When he was away, he would write her letters. She would usually write him back, even if it sometimes took a while. By the time Samuel quit school in Phoenix and returned for good, another local boy, George Correa, had started to visit the Monroe house too. It wasn't long before Samuel came across George and Daisy spending time together.

As Mr. Welch suffered from declining health, Samuel assumed an ever-increasing role in the business. No longer insistent on a city life, Samuel knew himself a worthwhile suitor for any girl in town. He certainly felt he was a better man than George. But Daisy never showed much interest in her "friend Sam," granting him no more than an occasional hug. "One day," Samuel convinced himself.

It shook Samuel to the core when he heard that Daisy kissed George at a friend's birthday party. The news made him physically ill. When he asked her if it was true, Daisy curtly replied that it never happened. Sensing he might lose her forever, Samuel apologized for accusing her so rudely. He chose to believe her, but would never shake that terrible feeling that she had lied, no matter how hard he tried.

When the Fourth of July came that year and Ketchum's barbeques were cooking, Daisy and Samuel made plans together. They sat on a picnic blanket eating small cups of ice cream Samuel brought to surprise her. Together again, the two watched the local display of fireworks burst and flash in the clear desert sky. Samuel hoped such a setting might spark some feelings and bring the two of them together. There was no place else on earth he would rather have been that night.

As Samuel parked his new car—proudly purchased with his own earnings—he climbed out, opened the door for Daisy, and stood there as she stepped out. He looked into her eyes and waited. He wanted so badly to kiss her, if only just once. He would settle for one kiss for the rest of his life, he thought. Just one. She stood for a moment outside the car and smiled, then said good-bye and thank you. She walked up the stairs to the porch and gave one final wave. Then she disappeared through the screen door. It snapped closed behind her. And like that, the night was over.

The following Friday after work, Samuel drove over to Daisy's only to learn that she had gone out with George. It became an increasingly common occurrence. She seldom seemed to find time to spend with "Sam" anymore. Of course, Samuel could have saved himself the trouble of those trips. He could have used the telephone, but he wanted to see her. Even if she already made other plans, the chance to see her, even for a minute, was worth the inconvenience. The fact that Samuel usually left her house feeling worthless and angry seldom entered into his mind until after the fact.

Samuel continued to devote his time and affection to Daisy, even as her blooming relationship with George moved from lies and secrets to common knowledge. For her part, Daisy continued to see Samuel on occasion, preserving their friendship. Daisy thought she was being kind and sweet. Samuel was always nice, and he could make her laugh. It was a game that she never took too seriously. Samuel refused to see the truth of it for some time. He clung to the thought that "next time" or "someday" they might be together, even as the facts were staring him square in the face.

Every once in a while, Samuel would decide to stop calling or stop visiting. He would count the number of days that passed, promising he would do nothing to contact her. Daisy would have to make first contact, he'd decide. She would do it if she cared about him. It was always much harder to do than he imagined. The fact that Daisy could go weeks without even saying hello to him was heartbreaking. "Not even a god-damned hello," he would mutter. Samuel had casual friends around town who would swing by his father's office on an average afternoon just to talk for a few minutes. There was nothing special about those friendships. Daisy was someone important to him, yet she acted so much like a stranger. Or simply like a person who didn't care much about him at all.

Samuel would break his pledges, of course. He would call Daisy up on the telephone, motivated by a resurgence of desperate optimism. She'd say hello in a friendly way, acting as if nothing was wrong. She always seemed not to notice how much time had elapsed since they last spoke. To make matters worse, Daisy would even talk about George, making comments about their time together and what the future might bring. It seemed deliberately hurtful. Samuel was no longer a man in her eyes at all, but an object of pity that operated in a different world than her own.

Set in his ways, Samuel endured this as long as any man possibly could. And he knew he was more than good enough for Daisy. After all, the Monroe family was "nothing special." Then he finally came to say, "Enough. No more." He still had his pride, after all. He would not spend another moment of his life on that "vapid, self-absorbed" Daisy Monroe. He no longer called her on the telephone. He made sure not to drive past her little house if he could avoid it. He was finished wasting his life on her.

Still, Samuel would slip at times. Just when he felt he had his jealous anger under control, old emotions resurfaced. He would dream about her calling him or coming to visit him. She would ask what was wrong, or where he had been all those months. That moment never came, though. Daisy seemed not to notice Samuel's absence from her life at all. That fact was very telling. He was away on a business trip in the city the day Daisy and George were married. But he always came home to Ketchum.

XVI

Samuel Welch's very public and provocative threat to destroy the mural—stubbornly calling it an act of vandalism—made the search for the mysterious artist all the more urgent. No one, however, had even the slightest idea who the artist might be. The whimsical observations and claims of Kathleen Morales were well known, but she offered nothing in terms of substance or concrete leads that anyone might follow. And after her spirited outburst at the town meeting, very few were interested in broaching the subject of the mural with her again.

Tyler spent the morning locked in his room at the Saguaro. He sat on his excessively soft mattress, sheets kicked down, with his computer on his lap, typing at a dizzying and obsessive pace. He was building his narrative piece by piece, as though a tower were being built block by block. And, since the previous night's encounter with Audrey Betz, he was unsure about his own role in the narrative.

The subtext of the tale was the author himself. Tyler had become involved in the events of the town. The line between author and character was blurred. Tyler had become one of a growing number of people touched by the mural. He would not, however, passively accept that role. On the contrary, he was working hard to excuse himself from it. He was an objective observer, he told himself, looking into the story of Ketchum dispassionately from the outside. But he'd never expected to find someone like Audrey. And as he wrote that morning in his motel room, Tyler was sure for a moment that he could hear the familiar sound of his small television playing somewhere in the background.

It was that same day that news broke about the identity of the artist. Tyler had hidden himself away in the motel and was not the first to hear it. A local man named Grady James had come forward. No one expected so sudden an announcement, given the failure of the town meeting only two days prior. In a short statement, he declared that he could no longer sit idly by and let matters continue as they were. A press conference was promptly scheduled, and the media in Ketchum was positively abuzz. Upon finally hearing the news, a flustered Tyler knew that he would have to revise his story a great deal. The ending to his tale was as yet unwritten.

Grady James had lived on the edge of town for a decade but was hardly prominent in the community. He'd arrived in Ketchum from Boston, accent and all, searching for artistic inspiration amid the rocky desert landscapes of rural Arizona and some affordable housing with space for an artist's studio. Watercolor was Grady's medium of choice. He had painted hundreds of landscapes—some large and many small—over the years. The perilous art market, however, never welcomed him.

Grady survived largely on odd jobs around town and government assistance. He tried teaching art classes, but he was a poor and impatient instructor, and few students had interest in working with him. Every now and again, he was able to sell one of his paintings. Two summers ago, he'd sold a large watercolor landscape to a dermatologist in Scottsdale who was redecorating the waiting room of his office. That was the typical fate of Grady's most successful paintings—not venerable public museums or elite private galleries in Los Angeles or New York, but waiting rooms, lobbies, and tacky family restaurants, thanks to their safe, pleasant, and unobtrusive nature.

There was nothing offensive, controversial, or revealing about his pretty pictures of a desert or a tree or a mountain or some rocks. The modern camera allowed anyone to document such scenes with the push of a button and print them to any size desired. Some would go so far as to say that Grady James was not an artist at all but an interior decorator of sorts. He documented what he saw in nature—typically in an idealized fashion—yet shared nothing of his imagination, himself, or his humanity. And like a family photograph, his works were framed and placed casually on walls of rooms where absolutely no one wanted to stay. For an artist like Grady, creating a work like the mural would have been nothing short of a revolutionary breakthrough.

Even before the press conference in Ketchum, the news about Grady's identity had spread quickly. The telephone at his house was ringing nearly nonstop. That had never happened before. There were calls from as far away as New York City, and art dealers left message after message. That never happened before either. None of them mentioned his watercolor pieces, though. It was only the mural that anyone was interested in talking about. It was the mural that everyone wanted.

Grady was able to decipher from the voice mail messages that people were seeing pictures of the mural across the country, exchanged via cell phones and digital cameras, posted to social media sites, in some cases. One call mentioned something about a video. A different caller inquired about commissioning Grady to do a mural for a city hall somewhere in northern California. Another message was left by a strange (possibly inebriated) woman in Oregon expressing her desire to pose nude for Grady at his studio. Still another message came from a school of art and design in Florida, asking about his teaching experience. In a single day, the life of Grady James was utterly transformed. He smiled and laughed out loud, alone in his house, listening to some messages multiple times.

The press conference was more than Grady expected. It had many of the circus elements that existed around the mural prior to the tragic accident involving the vendors. A stage was set up. On it was a table from which Grady would field questions from the assembly of interested reporters. George Correa would take the seat beside him, dressed in a suit and tie. Space had been designated for the media to capture perfect pictures. Rows of folding chairs took up several feet in front of the stage, and the fifty feet behind them was left wide open for standing crowds.

When George took the stage, he smiled and leaned toward a bundle of microphones. After greeting the crowd and telling two jokes, he offered prepared introductory remarks. He described the event as no less than an answer to the town's prayers, after the terrible damage done to the mural. More importantly, he said, it was the beginning of a new claim to fame for the town of Ketchum, still struggling to emerge from its copper mining past. The Boston-born Grady James, he explained, was a true son of Ketchum and a shining representative of their fine town for the world. "We might be a small town," he said, "but our people do big things!" He turned and raised a hand to the mural. There was laughter and applause.

Tyler could not help but cringe. He knew that the whole event might end in catastrophe. He was sure that George knew it too. The circus staged at the corner of Copper and Main rested on an unverified claim. Tyler wondered if George had ever even met Grady before that night. Simply wanting something to be true never made it so. The press was listening, though. There were multiple television cameras in town now and a dozen microphones and digital recorders sitting on the table in front of George as he spoke. Camera flashes popped like lightning every other second.

Grady sipped anxiously at a warm bottle of mineral water as he sat next to George. He kept forcing himself to look up and out at the reporters as he waited. But his head would inevitably drop back down. Sometimes he would futz with his clothing and seem to forget that everyone was watching. He wore a rustic buttoned shirt with long sleeves well suited for an artist specializing in rural landscapes. His hair was slicked back and tied neatly into a ponytail that hung down his upper back. The hair above his ears carried streaks of gray, revealing his age. And every so often, Grady would turn his head and glance up at the mural and smile as though he were very proud of his work.

When George finally concluded his monologue and ceded the spotlight to "Mr. James," Grady eagerly opened the press conference up to questions from reporters and all others assembled in the crowd. He had prepared no remarks or profound statement. The cameras burst into a momentary flurry, like a lightning storm, and he immediately turned to answering questions amid a chorus of clicks.

"What did you use to paint your mural? Is it acrylic?" one reporter asked.

"Is the weather going to damage it further?" another said.

"No," Grady said. "I think it should be fine, but I'll keep an eye on it. As for the medium, I used a mixture of different things. Ordinary house paints and some acrylics."

"How did you paint it so fast?" someone else shouted.

"Well, I knew what I wanted to do coming in. I actually did some initial drafting that no one noticed a few nights before. I just had to apply the paint, follow what I already had planned, and not second-guess myself. I thought someone was going to catch me too," he said with a big smile. "I was sure of it, but thankfully, no one noticed."

There was some laughter.

Tyler called out over the chuckles. "Why did you wait so long to identify yourself?"

"I wanted the art to speak for itself. It's really not about me. To be honest, if everyone hated it, I probably would have just kept quiet," he said, eliciting laughter.

Tyler did not laugh. He wrote studiously in his note pad. He was unconvinced and was annoyed that so many others there seemed to be buying his claims.

"When will you repair the mural?" a local woman asked with great concern.

"Very soon," Grady said. "I'll attend to it as soon as possible."

"What's next for you, Mr. James? Do you have any more works you can show us?" asked the pretty brunette from the television station.

"Well, as you know, I've been working with watercolor and selling my work for many years. Those works are available to anyone who would like to see or purchase them. It's only now that I've decided to make public the other techniques and different styles I've been developing privately for some time. So to answer your question, I think you'll definitely see more from me in the future."

"Do you have an agent now?" another reporter asked.

"Not yet," Grady said, smiling. "I've been getting calls all day, though, so I'll make those sorts of decisions in the coming days and weeks ahead."

George concluded the press conference with a surprise. Taking the microphone again, he smiled broadly. He'd been waiting for this. It was his grand finale.

"Ladies and gentlemen, while I still have you here, I'd like to make an announcement. As mayor of Ketchum, it is my great honor to announce plans for the construction of the Grady James Museum. Right here in Ketchum!"

There was great applause and a sudden hum of excited conversation in the air. Grady himself was wide-eyed and overwhelmed. Clearly it was the first time he had heard of it.

"This new building will house a first-rate gallery of Grady's paintings and will form the centerpiece of a new revitalized downtown," George said.

There was an even more enthusiastic round of applause now. Grady smiled broadly and put his right hand up against his chest. George smiled back at him and gave him a solid congratulatory pat on the back. The two men then stood, posing for the cameras, and Grady shook George's hand. Cameras flashed and clicked in another sudden burst.

As Tyler stood up to leave, intent on returning to the Saguaro Motel to work on his revisions, he saw the big figure of Abdullah Park standing alone in the back of the crowd with his arms crossed. He was easy to pick out. Approaching the golem, Tyler could already see the skepticism on his face.

"So, mystery solved, right?" Tyler said.

Abdullah gave Tyler a playful look of suspicion, arching his left eyebrow. "These people want to believe it," he said. "That still doesn't make it true. You can see why Grady's doing this."

"Well, they'll find out pretty quick if he can't produce anything to support his claims, don't you think?"

"Man, people believe way crazier shit than this. I had two Mormon missionaries come through my diner just last month. Tried to tell me how their little blue book came from some gold plates dug up on a hill in New York."

"What did you say?"

"I said you better order something or get out of my diner."

Tyler laughed.

"Look, how many people still think the world is six thousand years old? Or that we're the offspring of Adam and his incestuous kids? A lot, man. Here in the United States too, not just someplace like Afghanistan, where folks can't even read. People believe things because they want to believe it. Even if you put all evidence to the contrary in front of them."

"Yeah, I know. Is that so wrong, though?" Tyler asked.

"Yes. It is! My parents taught me not to lie. They said lying was a bad thing. But if you call people out, they act like *you're* the one acting wrong."

"It's only lying if the intent is to deceive someone," Tyler said. "Everyone can have an opinion."

"It's not about opinions. Not when people say they know the absolute truth. And that you don't. A person who makes a conscious choice to reject or ignore evidence that points in one direction for no other reason than they just want to believe otherwise? We don't allow that in the courts, do we?"

"No, we don't."

"So why put up with that bullshit everywhere else?" he said loudly. "It doesn't do us any good to let fairy tales and crazy old superstitions shape our society." There was a fire in his eyes.

Then there was a pause. Words were soaking in. Emotions settling down again.

"You're pretty deep for a short order cook," Tyler said.

"Like I told you, man, I've done a lot of things."

Abdullah was not the only skeptic in the crowd that night. Indeed, Samuel Welch was paying very close attention to these latest developments. As far as he was concerned, Grady was either an outrageous liar or the damned criminal who vandalized his private property. Either way, Samuel was going to press Mr. James for more information and act accordingly. He never cared for those worthless watercolors or the long-haired, welfare-taking man that made them. The fact that George took Grady's side and stood by his story on a stage in front of all those cameras was simply icing on the cake.

XVII

G rady James was all the rage the next day. The most fa- mous man in Ketchum. A public statement by Sheriff Weaver was made asking the media in town to respect his pri- vacy. Too many reporters had come knocking on his door. His voice mail was filling up with calls every hour. Someone was caught snooping in his backyard for artwork. His sudden fame was not so wonderful after all.

The crowds around the mural had quadrupled in size too, despite the loss of the grand mystery that once surrounded it. It was a state treasure, some began to say. Others went so far as to call it a national treasure. Still others announced a range of conspiracy theories about its origins. Some entertained ideas of aliens or spirits from Native American mythology, like kachinas. They insisted that no human being could ever produce something like it. One man even claimed he could see the face of Christ in the upper left corner.

As Tyler walked down to visit the mural again, he encoun- tered the foul stench of unattended garbage in the public trash bins. More and more rubbish and filth collected on the streets and sidewalks. So much attention had been given to the mural and the circus surrounding it that some people had neglected their ordinary day-to-day responsibilities. Tyler hadn't heard rumblings over any other interrupted services though, such as the mail or excessive employee absences. Business in Ketchum was good. He would investigate further. The possibility that the mural was lulling Ketchum residents into dangerous self-neglect added an ominous dimension to the story. Perhaps the beautiful mural was actually a nefarious Trojan horse of sorts, although he could hardly imagine anything so beautiful causing any harm at all.

The crowd at Welch's warehouse was bustling and exuberant and seemingly carefree. From what Tyler was able to overhear, some discussion went on about the exact identity of the human figure depicted in the center of the mural. Some suggested that it might be a self-portrait of Grady. Others saw many different people in the face of the figure, including lost loved ones and great cultural icons like FDR. It seemed that almost anyone could see something familiar in the face of the figure at the center of the mural. The man who saw the face of Christ began to insist that the figure in the center was Christ as well.

The one exception to this growing trend was Samuel Welch, who saw nothing but a stain on his property that needed a wash. He too came to the warehouse that day, sneering and staring at onlookers. He walked provocatively over the barrier erected to keep the crowds away from the damaged section. If he saw someone in the crowd drop anything, whether a gum wrapper or an empty water bottle, he'd point right at them and order them to pick it back up. "This ain't a damned park!" he barked at them.

Tyler decided it was time to talk to Samuel about his plans to whitewash the mural. He was skeptical that the threat was anything more than bluster. He couldn't imagine how anyone would want to destroy it. But Samuel was certainly a stern man who had already shown his anger and disinterest in pleasing his neighbors. He was a man who lived to defy expectations.

"Mr. Welch, when will you start painting over the mural?"

"Soon," he said. "Very soon." Samuel started walking the length of the warehouse wall.

Tyler stayed behind him like a bloodhound tracking a scent. "And you're doing this because you have a feud with Mayor Correa?"

"What's that?" Samuel said. He stopped and gave a small smile. A chuckle. "It figures that ol' Georgie would make this all about him. The man's a narcissist and a con man. You can quote me on that." He started walking the length of the warehouse again.

"And Mrs. Correa? What about her?" Tyler asked. "Is she as bad as her husband?"

Samuel stopped again. He paused. His smile was gone. The expression on his face turned very serious. "I think maybe it says something about her—that she chose a man like that."

"Is she the reason you have a feud?" Tyler asked bluntly.

"That's nonsense," Samuel said, shaking his head. "Now if you'll excuse me, I have work to do—unlike all these people apparently." And he walked away, reaching the back of his warehouse where the loading dock sits.

The work that Samuel was busy doing that day was planning. By dusk, he'd returned to the warehouse and summoned every remaining reporter in town. He issued a statement claiming that George Correa and Grady James were colluding in a grand hoax for their own personal gain. To prove it, he was challenging Grady to produce another work of art—publicly, in front of everyone—that could match the mural. That would settle it once and for all.

It was the first time anyone could recall hearing Samuel refer to the act of vandalism as "the mural." It did not, however, represent any softening of his feelings on the subject. Rather, it was only a strategic choice of words to reach an enamored public.

George didn't hesitate. He didn't even wait to confer with Grady. He saw the potential for a great public spectacle in the making and he was ready to put everything into motion. As most of the media was starting to return to their cities and next stories, they would have a reason to come back now or to stay and tell more stories about the town to the nation. It was perfect. It would happen immediately, George declared. And the work produced by Grady at the challenge event would serve as the new centerpiece for the museum the town was planning to build.

The sudden series of events took on a life of its own before Grady even knew what was happening.

Grady's humble home was located on the outskirts of Ketchum. It was on the opposite side of town from Audrey's home (the Argus Gord house). A dry riverbed ran through there, flooding sometimes during the seasonal monsoons, but little else of note stood near it. On very clear days, one could see very far out there and appreciate the vastness of the region and its birds and other wildlife too, especially in the mornings. Then the sun burned the effect off.

Grady had gone to sit alone in the dry riverbed that night. He sometimes worked on his watercolors down there during the winter months. However, on that particular evening, he was not working. Even if he wanted to work, it was too dark.

It was simply a quiet and secluded place to escape. Grady couldn't hear the sound of the telephone ringing there. No more strangers could come looking for him. No more of the same prying questions. There were only stars in the sky, and they asked nothing of him.

Alone, he smoked a hand-rolled, unfiltered cigarette. He sat on a stone, amazed at the events that had transpired over the prior twenty-four hours. Grady James went from an obscure and disrespected "starving artist" to the most talked about painter in the Southwest, perhaps the West Coast. Maybe, he dared imagine, throughout the entire country. He envisioned how his name was going to look chiseled over the grand wooden doors of the new museum. His body tingled with pride. It amazed him that the town would build it in his honor. He imagined how he would dress in a fine black suit and tie. Private gallery openings in New York and Los Angeles would surely follow too. Finally, it had all come true. The life of Grady James now had purpose. He nearly forgot that he was not the creator of the mural at all.

Back inside the house, there were new and important messages awaiting him on his voice mail. Those messages talked about something called the challenge. They described how he would paint a canvas before the entire town the next night. By the time Grady left his fantasies and seclusion at the riverbed and sat down to listen, it was too late to bring the grand spectacle to a halt. His chest suddenly felt very tight.

"What are you talking about?" he said, nearly shouting into the phone. "Art takes time," he rambled on, lecturing to the uninitiated. "This isn't finger painting. You can't just throw it down like some old sack."

After listening patiently, George calmly explained how everything would go smoothly. No one expected him to match the masterpiece at the corner of Copper and Main. He only had to show everyone his talent. He could do something simple, just for everyone to see. The publicity would be fantastic for him and, of course, for the town. It was a win-win situation, George insisted. The town would take care of procuring a fresh stretched canvas. It would pay for all the costs involved. All Grady had to do was show up and work for an hour or so. There was plenty of time to work on some drafts or some planning if that was his concern, George assured him.

Grady grew very quiet on the other end of the phone. A prolonged pause. When he finally spoke, a strange twinge of distress emerged in his voice. "Fine," he said with exasperation. Grady promised that he would come. He would do his best. After all, it was his moment to shine. It was his moment in the spotlight. He was a real artist, he reminded himself.

All his life, Grady James wanted to find fame and respect as a real bona fide artist. It had existential significance. It meant his life was worth something to someone. To the world. No more humiliating sales that banished his finest work to stuffy waiting rooms. No more cookie-cutter family restaurants—the antithesis of art and culture in every way. "I'm a great and talented artist," he reminded himself again. Everyone he ever knew—from the time he was a child—would know it. Now he would show everyone what he could do.

XVIII

On the day of the challenge, Tyler Anderson took an early lunch at Abdullah Park's diner. He sat at the counter as before and spoke to the golem at the grill over the sound of sizzling meat. Audrey Betz was waiting tables. She greeted him warmly, as though nothing unpleasant had happened between them. And Tyler believed that nothing had actually happened. It was entirely possible that he imagined the whole thing. His mind was prone to play such tricks. Perhaps she was simply too tired that night. Waiting tables was a thankless job. The influx of visitors to Ketchum had left her on her feet more in recent days than ever before. It would be foolish—indeed, narcissistic—to think that he alone could have been the source of her unease. Or her discomfort, or what he perceived as such. Or so Tyler tried hard to convince himself.

He smiled back at her. He spoke of inane things that were entirely safe and impersonal. It was only some minutes later—when chatter from an adjacent table regarding the challenge filtered into their own conversation—that the tone changed.

"Are you going to the event tonight?" Tyler asked.

"Yes. Well, I might," she said. "Depends on how busy we are." Audrey looked at Abdullah, as if awaiting approval.

"I'll be there. I'm not missing it for anything," Abdullah said, deciding the matter. "We're going to get right up there in the front for that train wreck, man. Five bucks says Grady passes out."

"You're terrible," Audrey said.

"You believe him?" Tyler asked.

"Sure. Why not? Someone had to do it. He paints."

"Sheep," Abdullah scoffed. "Turn your bullshit detector up."

"Whatever. The sooner it's settled the better. My feet are killing me," she said.

The table of tourists near the piano in the back required something. There were hands in the air waving frantically in Audrey's direction. She tried not to notice, but Abdullah gave a nod of his head in their direction.

Audrey sighed softly and left Tyler and Abdullah at the counter. She flipped on her smile and chatted personably with them when she arrived, as if they were her favorites. She showed no signs of discomfort from her feet or annoyance at the urgency with which they had summoned her to their table. They wanted iced tea refills, it turned out.

"Does she ever talk about me?" Tyler asked in her absence.

"Audrey?" Abdullah said, leaning over. "No. Why?"

"Just curious." Tyler looked down at the counter top. He felt Abdullah's gaze on him.

———

That night, a temporary stage was erected at the corner of Copper and Main. The roads were temporarily blocked by the sheriff, allowing for free-flowing pedestrian traffic and crowding. Great bright lights were propped up too. They shined down across the stage and on a large canvas with a metal easel standing in the center. There was a microphone too and a large box-shaped amplifier in a corner of the stage. Beside it rose a short row of stairs. Behind all of that, more lights were set-up to illuminate the mural, creating a dramatic backdrop for the night's events.

George Correa was there to oversee the progress. He was visibly annoyed. Not by the crowd or the workers, but by a particular town employee (one of the few) who failed to show up. Standing in for the absent man, George galvanized the work force and sent them to their tasks. Daisy, left in charge of media coordination, periodically updated him. No news came regarding the disappearing act of Tom Quinn, the head of grounds keeping and maintenance for Ketchum. Clearly not everyone shared George's enthusiasm for the spectacle taking shape at the corner of Copper and Main.

Samuel Welch, however, did share that enthusiasm. Indeed, he was tolerating the crowds and the bustle around his property well that night. He even wore a smile briefly. He was confident that humiliation would win the day. Samuel was happy to put up with the circus if it meant George would be publicly mortified. The bigger the crowds, the more cameras, and the brighter the lights, the better.

Tyler took a spot down near the stage, alongside the stairs leading up to the platform. All around him stirred energetic townspeople, including Doris O'Brien and Audrey, who mingled with tourists and reporters snapping pictures and talking into microphones and small handheld digital recorders. In the front, directly opposite the center of the stage, stood the community loner, Abdullah, much to the dismay of everyone stuck standing behind him.

In the opposite corner, Kathleen Morales engaged in an animated conversation with another woman. She was laughing as she explained how she'd mistaken Grady's trademark techniques for those of a former student. But she was quick to remind everyone that she had indeed recognized the technique as the work of a local. She *had* seen it before. She'd even bought one of Grady's watercolors last summer. It was on a wall in her kitchen by the pantry.

When Grady approached the stage, excitement surged in the crowd. It soon spilled over into wild applause. The artist had arrived. The tourists, in particular, treated Grady like an A-list celebrity—a star. He looked out over the crowd, smiled, and raised his hand in a grand wave.

Near the stairs, Tyler had a clear view of Grady's steps as he went up. They were heavy, shaky, and reluctant, despite the grand happy wave. It was understandable for Grady to be nervous, especially in a situation such as this. Yet those steps seemed to lead to the gallows, not a painting demonstration. Tyler recorded his observations in his note pad. The applause continued.

George stood comfortably in front of the microphone on the stage and clapped loudly. Just as the wild applause began to diminish, he turned to the crowd and encouraged them to match his enthusiasm. He smiled broadly as Grady drifted to his side. The two stood there under the warm bright lights. Then George extended his hand for a vigorous handshake in front of the cameras. There were flashes of light from the crowd. Blinding. Grady was invited to start preparing for the demonstration. George directed him to the brushes and materials assembled next to the large canvas. Then, clapping once again—urging a second round of applause—George turned back to the microphone and winked at Daisy in the crowd.

"Ladies and gentlemen, on behalf of the town of Ketchum, Arizona, I would like to welcome you all here this evening for a fine cultural event," he said.

Tyler watched Grady as the welcome remarks continued. Grady dug through long plastic tubes and metal cans of paint, as if unable to find what he needed. He held a large paintbrush between his teeth. He made a face that looked increasingly tense, as though trying not to scream. Grady's slouched back faced the crowd. He took his time, looking slowly through each of the supplies that were provided for him.

Perhaps, Tyler thought, he's missing something important. Or perhaps it was all part of the artist's process.

It was only George's final words—a third round of applause—that turned Grady around. Before the crowd, his face revealed a surprisingly blank expression. No smile or twinkle in his eye now. Gone was the triumphant waving artist who'd arrived only minutes ago. Awkward eccentricity was not unusual among people with exceptional artistic talent. The same was true of reclusiveness. Tyler recalled that his mother had once shared with him a long article about an artist named Henry Darger. She was fascinated by it and still brought it up occasionally in their e-mail exchanges.

Henry Joseph Darger Jr. was arguably one of America's most famous reclusive artists. Only three photographs of Darger were known to exist. A janitor, he lived alone on Webster Avenue in Chicago until, in 1973, he passed away at the ripe old age of eighty-one. It was only after he died that

Darger's landlord entered his apartment and discovered hundreds of drawings and paintings inside. Some of the works were illustrations of Darger's equally prolific and unusual writings. Darger's art, including his illustrations for the narrative called *The Story of the Vivian Girls*, are now housed in the permanent collections of the Museum of Modern Art, the American Folk Art Museum, and the Art Institute of Chicago, among many others. He never lived to see the fanfare.

The idea that Grady James was another Henry Darger— or a Vincent Van Gogh, who sold only one painting in his lifetime—made the spectacle of the challenge all the more alluring. Yet something was amiss from the start. Grady's entire demeanor had transformed. Gone was the smiling man soaking in the attention of the press and the townspeople. Now there was a slouching man. He stood in front of a canvas with shaking hands. His body was turned indecisively halfway toward the canvas and halfway toward the crowd. In his fingers, he held a stick of charcoal. His arm rose slightly before moving abruptly from side to side, as if he were tracing an image in the air. The movement was labored.

Over by the stairs, Tyler could see Grady's face as he began to work. Most of the people in the crowd could not. Tyler kept his attention on the artist, not the canvas. He noted the way Grady's lips were pursed. His throat strained to swallow. Moisture glistened on his forehead under the bright lights. He looked miserable up there.

Eventually, the charcoal started to scrape across the surface of the canvas. It left a long dusty black streak behind it. That was followed by a second streak, curving downward and back. With each gesture of his hand, Grady seemed to grow in confidence. Stroke by stroke he seemed to forget all about the great crowd amassed behind him. Soon it was only him and the canvas occupying the entire world. The pile of paints and brushes became orderly. He knew without thinking where each color or mixture of colors should be applied. No longer were his hands shaking. They were moving fervently and with absolute conviction. They could barely keep up with his commands. The canvas was being consumed by an outpouring of every doubt, heartache, and bit of loneliness that Grady had ever harbored in his heart.

Given the claim that he painted the mural in one night—encompassing the massive wall of Welch's warehouse—a time was approximated for him to complete the much smaller canvas. Having a time limit also offered audience members the chance to schedule their attendance at the event. They could take breaks to eat or even shop. Some visitors were already posing for photographs. To Grady's credit, the relatively short amount of time allotted did not appear to bother him once his hands stopped shaking. His brushes were working. He was embracing it.

The end result was a lovely expressionist landscape. The canvas erupted with a carefully selected palette of color, reminiscent of a more restrained Fauvist work, yet distinctly American Southwest in its subject matter and sensibilities. Nevertheless, if there was another Henry Darger hidden in the town of Ketchum, Grady James was not the one.

Grady stared at the canvas for a moment before setting his brushes down. He wiped his hands thoroughly with a towel. Behind Grady, illuminated for the first time at night for the evening's festivities, stood the benchmark that he had failed to reach. The mural loomed over the stage and belittled his efforts by its mere existence. When Grady turned to face the crowd, there was a polite round of applause from those who were still in attendance, and then a chorus of murmurs as they slowly dispersed into the night.

George quickly took to the microphone. He sung Grady's praises, proclaiming victory in the challenge issued by Samuel Welch. Few agreed with him, though, and Grady himself appeared defeated. He'd given all he had, and it was not enough. He tried to hold up his chin and pull his shoulders back with dignity, but his hands began to tremble again. His neck couldn't hold up the weight of his own head. He stepped toward the microphone for a moment, as if he intended to speak, but turned back, waved lazily toward the remaining people in the crowd, and retreated down the stairs and away into a waiting car. Tyler was prepared to ask a question when Grady passed him on the stairs. But when he looked into Grady's eyes, he saw everything he needed to know.

XIX

Abdullah Park's diner on Main Street was packed with patrons the next morning, the air still buzzing after the challenge. The tables were full, and people waited by the door for a seat. Behind the counter, the hot grill was covered with circles of bubbling pancake batter and rows of wrinkled bacon strips and piles of home fries doused in pepper and salt. The aroma of it all filled the air and made anyone within ten feet of the entrance stop to look inside.

Tyler Anderson was lured inside by the pangs of hunger, a drowsy thirst for a cup of coffee, and the possibility of seeing Audrey Betz again. Unfortunately, she wasn't there. Tyler took a padded stool at the counter. He swiveled and peaked around the room. Then he placed his order with a different waitress for a coffee and a short stack of pancakes. Tyler stared at her with a puzzled look on his face. She smiled back politely, but didn't know what to make of the journalist. He leaned slightly to the side, peering around her, to see if Audrey was somewhere else in the room. Maybe she was at another table. He wondered if it'd be too rude to ask the woman before him to get the other waitress. Probably. Maybe Audrey was in the back or preparing an order. She could be on a break too.

Abdullah watched their interaction from the other side of the counter. He smirked and dabbed the sweat from his forehead with a red handkerchief. It was always hot behind the grill. When the waitress recorded Tyler's reluctant order and walked away, Abdullah finally said hello. He extended his hand over the counter for a handshake, as if they were old friends now, and gave a good firm squeeze.

"Something wrong?" Abdullah said.

"Where's Audrey?" Tyler asked.

"She's out today. Called in sick. I could use the help if you feel like earning a few bucks."

Tyler smiled politely at Abdullah's joke and waited for a moment, distracted by the change in plans. "Is she over at her place?"

"I guess. Have you been there?"

"Where?" Tyler shot back, visibly distracted. He saw the nameless waitress bringing a cup of fresh black coffee toward him at the counter. The caffeine would help.

"To her place."

"Once."

The waitress placed the coffee down on the counter in front of Tyler and left.

"Look at you," Abdullah said.

"It's not like that," Tyler said. He dumped a splash of cream and some sugar in the coffee and stirred the concoction anxiously. The black turned many shades lighter. "I wish it was."

"She's single."

"I know," he said.

"So what happened?"

"We just talked about my story."

"That's all?"

"Conversations veer around like rivers."

"And?"

"And nothing. We talked. I left. End of story."

"Oh, man."

"What?" Tyler said.

"Remember what I said? About people believing in things," Abdullah said.

"Yes."

"Think about it." Abdullah tapped his forehead with his index finger.

Tyler nodded, mainly to be agreeable. He drank his coffee, which was still too hot. He didn't react, even though it burned him. Instead, he looked solemnly over at the front door. Seeing the people waiting there—tourists—he imagined a Norman Rockwell painting invaded by Disney World. He smirked, and took a smaller sip of coffee. He felt very skeptical about what Abdullah said. His life had never known romance. There was the temporary substitute. Or the drunken fling, but that was all. And those were few and far between. Never "the girl." Audrey was definitely "the girl." Thank goodness for imagination, he thought. And the hot pancakes that Abdullah had placed in front of him.

When Tyler noticed Abdullah was watching, he smiled. He raised his mug but said nothing, content to feast on his pancakes in silence. Nevertheless, his mind and imagination were entirely preoccupied. Maybe Audrey could see him as something more. It was not impossible. It was not total fiction. "Does she like writers?" he thought. "We are a weird breed." Tyler stared blankly at the countertop as he ate.

"How are those pancakes?" Abdullah asked.

"Amazing," Tyler said politely, after chewing.

Tyler raced through his breakfast at a record pace. He gobbled down the whole short stack of syrupy, buttery cakes and gulped two cups of milky brown coffee. He was tempted to have a third, but resisted. Hardly a second had passed without Audrey's smile or her laughter intruding on his thoughts. The two hours they spent together played out in his head. Images on a rapid loop—the highlights. He remembered what she liked, what made her laugh, the important details of her stories, and how he brought their conversation to a screeching end. He put his money down on the counter. Some pennies rolled in different directions. He slapped them down and told Abdullah to keep the change. "See you later," he said, and he headed out the door into the sunlight.

After a brisk and impatient walk back to the Saguaro Motel, Tyler climbed into his car and fumbled with the keys. It was like an oven inside. The car shook and sputtered for a moment as the engine started. In reverse, the car rolled out, nearly hitting some snowbirds with cameras around their necks. Then he spun the wheel back and headed out.

He drove toward the Gord house. He didn't think it was necessary to call ahead. It was best to make an appearance, he reasoned. Ketchum was a place designed for face-to-face conversations. However, it all depended on her being home.

He pulled into the dusty driveway. Rocks crunched. He drove to the back, where the door to Audrey's apartment was hidden away. The brakes creaked, and he turned the key and pulled it from the ignition, leaving the engine to tick as it started to cool. Tyler looked over at Audrey's doorway. He saw no sign that she was there. Staying put, he rehearsed for several minutes. He reviewed what he might say—pondering several options. Cool option. Funny option. *Sexy* option (if he had such a thing). He wondered now if he should have called her first. He pondered how he might phrase something—what topics to avoid. At the very least, he hoped to make her smile. One smile would do—a small victory.

Tyler knocked on the door with three solid taps in quick succession. Then he waited. Beneath the sun, the intense heat pounded down on the top of his head. He hadn't noticed just how hot it was outside. He began to sweat uncomfortably as the seconds passed with no answer at the door. A bead of sweat slid down his cheek. He took a white handkerchief from his pocket and dabbed at it. Then he hid it away quickly in his pocket. Tyler looked up toward Audrey's window, squinting from the sunlight, trying to see if she was peeking out in the same way she had before. He saw nothing though.

Tyler knocked again three times. He stepped further away from the door. Now he was easily visible from the window. Again there was no answer. He stood for a minute more and waited until more beads of sweat started to run down his face. It was so hot.

Tyler turned to retreat to the car. He had to escape the summer heat. He wiped the sweat from his forehead with the back of his hand. "So much sweat," he thought as he looked at his hand. He started to think about where Audrey might be. Maybe hiking? Did she hike? He didn't know. His feet were shuffling through the dirt of the driveway like they weighed fifty pounds each. When he reached the car again, desperate to turn on the A/C inside, he heard the sound of Audrey's voice.

"Tyler?" she said.

For a moment Tyler thought that he might have imagined the voice. He had a lively imagination. And it was very hot outside. Native Americans used to take vision quests in these desert hills. The Zuni had inhabited these lands.

"Tyler!" she said again, interrupting his thoughts.

Tyler looked back and found Audrey standing in the doorway. She stayed in the shade of the entrance, hiding half of her body behind the partly opened door. Tyler stumbled back around and tried to collect himself and look presentable. He wiped the sweat from his forehead and discreetly dragged his wet hand across his pants.

"I just came to check on you," he said, taking two steps toward her. "Abdullah said you were sick."

"Did you want to come inside—out of the heat?" she said, still not leaving the doorway.

Tyler could not, in fact, tell if she was sick, but he could see that she was not her usual self. She did not smile. Her eyes, always appearing older than she was, had faint but dark circles under them. In her visible hand, hanging down at her side, was a lit cigarette. A trail of milky gray smoke was wafting up and out the doorway toward him. He hated the smell of the smoke. It was better than those Indonesian cigarettes though, he decided. Those were awful things.

"I didn't know you smoked," he said as he came closer.

"Sometimes."

Inside the apartment, Tyler and Audrey sat at the table again. She asked him if he would like a glass of water, but he politely declined. Fearing the slightest offense, Tyler quickly explained how he had just come from having breakfast at the diner and how he was still very full and had eaten much too fast. Abdullah had told him about her illness, he repeated.

Audrey shrugged and sat down and put a fat glass ashtray down in front of her. Then she balanced her cigarette on its edge. She slouched in her seat and watched a straight line of gray smoke rise up to the ceiling at a constant rate. She said nothing.

Tyler watched her. Her lips looked parched. When she looked back at him, he lowered his gaze to the table. He put his hands on the tabletop in front of him, one on top of the other. "I should have accepted that glass of water," he thought. Tyler glanced back up at Audrey as she tapped the cigarette, letting ashes fall into the glass ashtray. He wiped his forehead very quickly and felt the moisture on his fingertips.

"How are you feeling?" he asked.

"I've been better."

"Is it the flu?"

"No," she said. "Don't worry. I'm not contagious." Audrey brought the cigarette to her lips, which had no shining pink lip gloss on them now. She took a deep drag, down to the bottom of her stomach, as if she were trying to fill her body with smoke. Then out came the smoke across the kitchen table in a ghostly stream, making Tyler lean back slightly and hold his breath.

"Is it something I did?" Tyler said as he came forward again.

Audrey was puzzled. "What? What did *you* do?"

"I don't know. Maybe I upset you with my questions the other night?"

"No. It has nothing to do with you," she said coldly. Audrey stood up. She turned and filled a glass of water at the faucet in the kitchen sink. When she turned again, she held the glass in her hand and took a small sip. She leaned back against the counter instead of returning to the table. "You'd know if you were the problem."

"I always assume the worst," he said, barely managing an uncomfortable smile. "My imagination gets the best of me. Good thing I'm a writer," he mumbled.

When Tyler was a boy, he frequently suffered from feeling like everyone was looking at him—wherever he went. He thought people didn't like him for whatever reason. Breathing, perhaps. His mother always told him it was nonsense. He was imagining things. But admittedly, he *was* an awkward looking boy—excessively skinny and too tall for his age. He had terribly crooked teeth too, especially the front two. There was a prominent gap between them that could almost hold a pencil. As a result, he learned to smile with his mouth closed, or not at all, so no one would see the gap. Older boys—even classmates with "normal" appearances—saw young Tyler as easy prey for teasing, although he was just one of many.

Tyler especially hated gym class. Held twice a week, it was a source of tremendous anxiety. Those dreaded shirts-versus-skins games? The Humiliation Games, he called them. No one ever hesitated to mention how they could see Tyler's heart beating, or to count his ribs. A teacher in a sixth grade computer class even referred to Tyler as "Bones" one day. It stuck. The boys in class adopted it. Then it quickly morphed into something worse. That terrible nickname didn't survive the year, but Tyler was still mortified. In his mind, it was only rare moments of compassion—curious and inexplicable—that seemed to make people tolerate him. It was safer to engage the world with a pen, he decided. And his interest in writing had the wholehearted approval of his father. That was certain. This mindset proved most debilitating when it came to women. He was always apologizing and trying to make things right, it seemed. Most of the time he made things worse. Tyler vividly remembered the time in seventh grade English class when the short pretty girl with the brown wavy hair turned to him and declared, "You are *so* ugly." A random act of unkindness.

Two years of corrective orthodontic braces and a slower metabolism remedied some of the insecurities with which he was plagued during those years. There were better times ahead, but Tyler grew up into an emotionally damaged man. Writing gave him a degree of confidence, especially in his professional life. Living on his own in the city—Phoenix—had been a fresh start too. He was far from anyone who knew him during those unhappy years. Yet his negative thoughts remained. It didn't matter how far he traveled.

"Can I tell you something?" he asked, expecting Audrey to agree. He hoped she would. "Remember what I told you—about my start in journalism?"

"The drug company," she said.

"Yeah. That's not the whole story," he said, and he paused, changing directions. "Believe it or not, I'm very fond of you. I hope my honesty proves it." Tyler's voice was awkwardly sincere. His face reddened slightly with embarrassment from his own words. "Good grief, what did I just say?" he thought.

Audrey was curious now. She returned to the table. Exhaling, she extinguished her cigarette in the fat glass ashtray. Ready now, she folded her hands in front of her. Then she listened as a lingering cloud of smoke drifted slowly upward to the ceiling.

"I told you about my father—how he raised me to write. Well, Dad suffered from heart trouble for most of my life. When I was in college, this doctor gave him some new pills to try. And everything was fine, at first. Then one day he collapsed at work. It was a stroke. A *major* stroke. He was comatose. The last six weeks of his life were spent in the hospital—hooked up to all these tubes and machines. I can still see it. Mom hardly left his bedside. I was nineteen when he died."

Audrey hadn't moved. She was listening quietly. Tyler looked across the table for any kind of reaction. Maybe a pouting lip. Some glistening moisture in her eyes. The expression he found, though, was surprisingly cold. She didn't extend her hand to console him. She didn't even smile softly with empathy. He was unsure whether or not she heard what he had just shared with her. Was she listening or too distracted? He looked down at the table wondering what to say or do next.

"I'm so sorry, Tyler," Audrey finally said, ending the ambiguous silence.

"There's more," he said, now ready to continue. "Those goddamned pills. Those were what did it—what killed my Dad."

"From the company?"

Tyler nodded.

"Oh, my God."

"I couldn't write fiction after that. It seemed so—trivial, I guess. I was so angry. *So angry.*"

"It's not too late though. Right?"

"I don't know. This is my life now. You really can't make a living like that anyway," he said, his voice trailing off.

Tyler's honesty had won him Audrey's attention for the moment. It was obligatory. That was the respect that the subject of death brought. Failure to show solemn respect was a great offense. Allegations of being heartless or cold or inhuman might follow. Tyler hadn't intended to corner Audrey in that way, but he had done it nonetheless. She couldn't dismiss him from the table so readily after that.

"I didn't come here to pry. But, why are you home today, Audrey?" he asked, hoping she'd reciprocate with her own honesty. "What's wrong?"

She looked at the floor and let out a deep sigh. "I really appreciate you sharing with me. You really didn't have to do that. I think—I just think you should stay focused on your story."

"Can I do anything to help?"

Audrey glanced over at him from across the table. She seemed to be caught in the midst of an internal debate. Her lips moved for a moment, as if she wanted to speak. Nothing came. Instead, she put a fresh cigarette between her lips, lit it, and inhaled deeply.

"You can tell me," he said. "Really. Tell me anything."

Audrey paused. She watched the smoke rise to the ceiling. "There's nothing anyone can do."

"Well, sometimes it helps just to talk about it."

"You don't want to hear it. Trust me."

"No, I mean it, Audrey. You have my undivided attention. My ears are at your disposal."

"All right." She flicked her ashes. "You know I'm from Phoenix."

Tyler nodded.

Audrey stilled, visibly reluctant to say more. Her hand was shaking.

"Today is…sort of an anniversary," she managed to say. Her voice was getting higher.

"How so?"

"Somebody died, two years ago."

"Someone very close, obviously."

Audrey impulsively flicked the ashes from her cigarette again. Then she inhaled. Her hand was still trembling. Her tired eyes began to well up with tears.

"I couldn't talk about my Dad for months," Tyler said. "I couldn't say a word about it." He scanned the room quickly to find a box of tissues, but found nothing.

"I thought moving here would help me forget," she said, as if voicing a complaint. "We were supposed to get married, Tyler." Tears now rolled down her cheeks.

"I'm so sorry." Tyler started to repeat himself. He cast around for something else to say.

Audrey put her hands to her face and took a deep breath. After one failed attempt, she composed herself, wiped the tears from her red cheeks. "Good God," she said. She sniffed and cleared her throat. "I need to stop," she said. "Sorry you had to see that."

"I promise it was all off the record."

Audrey smiled politely. She took a deep breath and cleared her throat. Then she picked up her cigarette without saying anything more. Very little was said between Tyler and Audrey after that. Before long, Tyler knew it was time to go. He walked around the table. Audrey stood up too, and Tyler opened his arms. She hesitated for a moment and then stepped into his embrace. He said good-bye as he hugged her and marched down the stairs. Audrey locked the door securely behind him.

Tyler sat in the driveway for several minutes. He could smell Audrey's cigarettes on his clothes. His hands rested lazily underneath the steering wheel, now hot to the touch. It was entirely possible that *that* was the last time he would see

Audrey Betz. What a terrible ending. He started to delete the little fantasies he'd been constructing since they'd first met at the diner. It was best to focus on his work—his pen and paper. That was worth something, he imagined, even if he remained unconvinced.

At that precise moment, the harsh business of writing interrupted his inner dialogue. The cell phone tucked away in his pocket began vibrating in short bursts. He immediately wondered if it was Audrey. Perhaps she wanted to say something more, a final word—something poetic. Or she wanted to know why he was still sitting outside in his car. No, it hadn't broken down, he would assure her.

But the little glowing screen read, Rebecca.

"I was just going to call you."

"How's it going? Almost done?" Rebecca said, straight to the point.

"Not yet," he said. "I don't have an ending."

Tyler spent the next five minutes assuring Rebecca that he understood his responsibilities. He understood that he'd have to pay for his room if he continued to stay in Ketchum. He knew that other news outlets were doing stories about the mural. He knew that he would need a unique angle. His story had to stand apart from the others. And he knew that there were other stories for him waiting back in the city. He understood all his responsibilities as an employee.

Rebecca disliked having a core member of her writing team away from the office for so long. And far out in rural Arizona no less. In a particularly excruciating moment, she even reminded Tyler why he was originally hired. It was way too much. Tyler listened patiently like a good employee, even if he was rolling his eyes in the car. When Rebecca was done, she briefly discussed some stories that she wanted him to cover. All of those stories were in the city—waiting for him.

When the call ended with a good-bye and a click, Tyler let out a sigh of frustration. He wrapped his fingers tightly around the hot steering wheel again. The heat no longer bothered him. He squeezed until his knuckles turned white. He knew that his time was up. His pilgrimage was coming to a close.

"She'll never let me leave the city again," Tyler thought heavily.

XX

Ketchum's once charming streets were soiled and dirty with neglect. Embarrassed, George Correa rolled up his sleeves and took matters into his own hands. The humiliation of the challenge two nights prior had left him anxious. He was eager to accomplish something tangible to appreciate with his own eyes. Daisy Correa—easily recognizing the signs of distress in her husband—encouraged him to take a break, at least for a day. George would hear none of it, though. There was work to be done, he insisted. And nothing seemed to him more urgent than the declining situation on the streets and sidewalks of Ketchum, where trash was building up by the hour. The overflowing, fly-infested bins were ruining the picture perfect small American town he wanted tourists to enjoy when they came to see the mural and remember when they left.

Keeping downtown (i.e., Main Street) clean was Tom Quinn's responsibility. He had never neglected it before. In fact, he hadn't been seen in days, perhaps even longer. All efforts to find or contact the head of grounds keeping and maintenance for Ketchum had failed. He stopped answering his phone. No one came to the door at his house. It was the most inopportune time for an otherwise reliable, longtime town employee to take a vacation or to quit his job. But it seemed that Tom had done just that.

On Main Street, Tyler saw George with a pair of sour-faced workers wearing heavy gloves and stained baseball caps. They chatted on the sidewalk next to a battered old pickup. A bundle of rakes, brooms, and a shovel lay beside a large plastic trash bin in the truck bed. George was pointing at something down the street. Another overflowing trash bin had grabbed his attention. It needed to be emptied and cleaned. The two workmen nodded and headed that direction, carrying a fresh garbage bag and a broom. There was still much work to do.

"I didn't know this was part of your job," Tyler said.

"You know what they say," said George. "If you want something done right…"

"Do you normally do this?"

"No."

"I didn't think so. Whose job is it?"

"Grounds keeping and maintenance supervisor. Changes the bulbs and such. It's a part-time position. Tom Quinn's been doing it for years."

"I don't think I've met him. There're no sanitation trucks to get these?" Tyler asked, gesturing vaguely toward one source of the foul stench. The garbage was forcing Tyler to breathe through his mouth as much as he could. He even felt the urge to pinch his nose. The people walking down the sidewalk were making wide turns around bins as well.

"It's cheaper for Tom to do it," George said quietly. "Toss it all into a dumpster. Then a truck comes for it."

"Where is he? On vacation?"

"I wish I knew," George said, swatting a buzzing fly away from his face.

George had called Tom's house several times, but there was no answer. Tom didn't have an answering machine either, he added. George went over to Tom's house last night, but no one came to the door. He'd also driven past the house several times, looking for some sign of life, but there were never any lights on. Tom had never caused a problem before. Nor was he known to take vacations, George explained. He stopped short of suggesting that something very bad had happened, deliberately trying to avoid the next logical step in the thought process. No one wanted to admit the possibility that Tom might have died in his house. Living alone, Tom's body would sit in the house, undisturbed and decaying for days. It was a terrible thought. George profoundly disliked such thoughts.

When Tyler and George arrived at Tom's house a little while later, Tyler having guided George to his car gently, the windows were dark as they'd been for days. There were no signs of life. It was just as George had described, the only sound a dog or coyote barking in the distance. Tom's pickup truck was parked in the driveway. The doors were unlocked. Assorted envelopes, fliers, and catalogs piled up inside the white mailbox out by the road.

Approaching the front door, Tyler thought about what he would do if he came across a body inside. Dead bodies reminded him of how his father had looked, his face pale, almost wax-like, his body motionless in an excessively polished casket. Tyler wrote a letter to his father when he was in a coma. At the funeral, Tyler tucked it inside the casket before it was buried. No one knew he'd done it, and when he discreetly reached inside the casket at the church, he'd unintentionally touched his father's hand. Against his fingers, it felt cold and leathery.

George knocked on the front door of Tom's house with three firm taps. A few seconds later, he tried again. Together they listened for any sounds inside. Nothing. George knocked a third time. Nothing. Tyler reached down and turned the door-knob. He found it unlocked. That was not entirely unusual in Ketchum. Still, it was rude just to enter someone's house. George called out Tom's name to announce their arrival as he opened the door. Tyler waited for a moment, listening to the barking animal in the distance. Then he followed George inside.

At the foot of the staircase, not far inside the house, George looked for any signs of recent activity or occupancy. Nothing caught his attention. The house was dimly lit. Rays of sunlight were entering through a few windows. George fumbled for a light switch before flipping it on. Still he saw nothing important. It was a modest but well-organized and clean house. No signs of disrepair. Tom had taken great care of it. In fact, it looked like Tom was intent on spending the rest of his life there.

"Anyone home?" George called out again. "It's George Correa."

Tyler and George stood frozen for a moment. They listened, but there was no answer.

"What now?" George said.

"Maybe you should go upstairs. I'll look around down here."

George took a reluctant step up. The wood creaked beneath his weight. He placed his hand firmly on the wooden railing. "I'll holler if I find anything," he said, turning back toward Tyler.

Tyler nodded. He watched as George went slowly up. As George's back disappeared and only his legs and then his feet were still visible, Tyler, not making a sound in fear of upsetting the eerie calm of the house, went down into what he found to be the kitchen. It was an older kitchen, with yellow flooring and flowered curtains. There were no dishes in the double sink. There was no food left out on the counter. There was nothing more than a salt shaker on the table. The refrigerator, which Tyler opened for inspection, was still stocked with food. There were pickles, eggs, a half-eaten package of bologna, and a carton of whole milk that had expired two days ago. Tyler left the milk where he found it.

Beside the twenty-year-old refrigerator, a drawing hung on the wall in a fake mahogany picture frame. It caught Tyler's eye immediately. Taking two steps toward it to get a closer look, he studied the fine lines of the charcoal portrait. It was a young woman with an exquisitely beautiful face gazing down at the ground. She was smiling slightly, as if someone had just complemented her to make her blush. Tyler didn't know who she was. He stared at the face for several seconds and almost expected her to look up at him.

"Tyler?" George shouted from somewhere upstairs.

"Yes?"

"Come take a look at this."

Tyler's chest tightened. His pulse quickened, and his heart pounded faster. He felt panic. His thoughts whirled. There was dread. A terrible image appeared in his head—his father lying in his casket. Like it had happened yesterday. The pale and wax-like flesh. Tom would be worse. Decaying flesh unattended by a mortuary staff for days. It was not something Tyler wanted to see. He didn't want that memory. This was not part of his job, he reminded himself. The police should be there.

"What is it?" Tyler stood at the foot of the stairs, reluctant to go up.

"Come take a look," George said.

It was a strange response from someone who had just found a dead body. He imagined a far more dramatic reaction. Some screaming at least. George would stand at the top of the stairs, hand over mouth. He would look sick. His face would go pale and maybe a bit green. Maybe he'd even run down the stairs and go charging straight out the door, spewing vomit as he went. But instead, the same eerie calm remained throughout the house. Tyler sniffed the air to see if there was a hint of death, but there was nothing.

"Coming," Tyler said. He climbed the stairs.

The second floor of Tom Quinn's house was darker and smaller than the first. Most of the doors were closed, preventing any light from coming into the hallway. He hadn't noticed a light switch on the wall either. Perfect. Tyler saw more terrible scenes playing out in his head, as if in a horror film. He was the lead character now. It was time to make a wrong turn. He could almost hear the ominous cello music. Down the hallway, George's silhouette stood in the doorway of the last room at the end of the hall. Sunlight poured in through a window. Tyler wondered what waited. He took a breath. He feared that the images would never leave his memory. The gore would haunt him forever.

"Is it him?" Tyler said.

"What? No," George mumbled. "Look."

Tyler's body immediately relaxed. His shoulders dropped two inches. His steps grew easy and he approached the door. George stepped aside and let him enter. Nobody occupied the room. No blood or terrible images. It was a cluttered drafting room. There were stacks of thick drawing paper. Spiral note pads were piled high in every corner. A large, hand-crafted drafting table sat against the far wall. An adjustable metal lamp and a canister full of sharpened pencils, sticks of black charcoal, brushes, and bottles of India ink were arranged on top of it. This was the studio of a busy and active artist.

In the center of the room was a tall but empty painting easel. Next to it sat a short metal stand. A heavily used hand palette, layered with dry strokes of paint, sat atop the stand. Alongside it were a dirty rag and an empty glass jar. The bare wooden floorboards of the room were speckled with accidental drops and dashes of paint in every color, giving it the look of a Jackson Pollock painting gone awry. And on the walls were tacked several sketches and detailed drawings and painfully performed portraits demonstrating exceptional artistic skill and technique.

"Did you know about this?" Tyler was staring at the sketches on the walls.

"No idea," George said.

As Tyler and George explored the room further, the magnitude of their unexpected discovery became apparent. The great skill and technique so clearly evident in the countless drawings and paintings gathered there were strikingly reminiscent of the mural, albeit on a much smaller and simpler scale.

"Now we know," Tyler said.

"What?"

"Why the artist never came forward."

"He must have left right after he did it," George said.

"Where? Where would he go?"

"I don't know," George said.

"Think he was afraid of getting caught?"

"No. I doubt Sam would have done anything. Probably just have him paint over it."

"Well, something scared him away," Tyler said. "Did he leave a note?"

"I didn't see anything." George looked around the room.

"He had to know someone would come looking for him."

"Nothing," George said.

"What about family?"

"Tom was an only child. His mother died years ago."

"Did he have any friends in a neighboring town?"

"No, Ketchum was Tom's entire life. I can't imagine him just leaving."

Tyler perused a stack of sketches piled up on a crowded bookshelf against a wall. Flipping through the stack—page after page—he found wonderful portraits of unknown people. There were animals and scenes of the Arizona landscape too. They weren't all masterpieces. Some were scribbles and lazy doodles. Furious eraser marks marred some drawings too. Some of them had failed. Erratic marks of pencils and sweaty hand streaks dirtied the surfaces. Some of the paper had been crinkled or torn. Pages were torn out, presumably thrown away.

"We should go talk to the sheriff," George said. "There's been a lot of new people in town recently."

"Think someone kidnapped him?"

"No," he said quickly. "I don't know. It's been days. People don't just disappear like this. Not Tom Quinn."

"Should we take some of these?" Tyler was holding a bundle of sketches in his hands. "People will want to know."

"Leave it for now," George said. "We'll deal with that later."

As Tyler went to return the stack of sketches to the shelf, he noticed another drawing. It depicted a dilapidated mine shaft at the foot of a rocky hill. Picking it up, Tyler found more drawings underneath it. There were several drawings of mines. All the same shaft. Tom had done a whole series.

"Where is this?" Tyler held up one of the drawings for George to see.

George studied it for a good ten seconds before he finally recognized it. "I know this. We used to hike past it. It's a pretty good walk from here."

"It's a real place?"

"Yes.

"Is it still in use?"

"No, it's been abandoned for decades. Those things are death traps."

"Is this the same one?" Tyler asked, pointing to a drawing pinned up on the wall.

"Looks like it," George said, stepping closer. "Yes, that's it."

"Tom must go there a lot. Can you take me to it?"

George agreed. He warned Tyler that he would have to walk a good distance, because there were no roads leading directly up to it anymore. And George was going to stay in the car. His hiking days were over, he said. Tyler assured him that he was prepared to undertake the hike alone, even if it meant going off-road and dodging rattlesnakes and cacti. George only had to tell him where to go and then wait for him in the car to come back.

XXI

Tyler carried a bottle of water with him as he climbed over a rocky hill and down into a little valley. He could no longer see the road or George's car. He was already starting to sweat from the heat, which seemed to radiate off the rocks. George had told him to go straight down the little valley until it veered around to the right. Then he was supposed to continue straight up another hill and down again, where the terrain flattened out before another outcrop of hills. This was a world apart from the city. Hard to imagine such a stark and desolate place these days. He could see how someone could disappear out there. The world so often seemed crowded to Tyler, and then he arrived here. The sun overhead was unrelenting, and Tyler stopped to drink some water before heading up into the hills.

George had said the old mine was one of several there in the hills. Tyler could follow the remnants of an old rail track once he got past the first rise. It stretched down from the mines to the far side of the hill, where an access road used to be. Nature had reclaimed it many years ago. Tyler took one of Tom Quinn's drawings with him. He hoped to use it to identify the mine he was looking for. It turned out that he didn't need it. The first mine shaft he passed, smaller than the one in the drawing, had caved in years ago. Two others were boarded up. Battered and rusty warning signs were tacked to them. Then he came to the largest mine of the lot. It was big, open, and clear of debris. It was clearly the one in Tom's drawings. Tyler now understood why George remembered it. It embodied the essence of an old mine shaft. Cut deep into solid rock, its entrance was framed by thick planks of timber and iron beams. Tyler was unable to see the end of it. There was only a deep darkness in the belly of the earth.

Tyler stood at the entrance and touched the inner rock of the chiseled walls. It seemed sturdy enough, but George had warned him not to go inside. All sorts of wildlife make abandoned mines their homes. Tyler could stumble his way onto some sleeping coyotes, a diamondback, a nest of scorpions, or go face first into the web of a black widow. He decided not to go down the dark passageway. Instead, he listened. Silence.

"Hello?" he called out. There was a slight echo but nothing else came back in response. There were no signs that someone had been camping there either. He saw no burnt wood or curiously organized stones. No traces of food. Tyler took another drink of water, noting that his bottle was now barely half full. Wary of the heat, he was about to turn around when he noticed a bit of rock jutting out from the wall of the mine. It was an unnatural shade of red. Blood?

The opening of the mine was large enough for Tyler to walk inside easily while keeping his head low. He was careful not to bump it or step into a web or nest of creeping crawling things of some kind. He needed a helmet. Light was lacking in the mine, even with the sun blazing down outside. He hadn't even thought to ask George for a flashlight. Nevertheless, Tyler could see that the unnatural red was actually part of something much larger. He stepped back and attempted to angle himself enough to catch as much light as possible. Now he could see it. It was a painting. It stretched dozens of feet down the side of the mine. The dusty rock surface was not an ideal canvas, but the painting was a beautiful expressionist work of angst and creativity. The paint had worn away in sections—some of it covered in a thick layer of dust—but most of it had withstood conditions well in the protection of the mine. Tom Quinn had not only drawn the old mine in his sketches, but used the mine itself as a canvas.

Curious about the full extent of the tableaux, Tyler ventured farther down into the mine. He stepped along the jagged rocks very carefully, listening for the slightest rattle in the dark. He again turned in such a way as to let as much sunlight through as possible. He now pressed himself to one side of the mine—keeping his head down and angled oddly—and tried to view the entirety of the painting. Up near the mouth of the mine was a profile of a man's head. His eyes and mouth were closed, his curious face serene and contemplative. Trailing behind the head, as if pouring into the mind of the figure, was an array of images, forms, and colors. They stretched back over twenty feet down the wall of the mine into the dark. Unlike with the mural, Tyler could see brushstrokes and droplets of paint collected along the ground. The cave painting was beautiful, but hardly immaculate. He could see Tom's labor in it. There was some sense of frustration in it too.

When Tyler reappeared over the hills and returned to the car—covered in sweat and holding an empty water bottle—George immediately confronted him. Tyler told him he'd found the mine but that no one was there. It looked like Tom had been there, he added. When George asked what exactly he'd found, Tyler said only that there were traces of paint and drawing tools that had been there for a long time, judging by the dust and the dirt.

He made no mention of the painting in the mine. There would be no circus there, Tyler decided. Tom could keep his sanctuary.

XXII

Tom Ludlow Quinn was born and raised in Ketchum, Arizona. He was the son of a union miner—a Mine Mill man—who reverently kept a framed photograph of Franklin Delano Roosevelt hanging in the family's house. Tom's mother, Anna, was a housewife and crafter, well known in town for her elegant seasonal quilts and lace. She'd always encouraged Tom—her only son—to avoid the harsh existence of the mines that later claimed Tom's father, whose official cause of death was "miner's consumption."

The mines built on the copper veins in the hills around Ketchum were owned by the Phelps Corporation. Business was generally good. Electricity was the life-blood of the copper industry, so the rapidly modernizing world improved profits. Copper was an excellent conductor, and every technological advance over the years had made it an even more important commodity. Workers in mining towns like Ketchum benefited from the demand, but saw little improvement in their living conditions. Management prospered, though.

At the onset, the work in the mines was usually relatively easy. Miners took the ore deposits near the surface. Over the years, the mines grew deeper. In turn, the work became exponentially more perilous. It grew so dangerous that many men left the mines altogether in search of something better. Living poor was better than not living at all, they said. For those who stayed (or returned), like Tom's father, the serious toll was evident on their very faces.

Hundreds of feet below the surface, the air turned moist and warm and filled with dust in the darkness. Sometimes, the air contained toxic smoke too, generated by chain-smoking miners. The chiseled, hewn, and sporadically glimmering walls of gray stone were held up by large thick beams of timber brought down from the highlands near Flagstaff. Iron rails, taking up precious inches of tunnel space, extend down into the bowels of the mines to carry heavy metal carts full of rock to the surface for smelting. And down where the timber beams were new and freshly installed, the possibility of a deadly collapse was much more acute and unnerving. The men were paid little for risking their lives each day.

Tensions between workers and management were always emerging. Whenever management tried to bring in immigrants (usually from Mexico) to work at a fraction of the cost, especially as scabs, mobs of white union laborers would run them out of town. Sometimes brutal violence erupted, worker fighting worker. The miners risked their lives every day in the bowels of the earth. Those men, so much younger than they looked, sacrificed much in the process. To have bosses try to undercut them and strip them of their modest wages was nothing short of a declaration of war.

Arizona became no stranger to harsh labor disputes between miners and wealthy corporate bosses. Even as early as July of 1917, the Industrial Workers of the World, or the Wobblies as they were known, organized hundreds of copper miners in the town of Bisbee, Arizona. The union gave the Copper Queen Mining Company a list of demands to improve the vile working conditions that the miners faced on a daily basis. Their demands constituted very reasonable requests, such as an end to rock blasting while workers were still in the mines. However, management refused to accept a single demand. In response, the union called a strike.

Virtually every miner in Bisbee walked off the job. Then, early on the morning of July 12, a massive armed posse organized by the county sheriff and Copper Queen management arrested over one thousand people. The posse marched them at gunpoint to a nearby baseball field. Later that morning, the workers and their supporters were forced into filthy cattle cars on the railway and deported to New Mexico. Despite efforts to keep the forced deportation hidden by the company, the union managed to expose these kidnappings, as the Wobblies called them. The story went national. In May of 1918, the US Department of Justice ordered the arrest of numerous corporate executives and members of the county sheriff's department for what they did to the miners that day. It's still known today as the Bisbee Deportation.

Tom Quinn's father came to Arizona long after the events in Bisbee. But those stories lived on among the workers as if they'd happened yesterday. When Tom was born, his father gave him the middle name of Ludlow, venerating the Ludlow Massacre. It was his way of honoring the men, women, and children who were killed by the National Guard and a corporate militia during the union coal miners' strike at Ludlow, Colorado, on April 20, 1914. Those were the types of stories Tom grew up hearing. As a boy in Ketchum, Tom learned to sing the folk songs of labor activist Joe Hill—executed by the state of Utah in 1915—long before he ever heard the old Christian hymn, "Jesus Loves Me."

XXIII

The sheriff's office on Main Street was next to Town Hall. The two buildings even shared a wall. George Correa passed it every day when he went to work. The stir created by the mural left Sheriff Dale Weaver busier than ever before. It was usually a sleepy job, devoted to traffic stops, domestic disputes, the occasional theft, or a teenage act of vandalism motivated by rural boredom. But the mural had changed the pace of it all in a hurry. Most of it was still traffic and crowd control, but it was a lot of work nonetheless.

Weaver wasn't the sheriff back when Argus Gord lived in Ketchum, and he was grateful for that. He was a friendly and optimistic man, prone to finding goodness in people, even when it's hard to see. Working in Ketchum meant that Sheriff Weaver could avoid the worst sorts of crimes, like homicide or rape. He managed to keep his hope in mankind largely intact. It wasn't always easy though—especially when he turned on the nightly news.

That afternoon, when George and Tyler arrived, visibly excited, with news of Tom Quinn's disappearance, Sheriff Weaver thought the two were overreacting. After all, Tom was a loner by nature. He always had been. He could have gone on a trip for a week or two without telling anyone. Maybe he wanted to escape the crowds. That was his right. Maybe he'd gone to Phoenix to see a baseball game. He loved baseball.

"Why wouldn't he tell anyone at work?" Tyler asked.

"Who does Tom work for?" the sheriff replied.

"The town."

"That's right. The town. He could have called you, George, but probably didn't want to bother you. Especially with everything going on. Hell, Tom is probably trout fishing in the White Mountains."

"With who?" George asked in disbelief. "His truck is still in the driveway."

"Look, if it'll make you feel better, I'm happy to put the word out. But I'm sure he'll show up. And later on, we'll all feel very silly."

"Dale." George stepped closer and glanced around the room. "I'm going to tell you something, but keep it to yourself." George leaned over and spoke in a mildly hushed tone. "We're pretty darn certain that Tom Quinn did it."

"Did what?"

"Painted it."

"Painted what?"

"He painted the *mural*."

Weaver smirked. He glanced over at Tyler. No smile. Weaver realized George and Tyler were truly serious. "We're talking about the same garbage man, aren't we?"

"That's the one."

"Hold on now. You're telling me that Tom Quinn is some kind of secret Picasso? Come on, Mayor."

"See for yourself, Dale. There's a room full of stuff over at Tom's house. The man is some kind of prodigy."

"Well, maybe not a prodigy," Tyler said.

"Huh? What do you mean?" George was baffled by Tyler's sudden betrayal.

"He's really talented. I just didn't see anything there that matches the mural."

"So it's his goddamned masterpiece! For goodness sake, you agree that he's the artist, right?"

"Yes."

"There, you see? Sheriff, go over and look."

"I'll take your word for it," the sheriff said. "I'm not going to snoop around Tom's house."

"I'm telling you. Tom Quinn is the artist, and something isn't right," George said.

"Fine. I'll put out an APB as soon as I can. We'll handle it. Tom isn't a lost child."

"He's not the type to just go missing for days either."

Tyler decided to leave George and Sheriff Weaver to their dispute. This was big news. He hurried back to his room at the Saguaro Motel, excitement in his steps. Tyler was the only journalist who knew the true identity of the artist. Grady James had excited a lot of people and fooled them with embarrassing consequences. But Tom was as far away from the spotlight as possible. In fact, if it weren't for those overflowing garbage bins, Tyler would never have discovered Tom's secret at all.

He held his cell phone in his hand. The screen was lit up and illuminating his face as he gazed down at it. His thumb rested gently on the 3 button, which was the preset speed-dial button for Rebecca's office in Phoenix. She'd told him to find a unique angle for his story. This was it. He'd done it. He'd surpassed all the other reports coming out of Ketchum. He had the exclusive story about the real identity of the artist. And he was a garbage man of all things. No one had even known he could draw or paint. It was the sort of stuff that Hollywood producers positively drool over. Yet Tyler didn't push the little button with the number 3 on it.

As he sat there holding the phone, he heard the eerie cry of a police siren in the distance. It grew louder. Then it came whizzing past in a sudden howling burst. It faded away as it moved down the road into the distance. How many patrol cars did the town of Ketchum have? Two, he guessed. Maybe three. They would never need more than three. Sheriff Weaver was headed somewhere fast. Tyler considered the possibility that George convinced Dale to look for Tom. "A salesman," that's what Doris had called him. Maybe they'd already found him. Or maybe they'd found his body rotting away somewhere. Left out like the garbage on Main Street.

Tyler tucked his phone away and hurried out to his car. The sound of the police siren was well into the distance now, barely audible. But he would follow. Even without the whine of the siren in the air, it would not be hard. There weren't many roads and Tyler already had an ominous feeling where he was headed.

Sheriff Weaver's patrol car was parked outside of a small house with an art studio in the back. There was another car parked there too. But there was no one in sight. As Tyler brought his car to a slow roll, he watched for signs of activity in the house. Then he parked along the road and started walking to the front door. It opened before he could reach it. George immediately came out and ushered him away. He did so quickly.

"What's going on?" Tyler said.

"Let's talk in the driveway," he said, quietly. He wasn't smiling now. Tyler walked with George. They stopped behind the cars in the driveway. George's face was pale. He was breathing strangely too. He started to lean back against the sheriff's car as if he needed something to support him. His knees seemed to strain under a sudden new weight. "Grady hanged himself," he finally said.

"My god," Tyler said. "Who found him?"

"A friend."

"Did he leave a note?"

"Yes."

"Did you read it?"

"No."

George was hardly able to speak. He took deep breaths. Tyler had never seen George like this before. Here was the man behind the stage curtains—shaken and disturbed. Tyler put his hand on George's arm.

"You okay, Mayor?"

"Yes," he said, breathing hard. He mumbled something else.

"What?"

"Please don't write about this," he said, louder.

Tyler wasn't sure whether he meant the suicide or his reaction to it.

"Did you hear me?" George said.

"I heard you," Tyler said. "But I can't just ignore it."

George wasn't sure whether Tyler meant Grady's suicide or his reaction to it. Nothing so tragic as the death of Grady James had occurred in Ketchum for many years—not since that Halloween night at the Gord house. That was many years ago though. Many in Ketchum had not been born yet or were too young to remember the tragedy that had happened in that house.

XXIV

The house once owned by Argus J. Gord was the source of some local interest well before the tragedy there. Imposing, it was among the oldest surviving buildings in Ketchum. Its distinctive architecture gave it a strange mystique. It could easily overstimulate imaginative young minds. Local kids often called it the gingerbread house, even though its walls were white, with a forest-green trim. It didn't resemble the rich brown color of a Christmas cookie at all. In fact, the house was associated with Halloween more so than any other holiday.

None of Ketchum's children had ever actually been inside the house. This left a void in their minds that was filled by their imaginations with bizarre and sinister fantasies. One popular story related that it belonged to a witch, although only the very young believed that story. The older kids had seen Mr. Gord around town or outside tending to his lawn enough to know that neither he nor Mrs. Gord were, in fact, witches. Nevertheless, the local kids continued to tell other stories that were equally outrageous.

The Gords had a son, it was said. None of the kids had ever seen the boy before. Some said they caught a quick glimpse of a barely discernible figure in the distance once. Others reported a blinking eye peeking out from the dark corner of an upstairs window. They all heard the terrible cries too, or so they said. And some of the kids swore that they knew a friend of a friend, or a distant cousin, who saw the boy's face one time and witnessed how inhuman it was. Some said it wasn't a real boy at all, but the ghost of a boy who died there long ago and still haunted the house.

On Halloween night in 1992, a group of local kids—ranging from ages twelve to fifteen—gathered around a cluster of palo verde trees across from the Gord house. Local trick-or-treaters seldom ventured there, especially at that late hour. But a dare was made. Each of the kids proved their courage by slipping across and circumambulating the Gord house alone. No running was allowed either. The most frightening part, they all agreed, was that moment when they reached the back of the house. That was the place where you fell out of sight from the others waiting across the street. It was especially dark. It was unfamiliar. Noises seemed especially unnatural. Several of the kids secretly planned to start running once they were out of view.

As the dare commenced, the eldest boy went first. He was brave and sauntered across the street as if bored by the challenge. In the trees, the others all watched as his dark silhouette disappeared around the side of the house. Tense seconds passed. "Where is he?" someone whispered. Soon he came marching around the corner and back across the street with his arms out. "It's not scary at all," he boasted. Then one-by-one, the kids scampered across the street. And one-by-one, they returned to the trees with their chins held high, unscathed, and hardly able to contain their giggles of excitement. "It was so scary," one of them reported. "I think I heard the boy," another claimed. There were only two kids left to complete the Halloween dare when fourteen-year-old Karen McKee went across the street in the dark that night.

Karen was the second-to-last one to take the dare. She was far more frightened than she would admit. She tried her best to walk across the road bravely, as if nothing bothered her, but her body was giving her away. Her steps were erratic and clumsy, and she had to keep lifting her chin as it swung down below her tense, nearly shaking shoulders. Karen had never liked the dark, especially in rural Arizona, where snakes and spiders and scorpions might lurk. She still used a night-light at home in her bedroom, although she hid it whenever her friends came over. The Gord house seemed like something out of a horror movie—the type of movie that her parents told her not to watch. She had no stomach for sudden scares or blood, but weekend slumber parties and her interest in boys inevitably brought those types of movies to her. She always wanted to be part of the group.

Karen walked carefully around the side of the house. She stepped heel-and-toe, so as not to trip or stumble over any rocks or shrubs. She took deep breaths and tried her best to think about other things. She thought about the boy she liked so much and how she wanted to kiss him. She thought about the summer camp she'd gone to visit last summer in Flagstaff. She swam every day for a week there. Before Karen knew it, she was doing it. She was turning around the back of the Gord house, out of the view of the other kids hiding across the street. The crickets, chirping away in the dark, seemed suddenly very loud. It was distracting. She thought nothing of the summer camp or the boy she liked now.

There was a doorway there at the back of the house that she could barely see. Her eyes began to play tricks on her.

Things seemed to shift and move. The sole source of light was the small sliver of moon in the sky overhead. She put her hands out, fearing she might trip on something. Her hands landed against the door and she felt her way around it. She could see the far corner of the house ahead and she felt a small tingle of relief bloom in her chest. Her fingers left the wood texture of the door behind, and she took two steps forward, but something confused her. The sensation of hands, bigger than her own, paralyzed her. There was a shape like a body in the dark with her now. Her eyes were not playing tricks. Arms were squeezing her and pulling at her. When she tried to scream, four foul-smelling fingers pressed down on her mouth and bent her nose to the side.

"Got you. Got you!" a man said with a slur and a giggle.

Across the street, Karen's friends waited. They stared at the corner of the house, looking for her to come around. She was supposed to come marching proudly around and back to the trees. They waited. One of them suggested she was only trying to scare them. Another one wondered if they should leave and go home. The one kid who had yet to complete the dare agreed with that idea. The eldest insisted otherwise. They all agreed to wait for two minutes more. When they dared to call out her name, a light went on, and Argus Gord came rushing out the front door with a flashlight waving in his hand. The kids, still hovering under the palo verde trees by the road, instantly scattered and retreated in a panic toward town.

In the back of the house, Karen struggled. The arm wrapped around her was so strong. The hand pressed down so forcefully against her mouth that it choked and muffled her attempts to scream, even to breathe. The back door shut behind her, and not even the moon was with her now. She was being dragged up some stairs. She could feel the wooden steps bumping painfully into the backs of her legs and her feet. She flailed desperately in the dark. The voice in her ear hushed her again and again, as if she were a crying infant, and when she tried even harder to scream, the hand across her mouth pressed down even harder and yanked violently at her head.

"No!" the man said. "No."

Her legs kicked and banged into the stairs and she was pulled up into the dark farther and farther. There was more hushing in her ear and small bits of saliva landed on her cheek.

That night, Karen McKee did not return home. Her mother started calling the homes of her friends (those she knew anyway) and the boy her daughter liked so much. With every additional phone call, her mother's voice grew more frantic, and her thoughts grew more and more terrible. Mr. McKee, meanwhile, had gone to drive around town and search for Karen. He drove slowly down every neighborhood street and called out her name whenever he could. He didn't care if he woke anyone up.

The kids who were with Karen were reluctant to say any-thing. But when Sheriff Danby, Dale Weaver's predecessor in Ketchum, arrived at the door to see one of them, the tearful confession was almost instantaneous. There was talk of the dare and older kids pressuring others and how it was a mis-take and how they were scared. None of the kids knew where Karen was now.

Sheriff Danby arrived at the Gord house that night. He came at an hour when he would normally be asleep in bed. He had never been called out to the Gord house before, and it seemed unlikely that the Gords had anything to do with a missing girl on Halloween. Nevertheless, he knocked on the front door and waited there on the big front porch for someone to answer. He would ask the Gords for permission to search the area.

"Yes?" Argus said after opening the door.

"I apologize for disturbing you at this hour, sir. But we have a report of a missing girl and she was last seen on your property."

"My property?"

"That's right. A group of kids were out here earlier. I believe they were up to some Halloween high jinks around your house."

"I see. Well, I heard some commotion outside earlier. I came out to the porch to have a look. Then I saw a whole group running off down the road. I couldn't make any of them out, though."

"If it's no trouble, I'd like to have a look around. Maybe she's hiding around in the trees somewhere. It shouldn't take long."

"Certainly Sheriff, but I—I'll come out and show you around. There's not much to see, really." Argus stepped out onto the porch and started to go down the steps. He jogged down quickly as if he were in a hurry. "Did you look around down the street?"

"Yes, sir. The father and I have been searching everywhere for this little girl. I imagine she's in a heap of trouble when she gets home tonight."

"I should think so," Argus replied. "Can I ask, what were the kids doing? I mean, out here. They didn't vandalize the house, did they?"

"Oh, no, sir. Nothing like that. I don't know if you realize it, but the kids think your house is pretty spooky. They were daring each other to make laps around it in the dark. Pretty innocent kid stuff, really. Do you have kids, Mr. Gord?"

"Yes, well, a boy. He's handicapped though. My wife and I care for him at home. He doesn't socialize with other children."

"I'm sorry. I didn't know that."

"Oh, that's quite all right. We manage."

Argus gave Sheriff Danby a tour of the property. They started with the front of the house. As they went, Argus made sure to point out his wife's flower garden so that nothing was trampled underfoot. Danby carried a large flashlight, and he swept the beam of light back and forth over the ground for any trace of the girl's presence. They found several sets of small footprints in the dirt. They went along the house and around the corner toward the back. Danby counted at least a half-dozen tracks, all of them from sneakers the size that kids wear. He did not know if any of them belonged to Karen McKee.

"Do you think she could have run away with the rest of them and gotten lost?" Argus asked.

"Maybe."

"There's not much back here. She could be out there, past the road."

"She could. I won't take up much more of your time."

Sheriff Danby continued to sweep his light over the rocky dirt with its hues of red and bronze—until he came across a sudden disruption in the tracks. There were prints facing every direction, and streaks, as though someone's feet had been pulled across the dirt rather than taking steps. There were new tracks too. They were larger than most of the others.

"What is this?"

"What?" Argus said, anxiously. "Oh, it's probably from me. I took a look around after the kids ran off."

Sheriff Danby turned the light toward Argus's shoes, which were leather and larger than the footprints in the dirt. "These don't look like your shoes," he said. When he brought the light back to the tracks, he could see that the long jagged streaks went directly toward a door in the back of the Gord house.

"What's in there?"

"Where?"

"The door."

"My wife is asleep, Sheriff. I'd really rather not wake her by going in and out of the backdoor. Our bedroom is right above here. You see that window?"

"The tracks lead right into that door. There are some awfully worried parents waiting up for their little girl. I think the least we can do is take a look. I'm sure Mrs. Gord won't mind."

Sheriff Danby stepped toward the door and placed his hand on the knob.

"It's locked," Argus said.

Danby turned the knob. "Looks open to me," he said.

"Sheriff—this is outrageous. I assure you, if there was a little girl hiding in my house, I would know about it."

Danby opened the door and aimed the beam of his flashlight inside. There were wooden stairs leading up to a room on the second floor. "Is there a light switch, Mr. Gord?"

"Sheriff!" he said.

"Karen?" Danby called out. "Karen?"

There was a noise at the top of the stairs, and another sound, as though someone was whining or crying in the dark.

"Did you hear that?" Danby said.

"I don't hear anything."

"Karen? It's Sheriff Danby."

When the only son of Argus Gord, whose name was Benjamin, reached the onset of puberty and began to grow bigger and stronger, he became harder for his parents to control. His mood swings and tantrums caused more and more damage. It was after a particularly bad incident that Mr. Gord decided it was best that his son have a separate living space, apart from the rest of the house. He could stay out of the watchful eye of the town too.

Mrs. Gord had always been uncomfortable with the idea of locking her son in the back apartment. So, on occasion—when she was the last one to leave—she would forget to lock it. Maybe she had a secret desire to see her son escape and disappear. Or perhaps she was simply repulsed by the idea of caging her only child like an animal. She used to pray for that child. Caring for a mentally handicapped son was always difficult, but when Benjamin grew older and became a young man, it proved nearly impossible. She could no longer physically control him, and his urges now led to embarrassing and disturbing situations.

Benjamin heard the children from his room that Halloween night. He had grown accustomed to silence and natural sounds of the night in his sparse apartment where he spent hours and hours alone. The sound of those kids shuffling around the house outside in the dark, one after the other, was something new. It excited him. When he crouched down beside his window, the moisture of his breath fogging up the glass in front of him, the small silhouettes of other kids—people he was barred from ever approaching by his parents—increased his excitement further. He had learned about games before. His mother played games with him, especially when he was younger. There was a game of tag they used to play when he still lived in the main part of the house. Now that he was put away in the back, he could still play. He would still play.

It was not Karen McKee specifically Benjamin was seeking. It was simply another accident of history. There was no grand hand (or caring eyes) guiding either one of them that night. Benjamin would have settled for anyone who came past that door, left unlocked. He did not understand why his father would get so angry with him, or why he was never allowed to play with others. He knew only his feelings and his loneliness.

When Benjamin grabbed hold of Karen, he took her resistance as something playful. He felt wonderful exhilaration in the sustained physical contact. He did not comprehend how much stronger he was than her. Nor did he hear her cries as anything more than something loud and shrill that would anger his father. Benjamin did not want his father to come out. He did not want a beating. So he wrestled her away into the door and up the stairs, all the while holding his hand firmly across her mouth.

Eventually Karen stopped resisting and moving at all. Her body became limp and heavy. Benjamin still kept his hand over her mouth. His hand was large enough that his fingers crept up over her nose. It was part of the game. He poked at her and tickled her, expecting her to twitch and curl up with laughter. Karen did not move. Thinking it was a trick, he continued. Benjamin squealed with glee when he could not contain his pride.

Then, when he grew bored, Benjamin lifted his hand and put it back down again. He tickled her and rubbed at her body. "Wake up," he said in her ear, giggling before and after. He poked at her face and under her arm. But Karen's head simply fell to one side. All his prodding did nothing to rouse her. Benjamin's face now started to change. He stood and paced around the room shaking his hands in the air. He hummed to himself in distressed tones. His father would be so angry.

Benjamin pulled Karen's body across the room to a closet and pushed it back against the wall. He yanked the blankets off of his mattress and threw them over her, trying to hide the body from the world. When her feet remained visible, he kicked at them. They didn't disappear beneath the blanket and he became angry, which made him shake even more and scratch at his face and chest in panic.

When Benjamin heard Sheriff Danby's voice later that night, he was lying down on his bare mattress. For a moment, he forgot what he'd done. He was tired and he did not move from his bed until he heard his father's voice too, irritated and arguing with the sheriff. He crawled off the mattress and walked over to the top of the stairs. The beam of the sheriff's flashlight shown directly on his face.

"Father?" Benjamin said. "Hello, father." His eyes were blinking and squinting from the sheriff's bright light. He raised his hands to block it out.

At the top of the stairs, Sheriff Danby found a nearly empty room. There was a mattress lying on the floor. There was a wooden rocking chair, scattered toys, some picture books, and a battery-powered radio. Some used dishes were piled beside the door. Then there was an adjacent bathroom and a closet with a curious bundle of blankets in it. There was a pungent scent too—body odor from a teenage boy—filling the air. Benjamin stared blankly at the sheriff as if he had never seen a policeman before.

In the days after the death of Karen McKee, Benjamin Gord was sent away by the state of Arizona to a special institution for neglected youth with mental disabilities. Argus was arrested on charges of abuse, child neglect, and obstruction. He eventually pleaded guilty. Argus was given a plea deal, although many in Ketchum felt he should have been charged with manslaughter. All charges against Angelica Gord, Benjamin's mother, were dropped. It was rumored that Argus had arranged it so in his plea agreement.

Mrs. Gord remained in the house for a month before she overdosed on a bottle of prescription sleeping pills. She survived. Argus's sister Ruth and her husband arrived from Tolleson to stay with her after that. She seldom left her bed though, and she would cry at random moments.

Beyond the house, the entire town of Ketchum seemed overrun with rumors and stories about the Gord family and the monstrous boy secretly kept locked away. For Angelica, the loss of her only child, the imprisonment of her husband, the overwhelming guilt she felt, the humiliation of all the malicious stories and staring eyes outside her windows were too much. Her simple world became a veritable hell, and she could not make any sense of it.

When Angelica was a young bride, she used to pray to God every night for a healthy, happy child. She always wanted a boy. She and Argus tried unsuccessfully for over a year. As time passed, the big beautiful house in Ketchum felt emptier by the day. She spent countless moments imagining what it would be like to hear the sound of little feet running down the long hallway. She longed to sing her baby sweet lullabies in the bedroom with the window that overlooked the flower garden. The day she learned that she was pregnant was the happiest of her life. She believed that God had heard her prayers and rewarded her patience. She decided to give that child a good Biblical name in thanks: Benjamin.

Angelica Gord never imagined that she would need to learn about the complex implications of nondisjunction or an extra twenty-first chromosome in Benjamin's DNA. Those were not things she was prepared for, nor had she read about them in preparation for such a momentous time in her life. She and Argus were sitting in an office at the hospital when they got the news. They did not understand what the doctor explained or why tests were being performed at all. She had given birth to a healthy baby boy, she insisted. Argus refused to accept anything the doctor said either. At home, though, the Gords were unable to continue their denial for long.

Having a child meant a great deal to Angelica. She always believed in the existence of a heaven—a blissful world yet to come—but the idea of dying and leaving no one to remember her was simply terrifying. And she could not find a purpose in letting time slip away, day-by-day, alone there in that house. There was Argus, and she loved him. He would die someday though. The odds, she knew, were that he would be the first to go to heaven. She would live alone in that big house. She would awaken every day to silence. Emptiness.

Angelica had asked God for a child and imagined that He heard her plea. She would not be alone. There was a deep sense of relief in that. Someone would remain after she was gone. Someone would remember her with stories and pictures, and it would be a kind of eternity for her. The news that her miracle child had Down syndrome was entirely unexpected. It seemed oddly dreamlike. She did not understand what it meant, and she could not help but ask if she had done something wrong. Had she displeased Him?

Angelica's deep confusion was intermingled with moments of blind faith and optimism. "It is a test," she would tell herself. It was a blessing in disguise. Those explanations were inevitably overtaken by dismay when her intellect overruled her heart, but the terrible fear that she was being punished still stirred. She, like so many others, had done nothing to deserve her misfortune. It was not an uncommon disorder, after all. It was still a child—a sweet, smiling child.

Karen McKee had done nothing to deserve her misfortune either. Neither did her family. "She was a sweet, shy, and funny girl," one teacher recalled at the pulpit during her funeral. Her only flaw, she added, was the schoolgirl crush she had on the boy across the classroom. It sometimes distracted her from her studies.

Benjamin had done nothing either. He was not an evil young man, nor any kind of monster, as some folks in town said. It was not his fault or his choice that he was born with an extra twenty-first chromosome. It was not Benjamin's fault that he was raised by parents ill prepared to care for his needs. It was not his fault that he had been born with the same emotions and urges of any other human being.

XXV

At Abdullah Park's diner on Main Street, Daisy Correa reluctantly explained to Tyler that she used to babysit Karen McKee many years ago. In fact, she knew all the kids who were out in the trees with Karen that night. It was the first time Tyler heard anything about the stories surrounding the Gord house. He wasn't yet sure why she was telling him about it now, except that the suicide of Grady James had reopened old wounds. Like many others, Daisy stayed away from the Gord house. The fact that Tyler was inside the apartment—the place where the girl died—surprised her. People from Ketchum would never go there, although some thoughtless kids still dared each other to go around the house on Halloween. Daisy knew that Audrey lived there, of course. She excused Audrey because she came to Ketchum from the city. If Audrey stayed much longer it might be an issue, though.

"We have tragedies and murders too, just like the people in the city. The difference is that we don't forget so easily," Daisy said.

"Well, I think there's just too much tragedy in the city," Tyler replied. "The more people, the more tragedy. You can't escape it, no matter where you go I guess. Like Grady James."

Daisy said nothing.

"Whatever happened to Angelica Gord?" Tyler said.

"She put the house up for sale. Left town with her in-laws. She used to go see Benjamin every week. As for Argus, well, once he left prison, he drank himself to death. Angry and bitter till the end. I don't think he ever went to see his son."

"Is she still alive?"

"No. She died about seven years ago. A few people went to the funeral."

"Not you, though?"

"No."

"Do you know the people who own the house now?"

"Yes. They're fine people, retirees with dogs. They know what happened, but prefer not to discuss it, as you can imagine."

"Could I ask you about Samuel Welch?"

"Sam?" she said with a look of surprise. "I suppose. What about him?"

"I understand he has a problem with your husband. It's been suggested that you're the reason for that."

"That's nonsense. It was ages ago. He used to spend time with me. Sam is just too involved in his business to give a hoot about anyone else. That includes my husband."

"Are you sure? Maybe there's more to this than you realize."

"Ridiculous. Small town gossip. That's what that is. Nothing more."

"Is he in love with you, Mrs. Correa?"

She scoffed. "Excuse me, Mr. Anderson," she said sternly. "You are a visitor to our town. I'm sorry if you find us all too boring as we are."

"Not at all."

"Please don't make things up then."

"I apologize. I didn't mean to offend you," he said, quietly. "If I could suggest it, though, I think you should have a talk with him."

"I think it's time to go," Daisy said, and she stood. She gathered her purse. "Thank you for the coffee, Mr. Anderson. Best of luck with your article." She left the diner.

Tyler remained seated at the little white table. He placed his head against the palm of his hand and pondered his next step. He wondered what Daisy had been like as a young woman, back when Samuel Welch was still courting her. Maybe Samuel still saw that young woman when he looked at her.

Tyler looked around the diner and noticed a man talking to Abdullah. The golem seemed serious and irritated. What was going on? Tyler stood and approached the counter. He recognized the voice now. His neighbor at the motel—the analyst, Dr. Wood—was the man talking to Abdullah.

"How was the Grand Canyon?" Tyler said as he sat down on the stool beside him.

"Oh—I got delayed. It's still on my itinerary though," Wood said.

Abdullah glanced at Tyler and then walked away without a word.

"Did I interrupt something?" Tyler asked.

"No. We were just chatting. He's an interesting guy."

"Makes a great burger," Tyler said.

"Really? I'll have to try one."

"You plan on staying awhile?"

"No. Lots to do, I'm afraid. You?"

"A little longer. I'm not done with my story yet."

"Yes, that's right. Your story. How's that going?"

"Fine. I think I might have found something to spice it up."

"Really? What's that?"

"Tell me what you think of this: 'Government spook active in small Arizona town.' Huh?" Tyler said, looking Wood in the eye.

Wood chuckled. "Oh, come now. I'm a world traveler, Mr. Anderson. I'm more interested in books and old archives than I am spying on anyone."

"Really?"

"I told you about Fischer, didn't I?"

"Yes, but I think it's a very long way to the Grand Canyon."

"It's on my way," he said, a bit annoyed now. "I have twenty days of vacation left and lots of places on my itinerary."

"But here you are. Still. Chatting with a cook named Abdullah."

"I've never been one to hurry. I'm a scholar for God's sake."

"I don't know. You're starting to smell fishy to me," Tyler said.

Wood smiled dismissively. "You see that picture on the wall?" He pointed to a framed photograph.

Tyler hadn't noticed it before. He looked closely at it now. It featured an oddly shaped stone about the size of a seated man. It was surrounded by thick green grass, and there were patches of green and brown moss on the surface of the stone.

"What about it?" Tyler asked, after a few seconds.

"They call that thing the *Derviš Kamena*—the Dervish Stone."

"Never heard of it," Tyler said.

"Of course you haven't," Wood said, amused by Tyler's response. "It's Balkan folklore—a fairy tale about a man turning himself into a goddamned rock. Hardly something you or I would care about. The question is: Why is there a picture of it hanging on the wall in this diner?"

"It's just a photograph. There are lots in here."

"Come on. Surely a good reporter like you can think of a few good questions to ask."

Before Wood could say anything more, there was a sudden electronic buzz in his clothes. He dug into his pocket, appearing annoyed by the interruption. "Excuse me," he said. He looked down at his cell phone. "Ah—excuse me while I take this," he said.

"Your NSA handlers calling?" Tyler replied.

Wood stood, shaking his head, and walked toward the front door. He left the faint scent of aromatic smoke behind him. Alone now, Tyler looked again at the photograph on the wall. It *was* strange. Then he glanced around the diner. Still no Audrey. But there was Abdullah headed directly for him.

"You know that guy?" Abdullah asked, anxiety in his voice. He leaned over the counter to hear Tyler's answer in a private manner.

"Not really. He was next door to me at the motel."

"The Saguaro?"

Tyler nodded.

"Well, he's some kind of spook."

"What did he say?"

"We were just talking. You know, the usual banter with a customer. But it went in a whole different direction. He starts asking about this picture. How I got it and everything."

"Where did you get it?"

"From a friend, man. Something wrong with that?"

"No. What'd you tell him?" Tyler gestured toward the door.

"I said I got it from a friend."

"What friend?"

"Oh man, not you too," he said, checking the door.

"Well, it is an interesting rock. More so than most rocks."

"This is the first time anyone has even noticed it."

"Really?"

"People come here to eat, man. Talk about sports or something," Abdullah said.

"He said it's from the Balkans. Where in the Balkans?"

"What?"

"The stone. Where's it located? What country?"

Abdullah rolled his eyes. "Bosnia, okay?"

"Bosnia? I work with a guy who was a foreign correspondent there for the *LA Times*. Years ago. He's a dick though."

"Whatever. Are you going to order something or what?"

"I'm thinking," Tyler said. He glanced again at the front door. "Did the government conduct an experiment on you? Is that why you're so big?"

Abdullah chuckled.

XXVI

I n 1993 Abdullah Park found himself on a flight to Rome. The world watched as Europe gave rise to a new horrific war on its soil. This time, the breakup of the Socialist Federal Republic of Yugoslavia in the Balkans had devolved into ethno-religious conflicts throughout its former territories, including Croatia and Slovenia. The central land of Bosnia proved to be the most infamous, hosting the most appalling atrocities in Europe since the Holocaust. "Never again," it turned out, was an empty phrase.

When Bosnia declared its independence as a sovereign republic in 1992, neighboring forces from Serbia and Croatia attacked. They wanted to secure land for their own states. To do so, they initiated a campaign to cleanse the land of its Muslim inhabitants, known as Bosniaks. When reports about the ensuing atrocities reached international audiences, many Muslim states and organizations tried to provide political, financial, and military support for their coreligionists. Most of them were legal. There were many humanitarian efforts to provide medicine and supplies. However, a few leaned toward more clandestine activities. Abdullah Park of Minneapolis managed to find his way into one of the latter.

A Somali immigrant in Minneapolis using the name Idris recruited Abdullah to join a small volunteer unit of foreign fighters, *mujahidin*, waging a jihad against the Orthodox Christian Serbs and Roman Catholic Croats. Abdullah was big and strong, and he had street smarts but no military background or battlefield experience. He believed the cause was just, though. He felt it in his heart. God, he believed, would bless the Muslims in their struggle. The Bosniaks were innocent. They were fellow members of the *ummah*, or worldwide community, that he adopted as a troubled teenager, who desperately needed help.

Idris, the Somali, told Abdullah terrible stories. Muslim corpses being stacked and used as latrines by Serb soldiers, priests blessing the death squads, the unspeakable horrors of the rape and concentration camps. Idris read from the Holy Qur'an, reciting verses that commanded righteous believers to fight anyone who attacked the Muslims, those who expelled the believers from their homes, those who persecute the Muslims for their worship of the One True God. Abdullah was always deeply moved. He asked himself how he could refuse.

An American convert to Islam, Abdullah always felt the need to prove himself among his fellow Muslims, especially to those born into the religion. This was a test. He would travel to a faraway land, return home as a hero, and defend his brothers and sisters in Islam in the process. And if he died in the war, he would be a *shahid*, a martyr, for God and His religion. Yes, God would reward him for his sacrifice, bestowing the infinite blessings of paradise on him. Eternity in the next life, Idris had reminded him, was far beyond any joy in this life.

Abdullah told his mother and closest friends that he was going away to study Arabic overseas on a fully paid scholarship. He'd won it, he said. Most thought it was a terrific opportunity, although his mother expressed some concern once she was sober. Others were amazed that the formerly troublesome young man, known as Christopher before his conversion, was so interested in learning and turning his life around. They had no idea that he was traveling to Bosnia. In fact, few of them had ever heard of Bosnia or knew anything of the conflict.

———

Sitting in the back of a late '80s model Fiat van, Abdullah stared anxiously at the backs of two heads belonging to Italian aid workers. It reminded him of the time, years ago, when he and two friends had stolen a car. He'd sat in the backseat, staring at the backs of their heads, terrified that the police would stop them. The Italians were paid to smuggle foreign fighters into Bosniak territory. This time it was Abdullah and three other men. Two were Arabs, probably North Africans, who spoke some French but no English. The other one was a Turk from Germany named Murat. He knew some English. Murat made small talk with Abdullah to pass the time. He seemed to know all about the history of Bosnia and eagerly shared stories about the once great Ottoman Empire.

The terrain across the border, between Croatia and Bosnia, was mountainous, and the van struggled loudly whenever going uphill. Sometimes the stink of diesel exhaust would creep into the vehicle and make it difficult to breathe. Abdullah would always try to hold his breath until it subsided.

The two Italians didn't seem bothered by it. The seats were uncomfortable too, and he could feel the springs poking him in the backside, especially when rolling over the copious potholes. It was hardly the heroic journey into battle.

The Dinaric Alps take their name from Mount Dinara, a limestone mountain peak that sits on the border that divides Croatia from Bosnia. The lands along the base of the mountains are flat, lush green plains wedged between jagged limestone cliffs and hills. The forests are full of tall beech trees and black pines, although the different armies had already started to destroy the forests to prevent anyone from using the trees as cover.

The van carried a shipment of rations, blankets, and medicine strapped in tight bundles to the roof. But hidden in the interior lining were six AK-47 assault rifles with several packets of ammunition acquired from Albanian arms dealers along the Adriatic coast. The Italians were taking Abdullah, Murat, and the Arabs to the town of Livno, where they would meet a new contact and travel toward Travnik for training. The weapons and ammunition would go with them.

The town of Livno sat in fertile green fields near rocky cliffs where battered medieval fortresses still kept watch. Like most cities in Bosnia, the rows of buildings and houses in Livno were bright white with red or burnt-orange tiled roofs that made them easily visible from afar. The few exceptions were the central Ottoman-era mosque with its silver dome and fat pencil-like minaret, the adjacent clock tower, and the drab gray modernist constructions of the Cold War years when Bosnia was a part of Yugoslavia. Winding through the heart of the town was the river Bistrica, which emerged from an enormous mountain cave called the Mali Dum, and ran down to form countless small waterfalls created by the rocks of the mountainous terrain.

Abdullah was immediately struck by the beauty of the city, even amid the disarray of the war and the grime of hopeless poverty. He knew that he was there to fight in a war, but he stared out the window at the waterfalls and the buildings as if he were on a tour. It was only when the van veered off the road and slipped into a narrow alley and quickly turned into a dark secluded garage that the grim reality of the situation snapped him back.

"This is our stop," said Murat quietly.

The van came to a halt inside. The door slid open with a loud thud, and one of the Italians directed the four men to climb out.

"Wait next to the vehicle," one of them said. The other Italian hurried back to the entrance and closed the big wooden doors. He was clearly less comfortable with the situation than his associate. Instead of coming back, he stayed for a moment, lit a cigarette and peered anxiously out into the alleyway through a small dusty window.

Abdullah, Murat, and the two Arabs stood against the wall with green duffel bags at their feet. As they waited, the Italian in the van carefully removed a panel along the interior and reached his arm all the way inside to remove the hidden cargo. First a bundle of dirty fabric came out, apparently some simple padding to prevent any of the contents from shifting too much. After that came the first AK-47 assault rifles. As each of the six appeared, the Italian passed it over to the four aspiring holy warriors waiting patiently.

The Arabs looked more than comfortable with the assault rifles in their hands. They spoke quietly but rapidly in Arabic.

They evaluated the guns, checking the sights by pointing them up toward the ceiling. Then one of them turned to Murat and Abdullah, smiled broadly and said, "Rambo," rolling his *r* and posing playfully with the gun. Then he broke out into a boyish laugh and continued inspecting the gun again.

When all of the AK-47 assault rifles and the packets of ammunition wrapped in plastic were removed, the Italian in the van replaced the paneling, climbed out, and slammed the heavy metal sliding door shut. "Okay! *Abbiamo finito*," he said to his associate still over by the entrance. "*Andiamo!*"

The Italian with the cigarette pushed the wooden doors again with a grunt. Anxious that someone might have noticed, he took a good look out into the alleyway, saw nothing, and walked briskly back to the van where he flicked the cigarette at the ground, climbed in behind the wheel and started the engine.

The other Italian turned to Abdullah and told him and his companions to wait there in the garage. He spoke in broken English and French and used a fanning gesture with his hands. When Abdullah nodded, he nodded back. He climbed into the van, slapped the side, and gave a wave of his hand. The van backed out of the garage and sped away down the narrow road. And the Italians were gone.

The Italians hadn't bothered to stop and close the garage doors. They seemed to be in a hurry. Not wanting anyone to see the four armed foreigners inside, Abdullah and Murat took it upon themselves to shut the doors. Then the four men were on their own. They had to trust that their handlers would come. They did not know who exactly was coming. Nor did they know when their contact would arrive. Abdullah tried his best not to think about it.

XXVII

As minutes turned into hours, the dirty interior of the garage grew darker. Abdullah Park could no longer see any other faces, and there was little to do. Sometimes the Arabs would try to communicate something using French words and a few gestures or body movements. They mostly kept to themselves though. Murat sat next to Abdullah on the floor, leaning on his bag, recounting more stories of Bosnia's Ottoman past.

"There is a town south of here, called Mostar," Murat said. "It is very famous because there is a bridge there. The name of the town, Mostar, comes from the word *mostari*, which means the bridge guards. The Ottoman Turks, they built this bridge, the Stari Most, over the Neretva River during the reign of the mighty Sultan and Caliph, Suleiman the Magnificent, in the sixteenth century. It is a high, arching bridge made of stone, protected by guard towers on each side, and it amazed many, many people. The Stari Most connects the two sides of the city, which was a place of different religions before the war. And every summer, the bravest young men used to jump from the bridge into the river below. Can you imagine? It is *very* high."

Abdullah thoroughly enjoyed Murat's stories. They made Murat sound like a well-trained tour guide, more so than a soldier. Or perhaps, Abdullah imagined, he resembled a very eccentric university lecturer. An art historian. The lost age of the great Muslim empire fascinated Abdullah. It sent his imagination spinning. In those days, Abdullah thought, he would have been one of a hundred thousand warriors marching into Bosnia. Not one of *four*.

"Do you know the story of the Dervish Stone?" Murat asked after a few minutes of silence, knowing that Abdullah did not. "There was a young dervish who lived near Tuzla. Every day he went to the cemetery. Every day. There was a tomb there. It belonged to a beautiful girl whom the dervish loved when he was a boy. Her name was Aiša. He would sit at her grave for an hour every day in silence. This went on for years. Then came a new war campaign by the Sultan."

"What Sultan was it? Suleiman the Magnificent?"

"No. Eh—I don't know, actually."

"What year was this?" Abdullah teased.

"Sometime in the sixteenth century," Murat said quickly. "Anyway, the Sultan called all the young men to join his army. But the dervish refused the Sultan's order. He would not go and leave Aiša's grave. When a Sipahi saw him one day, he struck the dervish with his bow and ordered him to go. So the Dervish hid. But he would still come out to visit Aiša. And the Sipahi found him again. The Sipahi threatened to drag the dervish to Sarajevo in chains. So finally the dervish agreed. That night, he came to visit Aiša's grave. He wept there in the dark. The next morning, the Sipahi and the soldiers gathered in the *meydan* (town square) to go to Sarajevo. When the dervish did not arrive, the Sipahi was angry. He rode to the cemetery with chains in his hands. But when he got there, he found only a large stone next to Aiša's grave, about the size of a seated man. They call this the Dervish Stone. Even today."

"The dervish turned into a stone?" Abdullah asked.

"Yes, *yani*, this is the story!"

Since the Arabs could not understand English, they intermittently sat and paced and spoke to each other in glottal, inflective spurts. Whenever a car or some pedestrians passed by in the narrow alleyway outside, the Arabs would suddenly go silent and raise their weapons, as if expecting an attack at any moment. Abdullah and Murat, eager to show solidarity with their Arab brethren, would belatedly follow their lead, even though it was only for show.

"Do you think they've fought before?" Abdullah asked Murat.

"Yes. Maybe Afghanistan or Algeria," he guessed.

Finally, after the men had spent several hours hiding patiently in the garage, a truck with a noisy diesel engine and bright headlights arrived outside in the alleyway and came to a screeching stop. A man climbed out and left the engine running. He approached the garage doors and started to pull them open.

The Arabs rushed to the dark corners of the garage with their assault rifles raised, frantically gesturing and making whistling noises for Abdullah and Murat to confront the possible intruder at the door. Abdullah's pulse began to pound in his ears as he scrambled over to the door and took a defensive stance with weapon raised.

When the garage doors separated, creaking every inch, and opened to the alleyway, Abdullah found a tall Slavic man standing there on the other side with a bushy beard, but no moustache, wearing a tight black stocking cap and a well-worn leather jacket.

"Assalamu alaikum," the man said with a deep growling voice.

"Walaikum salaam," Abdullah said, comfortable with the man's use of the traditional Muslim greeting. The Arabs, though, remained at the ready in their corners, awaiting further confirmation.

"My name is Samir," the new arrival said in English with a thick Bosnian accent. "I will take you to Travnik."

As they rode toward Travnik that night, Abdullah and Murat asked Samir about the war. They wanted to know all about the number of foreign fighters who were at the front. Hundreds, Samir said. They would be organized into a unit at the camp called *El Mudžahid*, he added. Samir spoke some Arabic as well, and he periodically asked the two Arabs short questions along the way to keep them involved. There was very little to do but talk on the road. Nightfall had made it almost impossible to sightsee the way Abdullah had done in the van with the Italians. He felt disappointed.

"What part of Bosnia are you from? Sarajevo?" asked Murat.

"No," Samir said. "I am from Višegrad, but there is nothing there now."

"What happened?" Abdullah asked.

"Things you cannot imagine," he said, gesturing to his head. "It is not an easy thing to talk about."

In the middle of the night, long after Abdullah had lost track of the hour, Samir's truck rolled down into a town situated comfortably within a lush, grassy river valley, surrounded by steep jagged mountains. Many of the buildings and monuments in Travnik were illuminated. Abdullah, unable to sleep, gazed out the window at the green dome of an Ottoman mosque with its towering minaret, at the curious *turbe* (tomb) of an Ottoman vizier along the road, and at the old stone fortress up on the hill. There were sudden pockets of people too, huddled around makeshift tents and spilling out from crowded buildings. As they rolled past one disheveled group, Samir explained that they were refugees.

The truck stopped outside of a storefront office near the edge of town with its lights still on. Two armed men outside the door smoked cigarettes in the cold night air. Samir, using English and Arabic, told the four to stay in the truck, and he stepped out. Abdullah watched and listened.

Samir spoke to the two men in Bosnian, and each gave Samir a manly hug and pat on the back. They laughed and smoked and stood about talking for several minutes, and then Samir returned to the truck. "Okay," he said without further explanation. He spun the truck around to a house sitting in the back, away from the road. They would stay there in the house for the night, he explained, and then they would go to the camp and join the others.

At around five in the morning, Abdullah awoke to the sound of a mournful Arabic chant echoing through the cold and still early morning air. It was the *azan*, or call to prayer, from a mosque up the road. He hadn't noticed it in the dark the night before. As he listened, he could hear other calls as well, breaking in at slightly different tempos and different volumes, creating a strange cacophony of Arabic phrases and melodic chants in the midst of the otherwise quiet Bosnian town.

As Abdullah rubbed at his eyes and sat up on the hard dirty cot that had served as his bed, he looked around the room. The two Arabs and Murat woke up from their sleep too. There was no sign of Samir.

Abdullah reached over and nudged Murat. "Hey, man, did you see a bathroom around here?" Abdullah's stomach was growling too. It made him feel nauseated, and he couldn't remember the last time he had eaten. He stood up, rubbing at his aching back and stumbled into the hallway to find his way to a small and odorous bathroom. When his stomach gurgled loudly, his thoughts drifted to hot juicy cheeseburgers with mounds of French fries and ketchup.

There was a knock at the bathroom door. Abdullah finished and opened the door to the two Arabs waiting impatiently outside.

"*Wudhu*," they said, making a washing motion with their hands. They wanted to perform the ritual ablutions before the *fajr* prayer, the first of the five daily prayers.

Abdullah nodded respectfully and stepped out of their way to return to the sleeping room. Murat had fallen back asleep on his cot. "Yo, Murat," he said in a hushed tone. When the man remained unresponsive, Abdullah kicked at his arm. It was not fitting for a *mujahid*, a holy warrior, to sleep while his comrades prayed.

XXVIII

Later that cold morning, Samir returned to the house with a bundle of cheese, some hardboiled eggs, and three loaves of bread. It was a simple meal, but given the circumstances, he'd brought a feast with him. Abdullah Park had never liked hardboiled eggs before that day, but he happily ate the one Samir offered without the slightest hesitation. It was smelly and rubbery and wet, but it was food and much appreciated.

As he happily ate, Abdullah realized that the egg, cheese, and bread in front of him might be his last meal ever. It was a morbid thought, but one he pondered calmly. Death was a very real possibility now. It was no longer a distant or an infrequent thing like it was at home in the United States. It was an everyday occurrence here. He realized the house where he was sitting might have been an overnight stop for many other young men who had long since died on the front. Martyrs, he reminded himself.

As the men finished their meal on the floor, a clean-shaven Bosnian dressed in military fatigues entered without knocking or announcing his arrival. "*Dobro jutro*," he said, his face bearing a hardened serious expression. He had wild thick black eyebrows jutting out above cold blue eyes.

"Komandant Enver," Samir said, climbing quickly to his feet.

The two men shook hands and spoke to each other in Bosnian. As the men spoke, they looked back at Abdullah and the three others still seated on the floor, chewing eagerly on bread and cheese. Abdullah assumed they were making arrangements to go to the training camp. He didn't stop eating to ask.

"This is Komandant Enver Halilovic of the Armija Republike Bosne i Hercegovine," Samir finally announced. Abdullah and the others put the food down, stood up in a line and straightened their backs out of respect. They looked ahead and said nothing.

The commander with the cold blue eyes stepped forward and shook the hand of each one as he went down the line. When he had inspected the last of them, he turned back to Samir and spoke to him again in Bosnian.

"He wants to know what weapons you have brought," Samir said.

Abdullah turned to Murat, who immediately broke formation and disappeared into another room. The others stayed in line and said nothing. Murat returned with one of the AK-47 assault rifles in his hands. He held it up and presented it to the commander. "We have six," he said proudly.

The commander took the weapon from Murat's hands. He looked it over, keeping the same serious expression on his face, and inspected its loading mechanism. When he gave it back to Murat, he turned to Samir and asked another question in Bosnian with a stern low tone.

"He wants to know if you have brought us any RPGs," Samir said.

The Bosniaks needed equipment and supplies more than they needed men like Abdullah or Murat. Pragmatically speaking, all the foreign holy warriors in the world were no use to them if they could not stop the Serbian tanks and artillery, despite what the most religious among them believed.

In an early attempt to suppress the fighting, the United Nations Security Council had imposed an arms embargo on the former Yugoslavian states. But rather than curbing escalation of the conflict, the real result was that the Bosniaks were left wanting and vulnerable to the far better-equipped Serbian and Croatian armies. Due to the arms embargo, the ethnic cleansing campaigns faced weaker resistance.

The dire need for equipment and supplies became especially evident when the four volunteers arrived at the training camp near Travnik. To conserve ammunition, an excessive amount of time was spent practicing troop formations and drills and hand-to-hand combat. They would likely never need all this, yet it fostered some camaraderie. There were men from Algeria, Saudi Arabia, Turkey, Chechnya, Egypt, Albania, Yemen, Iran, and several other countries training in the camp. A mélange of English, French, and Arabic served as the lingua franca.

Samir organized nightly study circles among the fighters to read passages from Islamic texts, especially the Qur'an and books of Hadith, and discuss their meanings as they pertained to the war around them. He was particularly fond of discussing Qur'anic verses about paradise and the eternal life to come. Sometimes Samir would gather groups of fighters to hear reports from the field, including eye-witness accounts of the atrocities committed against the Bosniaks in various towns.

One day, Samir brought a videotape containing footage from the Omarska concentration camp in the north. It was the same type of material that Abdullah was shown by Idris, his Somali handler back home in Minneapolis. It opened with footage of pale, emaciated Muslim men crowded into filthy warehouses, sleeping on the ground or staring blankly into the lenses of the cameras, almost too tired to blink. Most of the men had severe contusions on their heads and faces, signs of brutal beatings they had endured. Another clip showed a large ditch on the edge of the camp, hidden partly by overgrown grass and underbrush, where a dozen fly-covered bodies with their mouths hanging open had been haphazardly tossed, as though the place was a landfill for rubbish. These sorts of videos always resulted in weeping and defiant cries of "Allahu akbar!" It did not matter that the men were underequipped, because most of them had no fear of death (or so they said) and would face the entire Serbian or Croatian army alone if necessary.

XXIX

When Abdullah was sent into the battlefield, amid the black pines and mountain cliffs, he and Murat were organized into a unit where English was spoken alongside the obligatory Bosnian. The two Arabs that arrived at Travnik with them were assigned to a separate unit. Abdullah never saw either of them again. He often wondered what happened to them. Murat, though, was a constant presence in his life there. And his only friend.

The leader of Abdullah's unit was a quiet but stern-looking Bosniak from Sarajevo named Vedran. He wore dark green fatigues and a brimmed cap that hardly contained the thick mass of white and black hair that covered his head and threatened to overtake his forehead. His nose was long, wide, and pointed, and contrasted greatly with his small dimpled chin, giving the impression that he was perpetually frowning. And when Vedran spoke in English, he was difficult to understand, but Abdullah gradually grew accustomed to his peculiar speech patterns. Sometimes, the men would ask Vedran questions just to hear him pronounce certain words. Anything to do with human anatomy was usually good for a laugh.

Vedran's second in command was another Bosniak named Kemil. Unlike Vedran, he was more interested in smoking

Drina cigarettes than praying to God. Although a Bosniak, Kemil was not a religious man at all. He was assigned to *El Mudžahid* for his knowledge of English more so than anything else. Abdullah and the others respected him as their commander, but felt uncomfortable around him, as though they had no way to relate to him.

Once, before the unit was deployed to ambush a Serbian caravan on a winding valley road, Abdullah and the others gathered to make *du'a*, an informal prayer for God's blessings in their perilous endeavor. When Murat encouraged Kemil to join them, he responded rudely and lit another cigarette, as if he were annoyed at the delay.

"Who do you think God is? Superman? Christopher Reeves?" he said, mocking Murat. "Don't you think the people in the villages prayed? Did Allah answer them? Did he save them from the Serbs?"

Angered by the exchange, Vedran intervened and silenced Kemil by chastising him harshly in Bosnian. When he was done and Kemil ceased to speak, Vedran raised his hands and joined the others in the prayer. No one but the two commanders knew what had been said that day. Kemil simply continued to smoke his Drina cigarette and turned away to regard the terrain through a pair of binoculars he often wore around his neck.

Later that night, the unit came across a small group of exhausted and freezing Bosniak refugees hiding in the mountains not far from the ambush point. One of the refugees, a thin, balding man with deep-set eyes, had come all the way from the area around Mostar. He spoke no English, so Kemil acted as an interpreter for the unit and shared the grim news that the man carried.

"He says the bridge has been destroyed," Kemil reported. "The Stari Most, it was destroyed by a bombardment from Croat artillery."

Abdullah looked for Murat, fearing his friend and comrade would be devastated by the news, but found him asleep under a blanket that he had wrapped tightly around himself to keep warm. He would not tell Murat. It was better for him to believe that the old bridge was still there and as glorious as it was in the photographs in the books he kept at home. The city that Murat described from his imagination was more important than the actual physical place, Abdullah reasoned.

When Abdullah awoke the next morning at first light, now accustomed to having little or no sleep, he found Murat awake beside him with a cassette player in his hand. One end of a broken headset was placed firmly against his ear with the other hand. His head bobbed slightly to the beat.

"What are you listening to, man?" Abdullah asked, as he rubbed the morning grime from his eyes.

"Michael Jackson," Murat replied with a proud smile and a nod of his head.

Abdullah laughed, sat up, and looked around. He saw Vedran and Kemil reviewing a map spread out across a tarp on the ground. A few fighters in the unit were still wrapped up in their blankets, trying to catch every precious minute of sleep that they could, while others were keeping watch with guns at the ready along the cliff lines. The valley was no more than twenty kilometers away and the unit would reach its position in time for the noon prayer.

"*Inshallah*, today we will send many unbelievers to hell fire," Murat said as he marched beside Abdullah. They were traveling on a muddy trail that left thick layers of dirt sticking to the sides of his boots. Despite the words Murat had spoken, there was no hint at all of malice in his voice.

"Inshallah," Abdullah replied, piously affirming Murat's wishes.

Yet no matter how much Abdullah spoke of God, he could not shake the deep anxiety sitting in the pit of his stomach, or the hollow pain of his hunger, exhaustion, homesickness, or the brutal terrain on which he marched. He was tired of carrying an AK-47 around with him at all times, the bitter cold of the night, the dirt and mud on his clothes and skin, the sore muscles of his back from sleeping on the ground, the constant paranoia of an enemy attack or a sniper at any moment.

Abdullah and Murat were separated when Vedran positioned the unit on the rocks overlooking the valley. The nearest fighter to Abdullah was a skinny young Pakistani named Omar. He was so soft spoken that he sometimes seemed embarrassed at the sound of his own voice. The two of them sat there in their places among the rocks and buzzing insects and listened for almost an hour, shifting their weight from one leg to the other and occasionally twisting their backs from side-to-side to avoid cramping. Finally they heard the grinding metallic sound of engines approaching in the distance and echoing off the hills.

The first vehicle to appear on the road was a BOV truck with a heavy machinegun mounted on it. Abdullah could see the uniformed Serb, a soldier of the so-called *Republika Srpska*—Serbian Republic—manning the gun. It was the first time Abdullah had laid eyes on an enemy combatant within range of his weapon. But Vedran, speaking with his thick unintelligible accent, gave explicit instructions for them to wait until the entire convoy was visible. Otherwise, the Serbs might retreat and take a more dangerous defensive position that could imperil the mission.

The second vehicle in the caravan made a distinctly metallic and terrifying sound as it rumbled down the road behind the BOV. It was a Soviet-made battle tank. Abdullah needed no one to tell him his weapon was worthless against it. He would leave the tank to the comrade armed with an RPG launcher. Several others carried hand grenades. Still, a bungled attack against a tank could mean disaster. He felt a sinking in his heart, even if he did have God on his side—behind the battle tank came a transport carrying field artillery, an armored M-80 infantry fighting vehicle, and a pair of curious transport trucks full of armed irregulars.

Within seconds, a rocket propelled grenade came screaming through the air from the rocks to Abdullah's left and down into the roadway below. It crashed into the turret of the battle tank, sending a ball of fire and black smoke into the air, and it brought the entire convoy to an abrupt and confused halt. A volley of hand grenades followed, blasting the road like a meteor shower and the Serbs along with it.

"Allahu akbar!" Abdullah shouted as he fired his AK-47 down into the valley below.

The noise was deafening as the *mujahidin* launched their attack. The Serbs returned fire with their heavy caliber guns, sending fragments of rock and earth in every direction.

When Abdullah ducked down behind the rocks, bullets zipping and ricocheting over his head, he found Omar pressed down against the rocks, gritting his teeth, looking at Abdullah in terror. He was completely paralyzed with fear.

Firing his weapon again, but hardly aiming at all, Abdullah cried out with rage and adrenaline fueled excitement. An explosion at one of the vehicles drove him to stop and duck down again behind the rocks, although he wasn't sure why.

Omar was still pressed down in the dirt, cowering like a frightened boy who hoped the earth would absorb him.

"Get up!" Abdullah shouted. "Fight back!" Seeing the cowardice in Omar's eyes, Abdullah snatched away his weapon and fired it chaotically with his left hand. "Allahu akbar!" he cried out as the hot metal shook furiously in his hands.

A second rocket-propelled grenade came crashing down into the caravan and created another explosion that sent shards of metal and flaming rubber into the air. The M-80 infantry fighting vehicle, barely visible in a choking plume of black smoke, had been hit and severely damaged. Another volley of grenades followed, and soon, only the lead vehicle remained in the battle. The two trucks of irregulars in the rear of the caravan pulled back and fled up the road.

Kemil, his eyes ablaze, signaled the unit to advance down the hillside into the valley below, now thick with smoke and with flames dancing on battered metal. It was a dangerous maneuver, but the unit could take the remaining Serbs at close range and capture much needed supplies. At the very least, Kemil might find a few packs of Drina cigarettes or some cheap Russian brand to appease his addiction, or he might be able to take a grisly souvenir from the "Chetniks," as he called them.

Abdullah stumbled down the rocks and the hillside, slipping and trying his best to balance and aim at the caravan as he moved down into the valley. He fired periodically along the way with chaotic bursts from the two assault rifles.

Far off to the left, several *mujahidin* had sprayed the lead truck with machinegun fire. Two bloodied, uniformed corpses were slumped over along the back.

As Abdullah approached the smoldering remains, he tried to listen for any sounds of movement amid the carnage. His eyes darted from side to side looking for danger. He slowed his heavy breathing, aware that he may give himself away to a hidden Serb waiting to snuff him out. He filtered out the noises of his comrades too, storming down the hillside. He could hear his own heart beating like a bass drum.

A sudden burst of gunfire startled Abdullah. It shook him from his moment. One of the Serbs in the lead truck had moved from his position face down on the ground, and promptly received a bullet in his head from one of the *mujahidin*.

"Abdullah," a quiet distressed voice said. "Abdullah, my gun. My gun."

Abdullah turned, following the sound of the voice, and found Omar standing behind him, having come down from his hiding place. He was embarrassed to be seen by the others without his weapon and was quietly urging Abdullah to return it to him.

Abdullah handed over the AK-47, minus several rounds. And Omar quickly placed it over his shoulder, hoping no one had seen what had happened.

Elsewhere, Kemil shot an injured Serb twice in the chest with a handgun and went through his pockets. He found nothing and cursed and kicked the corpse. Murat was standing behind Kemil looking over the bloody, torn bodies of Serbs and the battered and burning vehicles. He scowled, and his eyes blinked excessively from the toxic smoke in the air.

And when he saw that Abdullah was watching him, his scowl went away, his chin lifted, and he gave an enthusiastic nod. He looked happy to know that Abdullah had survived.

Ten minutes later, the *mujahidin* slipped quietly back into the hills. They had taken some supplies from the soldiers in the caravan with them, including rations, ammunition, and a radio. The attack marked the first of what became a routine for the unit. Their mission was to harass, disrupt, and destroy Serb and sometimes Croat transports and supply lines into Bosnian territory. These guerilla attacks did not always go as smoothly as the first.

XXX

Time passed. On one bitterly cold day in the middle of January, Vedran, now struggling with a chronic cough, ordered Kemil to take some of the unit eastward. Their orders were to check on the condition of a strategic river bridge. It was rumored to be damaged already and it would need to be destroyed, if possible.

Murat, Abdullah, and six hardened and weary others joined Kemil on the mission that day. It was unusually quiet and birds could be heard chirping in the surviving treetops. The sky was clear too and the sun was warm on their dirty faces as they marched, even though the air was cold and biting. The conditions of the day put them at relative ease as they hiked eastward to the bridge.

"When I go home to Germany," Murat said quietly, "I'm going to get married, eat until I am fat, and move to someplace warm."

"Someplace warm?" Abdullah asked.

"Yes, like Spain maybe. I don't know. What is the warmest place in the USA?"

"Arizona, I think," he said.

"Maybe I will move there," Murat said. "To Arizona. Yes, I will marry a nice American woman and buy a house in Arizona."

"What would you do there?"

"Open a restaurant. I am a good cook. I make the most delicious kabob, even my sister says this!"

Abdullah hadn't thought much about the future. It seemed like bad luck to do so. He would leave it to God, he told himself. God's decree for his life could not be altered either way, even if he wanted to do so. "Inshallah, I'll come visit," Abdullah replied.

"Hey," Kemil snapped, as he stopped in his tracks. "Keep quiet. Pay attention."

The bridge was less than an hour away now. The danger grew with every step. Moving eastward meant moving toward the front line. There were no reports of Serb or Croat units in the immediate area, but communications were frequently disrupted, conflicting, and unreliable. Irregulars, in particular, were known to avoid detection and appear in unexpected places.

When the unit reached a hill where the bridge was visible through Kemil's binoculars in the distance, they sat down under the cover of the trees to survey the area and make final preparations. It was very cold there, and the wind whipped through the trees. A clearing some forty feet away was bathed in blinding sunlight, though, and once everyone had their orders, Murat went over to the clearing to warm himself before they advanced on the bridge.

Abdullah hadn't noticed Murat's departure. He often took the last moments before a mission to reflect on matters and pray for God's grace. His prayers had grown more labored and routine over the weeks, though. Sometimes he felt like he was only talking to himself. He had yet to see any sign that God was taking notice of his efforts at all. He certainly did not see signs of God's mercy or His power in the camps, the count-less burning villages, or the mass graves of rotting flesh they found. Abdullah tried though. He tried as best he could. He tried to pray and to believe that it all had a purpose. There was a hand guiding it all to a meaningful end.

That was the terrible moment when Abdullah heard the unmistakable pop—the loud, echoing pop of a sniper rifle firing from somewhere in the neighboring hills.

A sudden frenzy broke out. The others in the unit took defensive positions and tried to discern the direction of the shot. Abdullah looked and listened and saw the slumped body of Murat lying in the clearing in the warm sunlight. There was a jagged black hole in his head. Blood had sprayed out across his shoulders and back. It looked especially red on the rocks beneath him in the sun.

Abdullah dashed toward Murat's body. He paid no atten-tion to the terrible sound. It was a new sound. The hiss of hell. It grew louder as he ran into the warm sunlight of the clear-ing. He grabbed hold of Murat by the shoulders and started to pull. He was heavy. He struggled with the limp body. They had to make it back, to get to the tree line. But it was too late. The deafening explosion of a Serb RPG, erupted, shattering the air. It threw Abdullah. He went tumbling violently, like a rag doll, into the rocks and brown grass.

When Abdullah opened his eyes, the noise of war was all around him. Bright red blood covered his hands like gloves. Murat's blood, he thought, until he saw the blood coming from his body. A dozen deep lacerations on his arms; the result of shrapnel and small cold rocks tearing through his flesh. When he tried to move, hoping to drag himself back to the trees, he felt a sharp pain. More shrapnel was buried in the flesh of his thighs, his hip and his abdomen. Gritting his teeth, he pulled away from Murat's body. It was still lying there motionless in the warm sunlight.

Abdullah saw no angels. No golden hands came down from the heavens to help him. He felt no comfort. There was only desperation and mortal fear. He felt an animalistic will to survive coupled with a sheer adrenaline rush that pushed him forward, inch by inch to the trees. Gunfire. A bullet struck the rocks near his legs. "Can't stop," he thought. "Come on." He pushed closer. And then a hand finally came down to help pull him to safety. It was Omar's hand, shaking and afraid, knowing what had to be done.

XXXI

Rebecca held the telephone to her ear. She was calling Tyler Anderson one more time, but listening to an electronic ring tone again. There was no answer. She wouldn't leave a message. There was nothing new to say. She was doing her best to be patient—to breathe—and to remember what her therapist had said: "You can't control everything." She had stretched Tyler's travel budget to cover his lodging. She doubled the two nights that she initially promised. An act of kindness. In serving as managing editor of the *Valley Observer* for the last two years, she had developed a soft spot for the creative aspirations of her writers. Sometimes it was just lost in the business of things. It was a business, after all.

Rebecca worked long and thankless hours to keep the *Observer* afloat. When she was a student, she never imagined what corporate consolidation and the Internet would do to the newspaper business. She foolishly assumed it was a stable fixture of American life. Now she felt extremely fortunate to have a job at all. Many colleagues were not so lucky. She had many classmates who had no choice but to do other things in life.

Late each night, Rebecca went home from the office to a one-bedroom apartment five blocks away. She thought long and hard about getting a dog at one point, but decided that her schedule didn't allow it. Plus there was the pet rent. No new expenditures needed. Home was a place to sleep, bathe, and sometimes masturbate. Everything else took place in her office, including most of her meals. Sometimes even holidays. Last year, she ate a microwave turkey dinner for Thanksgiving at her desk.

Dating and romantic relationships were a thing of the past, despite her youth. Rebecca dreaded receiving calls from her mother for this reason above all others. To avoid the subject, she'd developed an ingenious blitz strategy utilizing a well-prepared list of a half-dozen topics to keep conversations on a predetermined course before suddenly ending the call. It usually worked like a charm. Her mother never knew what hit her.

On the morning that Tyler was investigating the whereabouts of Tom Quinn, Rebecca was attending an office meeting with the writers, staff photographer, and IT specialist. All the men at the meeting were older than Rebecca, except one—castoffs from sweeping budget cuts at news organizations up and down the West Coast. But Rebecca was part of a new generation, hired precisely because she had training and experience with online media. It was assumed that a young managing editor would help the *Observer* stay relevant amid the changing landscape. It would attract a broader demographic. The case had still yet to be made.

One of the most senior writers, a sour man named Harry Gleason, made little effort to hide his resentment. He had worked for the *Los Angeles Times* for many years and took every opportunity to question Rebecca's decisions. "At the *LA Times*," he frequently began his pronouncements. Some of the younger staff could do a good impression of him.

On that particular day, Harry was in rare form. He dismissed story suggestions with snide remarks. He squinted at a stain on the ceiling tiles, doodled in his notes, and scoffed when one of the other writers suggested an opinion piece on the new downtown Phoenix parking regulations.

"You have a better idea, Harry?" Rebecca said. "Let's hear it."

"At the *LA Times*," he said, "an opinion piece would address something readers actually cared about. No one's even heard of these new regulations."

"All the more reason to cover it, don't you think?"

"It's a nonstory. So what if someone gets another ticket next year. People probably won't pay them anyway. It's a small blurb at best."

"I think commuters care. The city council is betting no one will notice."

"Agreed," said Bruce, the writer who proposed the idea.

"Speaking of noticing," Harry said, "where the hell is Anderson? Is he excused from all staff meetings now?"

"He's still on assignment."

"What assignment? That art story in the boondocks? He should have wrapped that up in a day," Harry said.

"It's a developing story."

"Unbelievable," Harry said in a huff. "You let him get away with that crap?"

"I'm not letting him get away with anything," Rebecca said.

"Oh, really? And I suppose we're not paying for his costs?"

"Come on. You know he's her favorite," another writer added.

"Excuse me?" Rebecca said. "The budget isn't any of your concern. You do your job and I'll do mine. Sound okay to you?"

"Christ's sake—just ask the guy on a date. Save us all the trouble," Harry said.

There was a sudden murmur in the room. A line had been crossed.

"What did you say?" Rebecca said. Her eyes were wide, staring at Harry across the table. She put her hand down on top of the table, as if ready to push herself to her feet.

"Hey, let's not get personal here, okay?" Bruce advised.

"Try the bars, Becky. There're plenty of boys there that can help you out," Harry said.

"Hey, now let's—" one of the other writers started to say.

"Get up and walk out of this room. Right now," Rebecca said.

"I would love to," Harry said, adding a laugh for extra insult. He stood up and walked out of the conference room into the hallway of the ninth floor. The door clicked shut behind him.

Rebecca left the office early that day. It was very rare for her to take time for herself, especially when work was piled up on her desk. She had no idea what to do with herself. When Rebecca reached her car—baking in the sun—she stood with the key in her hand. Getting inside meant that she would drive home. She would get to her apartment and nothing would be waiting for her. It was still hours until dusk. Rebecca stepped away. She put her keys away. Then she looked around at the urban landscape of downtown. A coffee shop down the street was open. People with little white espresso cups were sitting at tables on the sidewalk under large umbrellas. Across from the coffee shop was a sports bar. There were flags from every Phoenix team hanging in the windows. She kept looking. She needed an escape—a place to let her mind clear. There was a movie theater that she knew. It showed old movies for two dollars a ticket, but she would have to drive there.

She chose to walk. It was an impulsive decision. She had no destination in mind. Her shoes weren't ideal for walking far. And it was hot outside. So hot. Rebecca simply walked. She went down the street, past the coffee shop, beyond the sports bar, toward an intersection filled with traffic. She stood in the shade of a storefront awning as she checked the street signs. Rebecca decided to go right because it was the easiest.

"What an asshole," she muttered to herself.

Rebecca started to walk quickly, as if she had somewhere to go. When she traversed an entire city block and reached another intersection, she chose to cross the street and not travel in a circle. She would go straight ahead instead. She came to a blue and white sign there. An arrow pointed in the direction of the city art museum. She followed it without thinking. She walked east for two blocks until a large modern building with tall tinted windows rose in front of her.

The Phoenix Art Museum sat on the Central Avenue Corridor, the north-south thoroughfare that cut through the heart of the city. The museum was originally designed by the well-known architect Alden Dow, who hailed from Midland, Michigan, and once apprenticed to Frank Lloyd Wright. Dow had once designed an entire town in rural Texas during the 1940s. He was the heir of Dow Chemical too. The maker of napalm.

The Phoenix Art Museum was completed as a part of a civic center project for Phoenix in 1959. The design featured many hallmarks of European modernism. It combined the simplification of form with the natural serenity of a desert oasis, complete with fountains of bubbling water. Tall date palm trees, otherworldly cacti, and palo verde trees dotted the museum grounds.

Rebecca had never been before. She knew nothing about Alden Dow. It was a fitting refuge, though—air-conditioned and quiet. No one would bother her—save the senior citizen guards who stared helplessly at all the visitors, making sure no one touched the art. In fact, Tyler's story assignment had made her more interested in the arts recently, especially paintings. Rebecca had gone to the Met and the Museum of Modern Art during a trip to New York City many years ago. That was largely the extent of her art museum experience. But this week she had spent time online looking up names of famous artists that she remembered. Picasso, Warhol, and Monet. Now there she was at the museum. This was perfect.

The interior of the museum was cold, well-polished, and sterile like a hospital. There were tall ceilings and an excessive number of circular light fixtures. The walls facing the meticulously manicured gardens were made of floor-to-ceiling panes of glass. The floors themselves were covered by burnished stone tiles of equal size and dimensions. The lobby was large and spacious as if enormous crowds were expected to come through it, its size forcing people to walk distances just to inquire about a ticket or closing hours from the front desk.

A woman with a plastic Phoenix Art Museum nametag on her blouse explained to Rebecca that a special exhibit was showing this month. An insert about it was placed inside the glossy visitor's guide, she further noted, slipping Rebecca the guide along with her ticket. As Rebecca turned away toward the galleries, she inspected the insert. It was titled Joseph Stella, and it had a subtitle as well—a Futurist retrospective. It was the last week that the exhibit would be on display in Phoenix. How fortunate.

The first gallery—located immediately to the right of the lobby—contained a menagerie of Southwestern and Latin American paintings. A smaller collection of less interesting black-and-white prints hung there too. Rebecca was drawn to one painting in particular. It depicted a Madonna and Child, but not in the faint, delicate sensibility common among European Renaissance masters. It was a nineteenth century oil painting by a Spanish-American artist whose name she did not recognize. The colors in the image were bold. Full of energy. The figures were outlined with thick lines and the perspective was flat and simple. It had the charm of folk art, but an inner complexity befitting an artistic master.

Rebecca's thought drifted to the subject of children as she studied the canvas. Her mother, she recalled, wanted so badly to be a grandmother. Last Christmas she'd expressed a wish to see Rebecca settle down. Rebecca had no siblings. Her mother's voice echoed so clearly in her head as she stood there in the gallery. The muscles in her neck and shoulders grew tense. She detested the idea of someone dictating the direction of her life. This painting embodied much of what she detested. It portrayed motherhood as the highest position that a woman could achieve. For God had made Mary neither a prophet nor the messiah nor the daughter of God. Nor did God take the form of a woman. She was only *the womb*. She was a perpetual virgin too, and she endured the vilest harassment because of it, or so the story went. Rebecca couldn't relate to the Virgin Mary at all.

Rebecca was proud of her job and the career she had built. Her mother had never graduated from college. She'd become a housewife. The world needed workers and educated minds, not more babies, Rebecca told herself. She'd read an article in the *New York Times* recently that cited UNICEF. It said that twenty-two thousand children died every day across the world due to poverty. The world couldn't care for the children it already had, let alone educate them and produce productive members of society. The phrase "be fruitful and multiply" should have been erased from the Bible as far as Rebecca was concerned. She refused to contribute to the problem—even to satisfy her mother, or anyone else. Humanity needed to get its priorities straightened out first.

Rebecca found the Joseph Stella exhibit two rooms down, beyond two glass doors. The entire gallery was awash with bright vivid colors. Many of Stella's paintings documented his interest in flowers. They stood out from the grand but mundane white walls of the museum with intensity. There were stretched canvases in every direction. Each one was lit overhead by angled tracking lights. A small white card with bold black print was affixed to the wall beside each canvas describing the work in English and Spanish. The cards included the date of completion, the title, dimensions, and the medium used. On the back wall, displayed in a well-measured row, Rebecca found a series of charcoal drawings of atmospheric scenes of industrial buildings, factories, and bridges. The contrast between those dark, gloomy drawings and the colorful organic forms displayed elsewhere in the room was startling. How strange.

Content to stay for a time in the gallery, Rebecca sat down on a bench in the center of the floor. She stretched her neck and tried her best to loosen her shoulders. Then she opened the visitor's guide and read from the exhibit insert. It contained a brief biography of Joseph Stella. An Italian-American, he'd died of heart failure in 1946. The short biography also described the distinct evolution in Stella's work. Over time, he'd demonstrated a fusion of modernist trends and a devotion to symbolism that sought to emotionally capture the vitality of the human spirit in the world around him. Described as America's foremost "Futurist" artist, it said that Stella's work championed humanity and creativity in all areas of life, including poetry, architecture, and cinema. Fascinating.

Rebecca was not alone inside the Stella exhibit that afternoon. Several other visitors came and went as they pleased. Some of them were clearly art students from the state university. The students camped out in front of pieces for a time and wrote in note pads. Meanwhile, other visitors moved slowly from piece to piece, pretending to appreciate each one. Sometimes they would stop and make comments to one another in hushed and respectful voices. Then they would keep moving to the next one.

There was one young man standing in front of a Stella painting titled *Flowers, Italy*. He wore tight black jeans and a gray hooded sweatshirt. He was tall and fashionably thin with a chiseled unshaven jaw and thick, gelled hair. He stood immediately to Rebecca's right and wrote in a spiral note pad. She figured him for an art student and probably five years younger than her. Rebecca started to look at his body as if he were part of the exhibit.

XXXII

Rebecca seldom had sex anymore. She had been single since her start at the *Observer*. There was no time to pick up boys in bars. Boys in bars were trouble anyway. The men at work were far from interesting, Tyler Anderson the lone exception. Rebecca's mother, she imagined, would relish the news that she wasn't getting laid. Her mother was so Catholic, Rebecca often told friends. The idea that sex was a sin was something Rebecca had always questioned. After all, human beings were biologically programmed to want sexual intercourse. It was an evolutionary trait designed to perpetuate the species. Why should anyone be punished with eternal damnation in hell for being biologically programmed a certain way?

"Excuse me," she said, her voice hushed.

The young man in the tight black jeans turned his head toward her.

"Do you know a lot about his work?" she said.

"Not a lot, but I've studied him," he said, approaching the bench.

"Oh great! Have a seat." She slid two inches over. "I'm Rebecca. What's your name?"

"Derek," he said and shook her hand.

"What's that painting called?" She pointed as she asked.

"That one, over there? *Brooklyn Bridge*. Do you recognize it? It's famous."

"I think so. No. I don't know. Maybe." She laughed.

Derek smiled.

"I wish I knew more about art."

"What do you do?"

"I work for the *Valley Observer*. Do you go to State?"

"Yeah, I'm a senior," he said, proudly.

"Can I touch your hair?" she said, randomly. "I love spiky hair." She held her hand out in the air, waiting for his consent.

He nodded and lowered his head slightly. Rebecca smiled and gently put the palm of her hand down against the gelled tips of his hair. There was a very subtle crunching sound. She slid two inches closer to him. The subtle scent of his cologne or his deodorant—she couldn't tell which—enticed her to stay put.

"Do you paint?" she said.

"I do. Want to see some of my work?"

Twenty minutes later, Rebecca was driving to the suburbs of Phoenix. Derek was seated on the passenger side. He was talking about something without pause. Rebecca tried to act as though she were paying close attention. Her mind was elsewhere. "Harry Gleason is an asshole," she thought. She could feel the anger and stress building in her chest. It was creeping up her spine. She ordered herself to stop thinking about it. She glanced over at Derek and smiled to let him know she was still listening. Then she imagined how he looked underneath his clothes. She wondered whether he had any tattoos or piercings hidden under there. What had he just said?

"Mm-hm," she said, vaguely. "No problem."

"It'll just take a minute. Pull into the one on the corner."

Rebecca had agreed to make a stop at a convenience store. It was on the way. The store was a block from his apartment. Derek went inside. Rebecca waited in the car, keeping the A/C running. Through the enormous storefront windows, she watched Derek collecting some items. When his hands were full, he stood in line behind a construction worker and an overweight teen buying an extra-large fountain soda. Rebecca wondered what Derek was buying. Condoms, she thought. Maybe beer. Or cigarettes. She hoped he wasn't buying cigarettes. She hated the stink. Her college roommate smoked. She hated it, even when her roommate switched to some type of clove cigarettes. Her roommate said they would smell better. It didn't really matter.

Rebecca glanced at the clock and checked her phone. No calls or messages. No texts either. No one at the office had even noticed she was gone. No word from Tyler either. She turned on the radio and leaned back in her seat a bit. She turned the dial. Ads mostly.

When Derek reached the front of the line, Rebecca started to feel self-conscious. She realized she might be undressing soon. What type of underwear had she put on that morning? She checked. Had she shaved her legs? She surreptitiously sniffed at her armpits. They smelled fine, despite the heat. She checked her teeth in the rearview mirror. Then adjusted her hair with a few quick swipes to add body.

Derek pushed the glass doors of the store open. He smiled and playfully swung a white plastic bag in his hand.

He did look good in those jeans.

"All set?" she said.

"We're good."

We? Had he bought something for her too? He seemed to imply he had something they both needed. She didn't know what she needed. She wouldn't ask either. That would expose the fact that she hadn't listened to anything he had said.

"Which way now?" she asked.

"Take a right. Down to the corner." He pointed through the windshield.

"Got a bunch of stuff there," she said, glancing over. The plastic bag from the convenience store contained many things.

"Just a few things. Gatorade. Newspaper—I'm working on a painting about the war," he said. "I got…some smokes."

Derek, whose last name Rebecca did not know, shared an affordable two-bedroom. He lived there with a roommate, another student, but he was away. His roommate had class until tonight, Derek explained. "He won't be back for hours."

Rebecca was thankful for that. She fucked and forgot for a while. Then she said good-bye and went on her way.

Harry Gleason was still a complete asshole. Rebecca was experiencing post-orgasm clarity. That was normal. She privately called it "momentary Buddhahood." It didn't mean her behavior was easier to accept. On the contrary, she knew it was impulsive and crude, even animalistic. That was the clarity talking, though. She also knew she was happy. It was pleasurable. It was human. Her choice of partners—a student she'd met only two hours prior—was less excusable. A judgmental inner voice was talking. It sounded remarkably like her mother. The clarity would go away, she knew. She would feel dirty for a little while too. That would go away. She would shower and change her clothes. The pungent smell of the cigarettes would go away. She'd go to sleep in her own bed with some fresh, clean sheets. Tomorrow, she would arrive at work knowing that the asshole Harry Gleason probably drank himself to sleep, alone, in a dark room. But what would she do the next day?

She checked her phone at a stop light. Her car sat idling in a wash of red, but her face was lit in electric blue. There were no messages. She never turned her phone off. She didn't even do that at Derek's apartment. No one from the office had called. No one checked on her whereabouts. No one had concern for her well-being. Nor had Tyler checked in from Ketchum. On her way out, Rebecca hadn't given Derek her phone number. There was no reason. He was a stranger again, and now she had work to do. There was always work to do in the city.

When Rebecca reached her downtown apartment, the mural had pushed to the forefront of her mind. The story was taking up too much time. Why had she let Tyler go? Perhaps she wished *she* could run away to the desert—somewhere beyond the concrete towers. Or did she favor him unfairly out of some affection? She despised the thought that Harry Gleason had recognized something that she had not. It made her sick and she shook the idea from her head.

It was true that Rebecca had fantasized about Tyler becoming a famous writer one day. She entertained the idea from the start. She could be the Gertrude Stein of her generation. It would make a good epitaph. There would be articles and books discussing her essential role in supporting Anderson's talents at a crucial time in his nascent career. It was a delicious fantasy. It was also necessary. It gave her everyday labors a deeper cultural purpose. It allowed her to endure the day-to-day grind. And the goddamned heat.

The imagined parallels between Tyler and the coterie of Gertrude Stein came with important qualifiers. Rebecca was well aware of Hemingway's fate. Indeed, so many great writers and artists have found tragic fates. The world seemed to devour them. The cruel world was too much for their sensitive minds. So many of them nursed themselves with alcohol, heroine, or whatever else helped them endure. Creativity could be destructive if the vessel that carried it was unprepared for the challenge. Rebecca had no desire to see Tyler take that path; to be swallowed by the abyss.

The complex relationship between neuroses and creativity interested Rebecca. She took a psychology course in college. She diagnosed her closest friends with a range of mental disorders, whether they liked it or not. She determined that the shy girl from Pomona next door suffered from social anxiety disorder. Her roommate was demonstrating signs of separation anxiety, constantly texting her boyfriend. Her political science professor? He had obsessive compulsive disorder because of the way he combed his hair and enforced really strict class rules.

Rebecca found the work of one theorist particularly fascinating. The psychoanalyst Otto Rank—a longtime colleague of Sigmund Freud in Vienna—devoted his time to the study of the relationship between psychology and the arts. Rank's first publication, released in 1907, was *Der Künstler,* or *The Artist.* He theorized that human neuroses are the result of a lack of creativity. Seeing life as a series of separations, Rank argued that human beings needed to separate or detach from the past in order to create new perspectives, beliefs, and choices throughout their lives. If this detachment process failed or broke down, then a human being became bound to his or her emotional past. In turn, those emotions became conflated with his or her identity. In Rank's scheme, great creative artists could achieve the greatest detachment from what existed before. This was true not only in the realm of aesthetics, but culture, belief, worldview, and so on. They were naturally progressive. At the same time, such supreme expressions of individuality and total creative autonomy were tempered by a conflicting desire for the individual to belong and find acceptance in society. This meant finding acceptance and an appreciation for their creative expression (painting, writing, music, etc.) by others. If the ability to achieve either one of these two goals failed to occur, the person was confronted by fear, doubt, guilt, despair, and neuroses ran amok. That's what Otto Rank thought, anyway.

Rebecca saw no worrisome signs that Tyler verged on self-destruction. Far from it. He didn't even spend time at bars. She imagined he was on the verge of great creative productivity. But the mere possibility that an onset of neuroses might soon begin motivated her to approve Tyler's request. She would send him away—out of the city. He would go to Ketchum for the story about the mural. He would be a Hemingway without the tragedy. But what was Hemingway without the tragedy? That voice in her head no longer sounded like her mother. It sounded like her own.

Rebecca sometimes thought about Tyler for reasons other than his writing. She did so despite the fact that he was not a very attractive man. He was not as handsome as the student she had met at the museum—whatever his name was. Tyler was not brimming with confidence either. She imagined he might apologize for the way he looked when he undressed. Or he would get embarrassed by sounds he made during sex. He was a good employee, though, mostly by virtue of his talents. Rebecca wondered if it was any less superficial to find someone attractive for creative talents than for appearances. Yes, she decided, it was more virtuous. The inner voice agreed. She was pleased.

After showering and brushing her teeth, Rebecca slid down between cool clean sheets in her own bed. It was time to close the door on the day. Tomorrow she would start fresh. Her mind would be clear. She turned off the lamp on her nightstand. Darkness. Rebecca took her cell phone from the nightstand. In the dark, she pushed a button with her thumb. The little screen lit up—electric blue. Still no missed calls or voice mail messages. No text messages either. She spun through her contact list with one swipe of her finger. There was Tyler's cell number. He was probably still awake. Maybe he was lying in his motel room bed looking at his cell phone too.

"How r things goin?" she tapped out slowly on the screen. But she hesitated when it was time to push send. Should she? Tyler might think she was being an annoying boss. He might memorialize her in his memoirs. She'd forever be known as that annoying boss at his first job out of college. Rebecca erased the text. She squinted in the dark. The blinking cursor was waiting on the bright little screen. Something else. "We miss u at the office," she tapped out. No, too personal. And she really meant *I* and not *we*. She deleted it away.

XXXIII

The sudden appearance of large buckets of paint outside the warehouse created great unease in Ketchum. Tangible agitation and excitement hung in the air like a toxic cloud. They were provocatively displayed—stacked in the form of a pyramid—and everyone could see the buckets. No one could miss them when coming or going down the street. Samuel Welch was sending a message to everyone. In short, he intended to live up to his word. He was willing to pull the whole building down if that's what he had to do. The vandalism was going to go, and nothing was going to stop him. Some thought Samuel had grown obsessed, in the most clinical sense, with the mural's destruction.

The telephones at the mayor's office—both of them—rang nonstop that morning. The calls poured in. As soon as one ended another would begin. Most came from outside of Ketchum. There were hundreds of agitated voices, each one desperate to express concern and outrage. Many also proposed possible solutions to the situation. A few people were helpful toward that end, but most were not. There was tremendous disbelief. Sometimes it robbed these voices of their coherence. Sentences came across the wires garbled and fractured by emotion. No one could understand why someone would destroy such a work of art. They had all forgotten that humanity had a long history of such acts. The mural, it was pointed out repeatedly, was helping Ketchum in so many immeasurable ways. "Tragedy" was the term many of the callers used, usually with soft, reflective tones.

One group of supporters started a petition. They'd posted it on a social media site on the Internet. There were 34,000 names or "electronic signatures" so far. It called for the Arizona state government to protect the mural as a landmark and state treasure. Any damage or modification would be prohibited by law. The goal was a hundred thousand signatures, however. That number was still a long way off.

Someone called the office anonymously and launched into a revolutionary rant about human shields and nonviolent resistance. Daisy Correa luckily let the call go straight to voice mail. Another caller suggested that someone buy the entire building from Samuel Welch. Perhaps the town could do some fundraising, a woman from Scottsdale said. They would have to act quickly though. Time was not on their side.

Samuel knew that no one in Ketchum could stop him. He'd always felt like the unrecognized ruler of the town. At least now people were finally recognizing the real order of things. Not even the intrusive power of the local or state government could thwart his plans. Certainly not a government led by George Correa. No, Samuel was a man with property to his name. He was well within his rights, he was fond of saying. He would never be pressured or cowed into anything by anyone. Push comes to shove, he had a clean shotgun he'd learned to use as a boy.

Making some calls the previous day, Samuel scheduled a group of freelance workmen to arrive at the warehouse that afternoon to whitewash the wall. They were from another town. The foreman said they could come in the early morning (when it was still relatively cool out), but Samuel preferred the afternoon. He had no intention of hiding this. He wanted people there. He wanted to see George's face. The idea of that pudgy smiling face deflating more and more as the mural disappeared under big streaks of white paint delighted him. Samuel didn't give a damn what anyone else in town thought.

Daisy would watch it happen too. She'd see her husband's hopes evaporate. She could do nothing to stop Samuel. That hollow, vapid woman would know how truly powerless she was when those men came to whitewash the wall. Ketchum was not the personal playground of the Correa family. Far from it! He owned that building. One of many, in fact. He was the one who would leave his mark. He had worked all his life for it.

XXXIV

Tyler Anderson joined the crowd of onlookers before the workmen arrived. The bag over his shoulder carried his laptop. Some handwritten notes were tucked inside too. He had skipped his breakfast, having chosen not to visit the diner. A Coke from the glass bottle vending machine at the Saguaro was a poor substitute, especially for his daily coffee. Tyler yawned and looked for a place to sit, anticipating that today would mark the end. It was the finale of his trip, regardless of whether or not Tom Quinn was found. He could almost feel it in the warm morning air.

The clicks of camera buttons coursed through the crowd like mechanical crickets. A hundred sunburned elbows jutted out before each round of clicks. Then they dropped, only to rise again with the next chorus. Dozens of shiny photo lenses aimed ahead, each pointing upward like a disorganized Roman salute. In front of them the colors of the mural were as radiant and bright as ever. The mysterious figure at the center, so majestic in its elegant form, seemed like a deity being worshipped. Beneath it was a throng of adoring pilgrims. The multitudes outside the warehouse even swayed slightly as if hearing a song that wasn't playing. But they still resisted the urge to bend their knees. The scent in the air was so thick too, one could almost taste it. Tyler detected the combination of coconut scented suntan lotion and true Arizona sweat. Maybe just a hint of menthol cigarette too.

No one seemed to notice when the work truck arrived. It pulled up slowly and stopped at the corner of Copper and Main.

Tyler watched the crowd. There were so many people there that morning. He couldn't count them. Many of the faces were new. One was a D-list celebrity from Los Angeles with a barely aged face, tucked and stretched and injected with fat cells and neurotoxins. She looked monstrous. Another was a popular motivational speaker. He appeared on the local PBS affiliate every pledge season. Tyler thought he was a grade-A bullshit artist. There were still a few local faces he knew. Dr. Wood still lurked about, as did the waitress from the diner who had no name. And the young man from the tree trunk bench stood back at the edge of the crowd.

"You're still here?" Tyler said as he approached.

"What?"

"You're still here. We met before—the other day over on the sidewalk."

"Sorry," he said with a polite smile of acknowledgement. He wasn't smoking now.

"So you decided to stick around," Tyler continued.

"Yeah—I did. I don't know. Things feel right here," he struggled to explain.

"How so?"

"Well, I'm not sure, actually. The way things are, I guess. The people here. I mean, look at everybody. No one's arguing or fighting."

"There was a fight. Earlier. See that big mark on the wall?"

"Yeah, but those guys were here to make money," he quickly argued. "That's not the reason we're here. This is like a focal point now. For people to come. I feel like this could really turn into something."

"Turn into what?"

"Well, we're thinking about setting up a community. Here in town."

"There's already a community here—Ketchum."

"I mean for people like me," he explained. "Like a commune."

"What do you need a commune for?"

"To find a purpose together. Figure things out and try to change things."

"A community," Tyler said. He'd almost used the word *cult*, but he'd bitten his tongue. "Then what?"

"I don't know yet," he said. "People just need to come out. See it first—the painting."

Their conversation was interrupted by angry shouting. It came from the work truck. A crowd had gathered around it on Main Street. Three workmen dressed in white overalls and hats had climbed out of the truck. They were met immediately by Kathleen Morales. A dozen others had joined her, bristling and looking for a fight. Together, they assembled a human chain with their arms locked together—they had clearly been practicing.

"No. We will *not* let you destroy this painting," Kathleen shouted. "Taliban! Over my dead body."

The others in the human chain started yelling too. They all shouted, "Taliban." The chants grew louder and louder. They initiated a collective maneuver as well. They bent and positioned themselves in a half-circle, keeping themselves firmly between the workmen and the mural. The workmen did nothing. They just stood there bewildered and confused.

Tyler pulled out his note pad. He scribbled a note about Kathleen's reference to the Taliban. She was referring to the destruction of the Bamiyan Buddha statues in March of 2001. The incident in Afghanistan made headlines worldwide. Footage of the explosions played again and again on every American news station. But he guessed that the three workmen had no idea why *they* were being called that name. They were simply there to make a day's wage. One of them was carrying a plastic thermos full of coffee.

Iconoclasm—the technical name for the deliberate destruction of a culture's own art—had shown its ugly, uncreative head many times in human history. During China's Cultural Revolution under Mao Zedong, the Red Guards destroyed countless irreplaceable works of art associated with the "Four Olds." In the *Bildursturm* (Iconoclastic Fury) of the sixteenth century, Protestant reformers stormed the churches of Europe, smashing statues of saints and icons. And in the fifteenth century, when the Byzantine capital of Constantinople fell to the Ottoman Turks, the grand mosaics in the domed basilica of Hagia Sophia were whitewashed with plaster. Iconoclasm was just now making its first appearance in Ketchum, Arizona.

The three workmen were befuddled, underpaid, and uninterested in confrontation with the people shouting at them. They stood at the corner in silence as Kathleen berated them. The human chain stretched out like a fence of sweaty flesh. One of the workmen finally raised his hands in the air. He motioned for them to stop. His pleas did nothing though. Rather, the line of interlocked bodies only grew more excited.

They grew louder and fiercer. "Taliban!" Kathleen shouted again.

One of the workmen broke ranks and retreated to the confines of the truck. Shouts surged from the crowd. Inside the truck, he put a cell phone to his ear and started talking. He was certain that they were at the right address. He could see the paint buckets waiting for them, just as he'd said there'd be. They had everything they needed to do the job. But he had no idea what to do. He hadn't expected an angry crowd. There might be a security issue. He was not going to put anyone at risk. The job would be impossible to complete. How could they even set up their ladders? "Mr. Welch," he said, "I think you need to get down here."

The commotion created by Kathleen attracted ever more people. One young woman—a massage therapist from Sedona—broke away from the human chain to tell the throngs of curious onlookers what they were doing and why. These men were here to whitewash and destroy the mural, she explained passionately. There were gasps and cries of outrage and incredulity in response. The chain grew longer with new sweaty bodies.

XXXV

Samuel Welch slammed down his phone. "God dammit," he growled. He jammed his favorite brimmed hat onto his head, locked his door securely, and marched out of his office—earlier than he had planned—onto Main Street. Samuel could see the workmen, dressed in white overalls, and the crowd on the corner as he approached the warehouse. He kicked wildly at a rock on the sidewalk at the sight of the protestors. He swore at the front of the unsuspecting post office. His anger grew as he got closer and could hear the chant: "Taliban!"

His mood had started to sour the night before. Resting comfortably at home, Samuel put his feet up. The nightly news was starting on the television. A tumbler of whisky on ice was cradled in his hand. There was a report on the bond market coming up. Then the rotary telephone rang. The clanging was metallic and abrasive. Samuel's eyes shot over to the clock on the wall. It was too late for telephone calls in the Welch household.

It was the call he'd wanted many times over the years.

"Doing your husband's dirty work?" Samuel said.

"George doesn't know I'm calling," Daisy said.

"I doubt that."

"Believe what you want, Sam," she said, exasperated.

"Well?"

"I need to know why you're doing this."

"What kind of a question is that?"

"Because no one understands. The town needs this," she said.

"I don't have to explain myself to anyone. Certainly not to you. It's my property."

"I know that."

"You believe in property rights, don't you?"

"I think you're making this personal. It's not right. This isn't about you or George. It's about the town, Sam."

"*The town*? Do you know how much this town owes me?"

"What will people think if you do this?"

"You think I care about that?" He chuckled. "I learned to stop caring a long time ago."

"I don't believe that," she said. "This place is your home."

"I'm not the boy you used to know."

She said nothing.

"Are we done here?" he said.

"What if we raised enough money to buy the building?"

"Building's not for sale, Mrs. Correa."

Samuel shook his head at the memory of the call as he reached the corner of Copper and Main. Sheriff Weaver was standing between the workmen and the mob, trying to calm everyone down. He was struggling to keep Kathleen and her cadre—still chanting, "Taliban"—under control, but the sheriff was entirely unequipped and wholly unprepared for this sort of crowd control. His sweaty, shaking hands gave his inexperience away.

Meanwhile, the three workmen—their task delayed by the mob—were seeing the mural for the first time. They had only just arrived in town. Only one of them, the one who'd called Samuel, had visited Ketchum before, but it was years ago. He had painted the walls of the new pizza shop on Main Street. Now he stood quietly beside his fellow workers. Looking up at the wall, they hardly seemed to notice the screaming faces in front of them anymore. Their ears grew deaf to the voices calling them terrible names. They were entranced by the mural's beauty.

"What the *hell* is going on here, Sheriff?" Samuel barked.

"Did you hire these men, Mr. Welch?"

"Damn right," Welch growled. "In case these people didn't know, they're all standing on private property. Owned by me. Maintained by me. Controlled by me," he said, taunting the crowd.

There was a smattering of boos. A hiss. Someone in the crowd lobbed a warm plastic bottle of water in Samuel's direction. It landed harmlessly to the ground with a thud but elicited cheers.

"That's enough," the sheriff said, facing the misbehaving crowd.

"Trespassers. I want everyone off my property, right now," Samuel yelled. "These men have a job to do."

The workmen seemed to shrink in their places. Their chins fell to their chests. None of them would look at Samuel.

"Well? You here to work or not?" Samuel said.

"Mr. Welch, we can't set up with this crowd here," one workman explained.

A sudden eruption of shouting buried Samuel's response, and his lips seemed to move without sound. The sheriff fell back two steps before recovering. The crowd pushed forward, held back only by the interlocked arms of the human chain. Worse things than warm water bottles would be thrown soon.

"Get 'em under control, Sheriff," Samuel said.

"I'm trying, Mr. Welch. Everyone step back!"

"Are you sure, sir?" a workman said to Samuel, leaning over to his ear.

"About *what*?" he said impatiently.

"You want to paint over this?" the other workmen said as he gazed up at the mural.

Samuel pretended not to hear the workman's question, but his jaw tensed as if he wanted to punch the man square in the face. He adjusted his hat instead and wiped away the sweat collecting on his temples with a white handkerchief pulled from his pocket.

"I won't do it," the third workman abruptly declared.

"The *hell* you won't," Samuel snapped back at him. "Pick up that ladder! Sheriff, get these people out of here. Every single one." Samuel took a step toward the crowd. "You're all trespassing."

"Your attention please," Sheriff Weaver said. "Step away from the building. Move across the street." He gestured with both hands in the air. "This is *not* a request. I repeat, this is not a request. It *is* an order!"

"Taliban!" Kathleen yelled. Little bits of saliva were collecting at the corners of her mouth. Cheers followed her. Her frizzy hair appeared even wilder than usual—the Medusa of Ketchum. It shook as she spoke like it was angry too.

"Ms. Morales," Sheriff Weaver said. "Across the street."

"This is outrageous!"

"I don't like it any more than you do. But please go across the street."

"Sheriff, history will remember you," she said, her voice cracking. "Wearing a uniform is no excuse. Don't let *him* do this!"

Sheriff Weaver sighed and ordered Kathleen across the street again. He wanted to go home. There was nothing he wanted to do more. He managed to usher dozens more across Main Street. Then he herded the remaining crowd back from the warehouse by several yards. It was something to call progress. There was some space in front of the mural now, barely enough to give the workmen access. But the lines were fragile, and the space could refill with a sudden surge at any moment.

Tyler escaped the crowd to watch the stubborn herd from afar. Timing his movements, he gradually approached the work truck. He regretted bringing his laptop. The part of his shirt where the strap of his laptop bag draped over his shoulder was now soaked with sweat. The bag was cumbersome and seemed to get heavier by the minute. Still, he watched.

"Start moving those buckets of paint," Samuel barked to the three workmen.

The first looked down at the ground, sighed, and walked begrudgingly toward the stack of white buckets. The second workman hesitated. He turned to look at the third, who did not move. The two stared at each other and said nothing, each seeking some support or guidance.

"Well? Are you here to work or not?" Samuel asked, impatiently.

"Don't do it!" a man in the crowd cried out.

"Please!" a woman said. More voices cried out after her.

"Mr. Welch, I—"

Samuel threw up his hands. "God dammit, get out of my way!"

In a rage, he stormed over to the stack of paint buckets. He rolled up his sleeves and grabbed the top bucket by the handle. It was full and heavy. He grunted as his arm awkwardly brought it down to the ground. There was a sudden twinge in his lower back, but he refused to show any discomfort. The lid was firmly on and sealed tight. Samuel grimaced as the lid resisted the impatient scratching of his arthritic fingers. "Give me a screwdriver," he said. He dabbed the sweat from his face with his handkerchief, then extended his hand and glared at the first workman.

"Don't you do it. Don't you touch that painting!" Kathleen shouted. She had crept back up to the truck.

Sheriff Weaver immediately closed in and caught hold of her arm. He begged her not to force him to arrest her. "Ms. Morales, you've lost."

Kathleen writhed helplessly in the sheriff's grip. It seemed to diffuse her rage and embarrass her. "Are you really going to let this happen?"

"I have no choice. I don't like it any more than you do," the sheriff said, as if asking for forgiveness.

The first workman handed Samuel a screwdriver from a large toolbox in the bed of the truck. Then he stood next to Samuel, awaiting his next move or order.

"This is madness!" Kathleen cried out.

"Don't do it!" someone else shouted. Many others cheered at these words.

Samuel jammed the tip of the screwdriver under the edge of the lid and popped it open. Drops of white paint splattered across the ground. There was silence, then a collective gasp. Samuel stopped to look up at the ocean of faces in front of him. All of them were frozen in disbelief. Samuel was looking through them now.

Tyler wished he could tackle Samuel at that moment. He would rip the bucket of paint from his hands. Hurl it away. The crowd would cheer. Audrey Betz would run into his arms. But he did nothing. Instead, Tyler pushed his feelings deep down and stood there watching. He was there to write a story, he reminded himself. He was not there to participate in the affairs of this town. He had to go back to the city. After all, it was just a painting. Tom Quinn could paint another one. He'd make another one someplace else to replace it. If anyone ever found him.

"This is over," Samuel shouted. He swung the bucket of paint down low to his knees. He jerked his old body upward and pushed the bucket into the sky. His hands held firmly to the edges of the bucket as a rush of thick white paint erupted into the air—a terrible, low-flying, wet cloud. And with a painful splat, the white paint collided with its target. It met the surface in a chaotic continental shape, spreading out across a lower portion of the mural and dripping down over its once radiant colors.

There was a chorus of cries from the crowd. A scream. "Oh, no," several people shouted, almost in unison. It was a cry of horror. Some people snapped pictures of the tragic scene, but most couldn't believe what they were seeing. They stood like statues.

Samuel bent down again and swung the bucket upward a second time. He grunted and a smaller amount of paint struck another section with a splat. When the bucket was empty, he tossed it to the ground. He marched over toward the stack again. He snatched up another one. His cheeks were flush. He could no longer hear anything from the crowd. The minutes rolled like a silent film in front of him.

Another bucket of white splattered against the mural. Every dash of paint felt strangely painful to Tyler, but still he did nothing to stop the events occurring in front of him. Nor did anyone else stop Samuel, although Sheriff Weaver admittedly had something to do with that.

"Get a roller and get to work," Samuel barked at the first workman.

The man hurried over. He gathered a large roller and a long handle from the truck. "Help me with the ladder," he said to the second workman, who obliged and carried it behind him to the wall. The third workman stood there watching.

"There," Samuel shouted at the crowd. "You can all go home now. Go on!"

The first workman affixed the roller to the long handle and started to spread out the paint with long, even, and sweeping strokes. More and more of the masterpiece at the corner of Copper and Main disappeared with every stroke and streak of the workman's roller.

Sorrow descended on Ketchum, Arizona.

As the mural was swept away under long glistening white streaks, the people who had gathered at the corner began to quietly disperse. Many looked defeated. They said nothing. Their bodies slumped over. Their steps dragged along the pavement. They were heartbroken and lost.

Tyler watched men and women and children drift out onto the street and away to rows of parked cars and unknown places in the distance.

"Where are you going?" Tyler said to the young man from the tree-trunk bench.

"Phoenix," he said, his mood visibly changed.

"Just like that?"

"It's gone."

"And everybody else?"

"We're all leaving."

"The town is still here. You're ready to just leave it for the city now?"

"I guess. I don't know."

"Well, I hope you find whatever you're looking for."

"You too," said the young man, and he walked away, adrift once more.

As the sea of backs with slumping shoulders marched away, Tyler saw one face against the tide coming toward him. George Correa. He held his chin high, but his expression was firm and serious. The jovial salesman was missing now. When George worked his way up to the warehouse, he stopped some ten feet from the edge and watched the workmen—all three of them now—climbing two ladders and submerging long rollers into open buckets of ivory white paint.

Samuel stood beside the wall with his arms crossed. He was carefully supervising their progress and pointing out any spots that the workmen missed. When he finally turned his head and saw George standing there, he said nothing. Tyler expected a confrontation—maybe something that started with words and ended in blows—but nothing happened. Neither of the old enemies said anything. Samuel turned back to the warehouse and the workmen. George simply stood there for a few more minutes—just watching—before going quietly back down the street.

With the enormous crowd nearly gone, Tyler stepped away from the work truck. He sat down on the curb across the street, where he watched the last bits of vibrant colors disappear one by one. He watched the figure in the center of the mural, which had fascinated so many, disappear too. First it lost its legs and its waist. Then it lost its arms and torso, and finally its mysterious face. In a matter of hours, the entire wall was an enormous field of white, bleak and empty. Tyler was the only one left watching when the last inch of the mural was erased with white paint. Ever the writer, in those final moments, he wrote down his thoughts in his note pad.

XXXVI

The sun was slipping below the horizon. The once clear blue sky was a wash of orange and pink. Walking alone, Tyler Anderson found the sidewalks of Ketchum deserted. Only the two lanes of Main Street were busy now. Cars, trucks, and RVs with different colored license plates from various states now fled. They were leaving the wilderness for the urban sprawl of the cities and the suburbs. They would probably never come back, Tyler thought.

Abdullah Park was watching the caravan too, as if it were a somber parade. He stood outside the diner, apron sullied, with his arms crossed. His big body cast a shadow out over the now empty sidewalk. His face unexpressive and seemingly emotionless.

"It was good while it lasted," Abdullah said, not taking his eyes off the caravan.

Tyler took the spot next to him on the sidewalk and watched the caravan. "I just wanted to say good-bye," he said. "I'm leaving in the morning."

"Back to the city?"

"That's right. Home sweet home." Tyler turned and extended his hand to Abdullah.

"Don't forget to mention my cooking," Abdullah said, shaking Tyler's hand. "I'm going to check. Don't think that I won't."

"I'll miss your burgers."

"You want one for the road?"

"No, thanks. I'll come back someday."

"Anytime, man."

"Has that guy, Wood, been back?" Tyler asked, seriously.

"You mean the spook? Nah, I think he took off with the rest of these folks."

"I guess he didn't want to be in my story."

"Imagine that. Someone in the government avoiding the press."

"Let me know if anything comes up."

"Yeah, sure—don't worry about me though. I've run into worse."

The two of them stood there silently for a moment. Cars passing.

"Just between us, what's the real story behind that picture on the wall? The one of the rock."

"The Dervish Stone," he said.

"Yeah, that's what Wood called it."

"It's a reminder of a friend. His name was Murat. Before he passed, he told me how he wanted to move out to Arizona."

"Why Arizona?"

"He wanted to go somewhere warm. Someplace with lots of sunshine. So what better place than here, right? He said he was going to cook, but honestly I never even saw him fry an egg." Abdullah smiled and drifted away in thought for a second.

"Is that why you came out here?"

"That's one reason," he said without further explanation.

Tyler waited for more details, but none came. "Well, take care, Abdullah," Tyler said, stepping away in the direction of the motel. "Next time, I want to hear the story behind those scars."

"Cooking accident," Abdullah said.

Tyler smiled and gave a final wave.

"Wait a second."

"What?" Tyler stopped.

"Let me tell Audrey you're leaving," Abdullah said, and he disappeared into the diner.

Tyler was alone on the sidewalk. He didn't know she was back. There was a sudden rush of anxiety in his chest. "Breathe," he thought. "Or I could just leave." But before Tyler could retreat, Abdullah returned with Audrey in tow.

"Safe travels, man!" Abdullah said with a nod, a smile and a wave. Then he left Tyler and Audrey together outside. The caravan of cars and trucks was proceeding slowly past them like a mechanized river.

"You're leaving?" Audrey said. Her hair was tied up in a ponytail. Her lips were pink and glistening. She seemed like her old self again.

"Yeah—Sorry, I didn't know you were back," Tyler said, gesturing toward the diner. He took several steps toward her.

"First day," she said. "Were you going to stop by my apartment at least?"

"Yes," he said, lying. "How are you feeling?"

"Better, I think. One day at a time," Audrey said. "So, you finished the story?"

"Almost," he said. "I'll work on it tonight and send it to my editor."

Jeffry R. Halverson

"I can't wait to read it," she said. "We'll frame it and put it up on the wall." She smiled.

"I'd be honored," he said, and returned the smile.

They both fidgeted awkwardly in silence for a moment. This was his chance.

"Listen, before I go, let me give you my number," Tyler said. "In case you ever want to talk." Tyler pulled his note pad out of his pocket. "Can I borrow your pencil?"

"Of course," Audrey said, pulling it down from her right ear.

Tyler scribbled a ten-digit number. He pulled out the piece of paper and handed it to her. It didn't matter if she ever called. He had still given it to her.

"I'll call you."

"You don't have to," he said, handing the pencil back.

"I said I'll call you," she said, firmly. Then, as she was about to put the pencil back behind her ear, she said: "In fact, give me a piece of paper."

Tyler tore a small piece of paper from his note pad and handed it to her.

"Turn around," she said. Audrey put the paper on Tyler's back and began to write. "There," she said. "Just in case *you* want to talk."

Tyler smiled and turned around. Audrey was smiling too. She handed him the piece of paper with her phone number on it and he tucked it into his front pocket. The note pad went into his back pocket.

"Or, you know, if you ever decide to come back to Phoenix. Give me a call, okay?"

"I will," she said.

There was a second momentary round of fidgeting.

"There's one more thing," he said, remembering. "Your apartment."

"Yeah? What about it?

"I was talking to someone about it."

"That's random," she said with a laugh.

"Well, there's some history there. Did you know that?"

"You mean about Karen?"

"You know?"

"Of course," Audrey said.

"Pretty dark."

"Yeah. It was a bit unsettling at first."

"I can imagine."

"Some people think I should move, but I'm not going to."

"Why not?"

"Well, the rent is great for one. But seriously, I feel like it's important to stay. When I first heard about it—what happened there—it scared me. But, after a while, I thought: She was this girl who never got to do anything. She never *lived*."

"She was fourteen," Tyler said.

"Exactly. Think about everything you did after you were fourteen. It's so crazy."

Tyler imagined that Audrey had had a much more exciting life as a teenager than he did. Nevertheless, her point hit home.

"I guess I want to live part of my life for her. And I don't believe in ghosts. I just mean, try to share it with her. Maybe in my heart—I don't know. Am I ridiculous?"

"No," he said. "Not at all."

———

It was dusk now. There was barely enough light to see the contours of the tall warehouse against the sky. The street lamps on Main Street illuminated sections of pavement in electronic orange. The Saguaro Motel, down the road, was almost empty. Tyler was one of the few who remained. When he passed through the parking lot, he found his old sedan sitting there alone in the dark. It was still radiating heat from a long day under the Arizona sun. Tyler listened to crickets chirping in the nearby bushes. The faint sound of a television in a room somewhere. And the humming engines of one final but thinly formed caravan of cars and trucks passing down Main Street and fading away into the darkness of the desert.

Tyler stood there in the parking lot for a moment. He watched the red glow of the taillights until they slipped out of sight. Then he looked down at his watch and turned toward his room. Rebecca mentioned a story about a dispute over traffic cameras. It didn't interest him. He would start on it tomorrow though. He would still have time in the afternoon. Before he could unlock his door, key in his hand, the beams of car headlights flashed across the motel. A car had slowed to a crawl and pulled into the parking lot. Tyler looked back but could not see the driver's face. He didn't recognize the car either. The bright headlights made it difficult to see. The car came to a stop, and the driver rolled down a window.

"Excuse me," a man said. "Can you tell us where to find the painting? I'm not sure what it's called."

"The painting? I'm sorry. It's gone now," Tyler said, approaching the window.

"Gone?"

"Yeah. It was down the street," he said, gesturing with his hand. "It's not there anymore though."

"You're kidding? We came so far to see it. What happened?"

Tyler hesitated. He thought about the man's question for a moment. "People being people."

XXXVII

The morning after Samuel Welch became the most hated man in Ketchum—more so than even Argus Gord for those who remembered—he awoke even earlier than usual. The sun was still just emerging over the horizon. The rest of the morning was routine. Samuel made his bed the same way he always did. He dressed and went to the kitchen, where he prepared two fried eggs for his breakfast. He ate them between two dry pieces of toast. His mother used to serve him eggs that way when he was a boy. And as he sat at the kitchen table, he sipped a cup of hot black coffee and listened to arguments on a radio talk show. The station dial was already set when he turned it on.

Samuel's house used to belong to his parents. Its grand scale was rivaled only by the Gord residence. He was comfortable in the belief that it was the best house in town, even if he was alone in that belief.

When he stepped outside onto the front porch, Samuel discovered that someone had thrown a beer bottle at his house overnight. It struck a wall and shattered into dozens of pieces. He hadn't heard the crash at all, just slept right through it. Samuel stepped back inside and retrieved a small hand broom and dustpan from a closet. He grumbled as he returned to the porch and promptly swept up the thick glass shards. He gave a hard look down the street as he swept. When he was done, he continued with his routine. It was still a fine morning in Ketchum, he thought.

Samuel would tour his properties in town that morning. He toured his properties about three times every month. The summer air was still reasonably cool at that early hour. It was comfortable enough to take a slow leisurely walk through Ketchum. The morning birds were active now, chirping from the tree branches and the power lines. The streets and side-walks were empty and back to the way Samuel liked them. The hills looked grand and picturesque in the distance too. The morning light made them look wonderful. And he recalled fondly his many hikes in those hills as a young man.

The first stop on his tour was a small building that he leased to a mildly successful pizza shop. It had moved in a few years ago. The shop was located on the corner of Grey and Main. Samuel ate there once but never again. Too greasy. Then there was the office building next door where the local bank has stood for years. He was a frequent visitor there, and he knew all the employees by name. Samuel used to own the drug store building too, but he sold it to the pharmacist in 2003. He had never stopped checking on it though.

Samuel left the big brick warehouse at the corner of Copper and Main for last. He wanted to savor it—his bold and defiant victory. He was going to bask in the glorious white wall and its stark emptiness. He would let the void wash over him like a purifying light. Unlike the rest of the town, Samuel slept very well. He felt rested and energized. There was an inner quiet that he hadn't felt for a very long time. And he walked proudly down Main Street.

For the first time in weeks, no one was loitering on his property. There were no festivities; trespassing, camera-carrying tourists; or smiling mayors shaking hands. No one selling his town to the media. That regained sense of control left Samuel feeling relaxed. His shoulders and back felt wonderfully loose. He would go to his office after lunch and check his mail, he decided. Perhaps he would go to the diner for a slice of pie. His favorite pie was apple, and it was usually served with a side of vanilla ice cream. He would sit alone at the end of the counter and leave a 10 percent tip, as he always did.

Samuel found himself starting to smile when he neared his final stop. The corner of Copper and Main. He felt like a child coming down the stairs on Christmas morning. The warehouse ahead appeared even bigger and taller than usual. It was a fine building to own. It was obvious why some jealous soul chose to vandalize it. Everyone in town wanted to own his warehouse.

Samuel reached the front doors and looked closely at it. He inspected the wood for any scratches or damage. He inspected the ground too, looking around on the pavement. He checked for any sign that vandalism had occurred overnight. He found nothing. Everything was as it should have been, and he felt strangely disappointed. At least there was nothing to clean up. One less chore to do. It meant he'd get to that apple pie sooner rather than later.

Samuel took a deep breath and made the wide turn around the corner toward the side of the warehouse. His steps, so eager, suddenly slowed. His eyes widened. His mouth came open like the hinges of his jaw had gone loose. Now, with a full view of the warehouse wall, his feet froze and his knees buckled. His mind turned inward, quickly filling with questions.

Had he gone mad? "This is impossible," he mumbled. His eyes strained and blinked repeatedly, as if trying to see more clearly. They were deceiving him, he thought. His hands, shaking slightly, rubbed at his forehead and pushed along the sides of his head. "Impossible!"

———

Tyler Anderson left the Saguaro Motel that morning after dropping off his key. Doris O'Brien was waiting for him at the front desk. She said good-bye in her own awkward way, insisting on taking a few minutes to discuss what Samuel Welch had done. She was so unhappy, she said. And not just because it was bad for business either. There was something deeper and far more profound that afflicted her, she explained.

Tyler nodded, commiserating for a moment. It took several tries for him to manage his escape from the lobby.

He walked out to his old sedan, sitting alone in the parking lot. He hoped it would survive the journey home to Phoenix. The tires looked fine, and there were no ominous puddles underneath the engine—good signs. Tyler tossed his bag in the backseat and slipped in behind the wheel. He yawned for a moment and took a deep breath. He hadn't slept well at all last night. Tyler now greatly resented that there was no complimentary coffee at the Saguaro Motel. He had grown accustomed to such luxuries in the city. That omission was more glaring now that he had no time to visit the diner for a cup. Audrey entered his mind for a moment, but he managed to shake her back out.

Tyler had orchestrated an early start that morning so he'd still have time to visit the office when he reached Phoenix.

There was work to do and errands to run. No sense in delaying the inevitable, he thought. The city held its residents to certain obligations. And there was always the possibility that the desert would delay him. It was known to do that on occasion, sometimes with dire results. His old car had fallen prey to it before.

Rebecca received Tyler's completed story in an e-mail late the previous night. She wrote him back immediately. She suggested a meeting in the late afternoon. Tyler suspected that Rebecca intended to lecture him about being away too long. That didn't worry him, though. She would see things differently once she read the story. It was great writing. The best writing he'd ever done. If Rebecca thought the track expansion story was good, she would think the story of the mural was pure genius. Admittedly, it was still too long for publication. He would need to edit and cut it down some. No matter though. Maybe he could convince her to publish it in segments, like the old serials of papers past. Either way, he was proud of his work. There was some comfort in that.

Tyler was driving down Main Street when he caught sight of Welch's warehouse ahead. Despite his drawing closer second by second, Tyler's brain failed to fully process the data being sent to his eyes, as if he were moving farther away and not closer. The impossible was not something that Tyler typically encountered in his 1997 four-door sedan.

The colors of the mural were ablaze. They overwhelmed the wall's surroundings; the town itself seemed to collapse into total insignificance on its periphery. At the center of the mural stood the great and mysterious figure that Tyler had watched disappear the day before. The small hairs on Tyler's arms and neck reared up. His car swerved as his eyes failed to look away from the miraculous image. He steadied the car and slowed down to a crawl, taking solace in the fact that the street was largely empty.

Tom Quinn!

Tyler pondered the possibility that Tom had watched everything in town unfold from afar and had returned under cover of night to repaint his mural. How though? It was impossible. But Tom had created it in a single night the first time. Why not again? But the white paint. That would contaminate it. Alter the colors. It would change the layout. Wouldn't it? The white paint couldn't have dried by nightfall. It was absurd. The wall is too big. And the mural looked exactly the same. "Exactly," he whispered.

As his car crept closer to the corner of Copper and Main, Tyler spotted the slumping figure in front of the warehouse wall. The man was on his knees, gazing up at the impossible. He was entirely alone. The crowds had not yet returned, still unaware of the impossible event. Who was it? As Tyler got closer, he realized it was Samuel Welch. He wondered if Samuel was having a heart attack. He didn't look well at all.

Tyler parked the car and rushed over, unable to resist looking up at the mural again and again as he approached. It was exactly the same. His mind raced to find an explanation but found nothing. It was simply impossible. Only the reality of what he could see made any sense. Or what he thought he could see. Maybe he was seeing things. But Samuel needed his attention.

"Mr. Welch?" Tyler said. "Are you all right?"

"How?" Samuel whispered, unable to say anything more.

Tyler stood beside him and looked him in his eyes. He found a startling change in Samuel's face, as if it had softened somehow. There were tears in the eyes that had been dry for decades. Tyler saw little trace of the stubborn, confrontational businessman he saw so often during his time in Ketchum. The man on the ground was confused. He was tired and had no interest in arguing with anyone.

"You see it too, don't you?" he said. Samuel feared that his sanity rested on Tyler's one-word answer to this question.

"Yes," Tyler replied. "I see it too."

It was no hallucination. Tyler approached the mural for a closer look. He had the irresistible urge to touch it. On the ground at the bottom of the warehouse wall, there were small droplets and splatters of dried white paint from the day before, traces left behind by the three workmen Samuel had hired. Yet, as he looked further, Tyler could not find a single drop or splatter of color there.

He searched for answers as his eyes continued to scour the ground. He tried to imagine every possible scenario. Enormous tarps, maybe. But there were bigger problems of logic. It was too dark at night for anyone to have done this. No one would ever be able to see what he was doing, especially in a work that required such precision, such attention to color, and so little time. Even night-vision goggles didn't explain it. Those devices saw the world in a wash of green. Maybe it was an enormous print glued to the wall. Yet he saw no edges or wrinkles or seams in the mural.

"Do you know Tom Quinn, Mr. Welch?" Tyler asked.

"Quinn?" Samuel said, a puzzled look on his soft face. "The maintenance man?"

"Yes, that's him," Tyler said. "Tom Quinn."

"His father worked in the copper mines; my father was a shareholder."

There was the connection, Tyler thought. "When was the last time you saw him?"

"I don't pay him any mind," Samuel said, in no condition to think too much.

Tyler turned back to the mural, stepping even closer to inspect the paint and the brushstrokes on the wall. There was not a single hurried or haphazard brushstroke in sight. "This should have taken months," he mumbled. Even the wound inflicted on the mural by the bickering vendors was repaired flawlessly, as if it had never happened. Nor was there even a ripple in the surface of the mural at the places where the paint had been scraped away.

"How did you do this, Tom?" Tyler said, as if speaking to a ghost. He heard nothing in return. But he was struck for a moment by the odd sensation that he might actually receive a response. Tyler waited and listened to the wind, as if a word might materialize out of thin air.

There was the sound of a car passing by on the road—then the sound of brakes being punched and a door opening. Tyler turned and found a local man—whom he didn't know—standing there in awe, right in the middle of the street. The man looked up at the mural, barely noticing Tyler and Samuel at all.

Now there were voices too—quiet and hushed—from a different direction. They came from two women walking toward the warehouse. Their arms were linked, as if they were escorting each other to an altar for worship. They were overcome with emotion. Their heads were tilted back. Tyler knew it was only a matter of time before more—crowds—would return. Meanwhile, the city was waiting for him.

Tyler needed answers, but had so little time to find them. He stood staring at the mural, searching for a sign. Any sign. A clue. Anything that might illuminate what he was witnessing. That was the moment when Tyler turned inward to the place where he found the words and ideas for his stories. There he felt a curious sensation. He felt as if he were no longer standing there alone. No, he felt that someone was now next to him. He turned his head in each direction. More people had gathered at the corner, but no one was near him. Not even close. Puzzled, Tyler reached into his back pocket. He pulled out the small note pad that he carried with him. Taking a pen from his pocket, he tried his best to transcribe the strange sensation he was feeling into words. It came out slowly. First a few words and then a sentence and then a torrent of ink and prose. "For Tom Quinn had done what no one thought imaginable; he transcended the abyss," his last sentence read.

Tyler stumbled back when he realized what he'd written. He looked up at the mural again, now astounded more than ever before. The mural *was* Tom Quinn.

His flesh, bones, and blood were now immaculate streaks of azure, pepper red, olive, amber, and a thousand other colors. A transformation beyond Tyler's understanding of physical reality had taken place. The billions and billions of atoms that once formed the man known as Tom Ludlow Quinn had been reorganized into the immaculate image that the town knew simply as "the mural." And it had reasserted itself, overtaking the unwelcome addition of white paint imposed on it by Samuel Welch. Was it alive? Or was the creative will behind it simply unyielding?

When George arrived on the scene, disheveled and excited, there was a smattering of applause. It came quite spontaneously from the bewildered townspeople at the corner. George raised his hands in the air when he saw the mural, as if celebrating a victory. He was smiling like an enormous schoolboy. He turned to everyone at the corner, shaking their hands and saying ambiguous niceties that deflected the fact the he knew nothing of how or why the miracle at the corner of Copper and Main had been restored. People were thanking him too. They mistook George's confusion for modesty.

Only Tyler knew the truth about the mural, and about the German painter Otto Fischer as well. He watched the entire scene at the corner with ambivalence. He said nothing to enlighten anyone. They would never understand. How could they possibly? He'd yet to find the words to fully express what he'd found out for himself.

"Mr. Anderson," George said as he hurried over. "This is incredible! Can you believe it? Have you seen Tom?"

Tyler said nothing at first. He was unsure exactly how to respond. How could George ever understand? Tyler opened his mouth, as if he might speak, but stopped short of saying a word. He looked at the mural and again at George. "He never left," Tyler finally said.

"Sorry?" George said. He waited for further clarification, but Tyler just walked away.

"Where's Tom?" George said, his voice louder. "Mr. Anderson?"

"Take care of Mr. Welch," Tyler said, looking back over his shoulder as he went.

XXXVIII

The road westward toward the city was quiet for miles. The traffic was mercifully sparse in both lanes. But Tyler knew that things would soon change. There were five million people gathered ahead. For the time being, Tyler simply looked out over the rocky desert landscape. The sun was beating down on dry shrubbery, and two sun devils were spinning in the distance. The return trip across the desert was another journey. And he was a different traveler now.

Tyler drove alone in the company of his thoughts. No radio. Just the metallic hum of his stalwart sedan's engine. He slipped into several inner dialogues, but these conversations were new. The transfiguration of Tom Quinn had changed everything. The implications were taking shape in Tyler's mind. What miracles humanity could achieve if their attentions turned inward, Tyler thought. What if? It almost seemed like a dream. "Imagine—just imagine—if people embraced the true potential of their creativity," he thought. Every great achievement, masterpiece, and breakthrough originated within. Yes, people using the creative genius within—guided by empathy for their fellow man. No, *human*, really. Tyler felt an emotional swelling in his chest. Was this some kind of faith? It didn't sound like a religion. Humanism. That's all it was.

Along the westward highway, Tyler passed what he'd seen only days before. The white crosses—pilgrim shrines—affixed along the shoulders of the road. The places where fragile lives were lost over the months and the years. The tall saguaros, rocky outcroppings, and the changing colors of the soil and the landscapes. *The gas station.* The place where the old man, Gus, had first told him about the mural. He watched it pass by. There was no time to waste.

Tyler shifted lanes on the highway to avoid something roasting in the unrelenting sun. The metallic hum of the engine grew louder as he accelerated. The mess on the road may have been a snake once. Or a bird. It was unrecognizable now. Just a pressed mass of tarry meat and bone.

"There's so much suffering in the world. Nature's a godless place," Tyler said.

"There's a lot of beauty too," he imagined Gus saying.

"It's an illusion. Temporary. Subjective," Tyler said.

"Don't you see the Creator in it?"

"No, I see the opposite."

"El Diablo?"

"No," he said, laughing. "Not exactly."

"You're so cynical. You're much too young for that. There's joy in faith. Community. Have you read the scriptures?" Gus asked.

"Yes," Tyler said. "Many times."

"Then you know its powerful stories. Like Hagar and Ishmael in the desert. How He saved them—"

"Now people dig wells and save themselves. Let's be honest, all we have is each other."

"How do you know? How do any of us know?"

"I know we should focus on each other. We can accomplish so much."

"I've seen what humanity can do," Gus said, ominously.

"You're right," Tyler said. "But don't let that blind you. We're bigger than that."

"Ever think we're hard wired for destruction?"

"No, we're just misguided."

"Well, we have an awfully long way to go," Gus said. "A long way."

"We can do it though."

"I'll stay where I am. Out here," Gus said. "Just in case."

"Maybe you should come in. Lend a hand."

"Maybe someday. Where will you go now?"

"The city."

"What's it like there?"

"Things are hard. There's a lot of work to do."

"I heard you say it was like a prison there."

"Some places. Sometimes."

"And now?" Gus said.

"It's changing. People change. I changed. Everyone can change."

Gus finally agreed.

As Tyler emerged from his inner dialogue, he realized how much time had passed. There were signs now. Signs of the city. Tyler slapped a button on the car radio. There was static initially, a pop, then a mangled voice. He turned the dial slightly to the right. Another turn. Slowly. A song started to emerge out of the static. The broadcast grew clear. Tyler was even closer to the city than he realized.

XXXIX

In the cooking concrete fortress of Phoenix, the main hall-way of the ninth floor appeared different. When Tyler stepped out of the elevator and onto the square blue tiles again, he found it easier to breath. It was brighter too, and he glanced up at the white ceiling overhead. The lights looked the same. Neon. He wondered if someone had installed new windows. He was sure that the air was fresher too. Perhaps the vents were cleaned. New filters for all that dust. Someone had done something.

Even the elevator caught Tyler's attention. Strangely, it seemed rather miraculous. Had it been polished? It was the same elevator. He had gone up and down in it countless times before. Yes, it had the old coffee stain on the carpet, right below the panel. It sort of looked like Florida. There was a cracked ceiling tile overhead—possibly a rare umbrella wound. The elevator made unsettling noises when one first stepped inside. It was all the same. Yet Tyler saw something new in it now.

Yes, it had an applied use—a menial one—but what an invention! The elevator transformed the world. People could live and work vertically rather than constantly expanding outward. Otherwise people would expand until no land on earth was left. Tyler had contemplated the broader implications of human population growth before. And if humanity extended its lifespan—if people stopped being killed in pointless wars—everyone would need someplace to live, work, and create. They would have to go up. They would live in enormous towers. They wouldn't need polluting vehicles to go from place to place. Elevators would transport them. Could elevators work on solar power? Someone would figure it out. He had faith in his fellow man. That wasn't his role to fulfill.

Green tiles.

Tyler stood outside the door to Rebecca's office, ignoring the room with cubicles across the hall. He looked down at his shoes. His leather shoes looked the same—the scuffs and the dullness of the brown leather. Bits of dirt. That wouldn't do at all.

Looking at his watch, Tyler saw that he still had fifteen minutes before his meeting. He swiveled on the green tiles and hurried back down the hall toward the elevator. Blue tiles. The clapping rhythm of his shoes was fast and loud. The elevator had yet to move to another floor. Lucky. It opened immediately when he smacked the down arrow on the wall. It rang. He was sure he had seen a shoeshine stand. It was somewhere close. Where? He had passed it countless times. Coming and going. What time was it?

The elevator emitted another high electronic ring. It reached the lobby. The doors slid open. Tyler rushed out in a blur. He dashed toward the front doors, nearly knocking over Harry Gleason, who cursed angrily as he passed. Now Tyler remembered. There was a newsstand. One block north. He'd bought a magazine there on his way to the airport once. The shoeshine stand was right next to it. Tyler jogged. He danced around busy, well-dressed pedestrians. The heat was already making him sweat. He ignored the red hand of the do-not-walk sign on the corner. He reached the next block. Now he could see it. The shoeshine stand was ahead, jutting out slightly from the big buildings behind it.

Sitting on one of two elevated chairs, the shoe shiner was reading a newspaper. His legs were crossed in a leisurely manner. Slow morning. Hot too. Then he saw a businessman carrying a black briefcase. "Sir, your shoes," the shoe shiner shouted. The man walked faster. "Sir!" Eyes down, the businessman ignored the shoe shiner. When a whole group of businessmen walked by—arguing loudly about politics—the shoe shiner shamed them too. None of them stopped, though.

"Excuse me," Tyler said, out of breath. "I'd like a shine." Beads of sweat were running down his forehead. He wiped some away with his fingertips.

"Yes, sir," the shoe shiner said, tucking the newspaper under his chair. He hopped down onto the sidewalk. Then, reaching to the side, he dragged out a box of supplies. "Have a seat," he said, gesturing with his free hand toward the two chairs. The man dug into the box. He picked out a shoe brush and a clean cloth.

Tyler sat down in the second chair. "I don't have much time," he said.

"Understood," the shoe shiner said, and he flashed a bright smile. He began with the shoe brush. He buffed the leather of Tyler's shoes with the clean cloth. Then he took out a tin of brown polish. He applied a small amount of the polish with a different cloth—popping it between furious rubbing motions. "I'll have these looking good as new," he said with pride.

"I've never had them shined before," Tyler admitted.

"I can tell," the man said with a chuckle. "Good thing you came to see me. I always say, the shoes make the man."

"I've got a meeting in a few minutes," Tyler said anxiously.

"Yes, sir. Almost done."

"My father bought me these shoes," Tyler said, unaware of why he was saying it. He was not accustomed to volunteering personal information about himself.

"Fine pair of shoes, sir. A fine pair," the shoe shiner said with a nod. A final pop. "There you go." He stepped back. "Shining like new."

Tyler looked down at his brown leather shoes. He was amazed. His old shoes were transformed. He was dressed in fine business footwear now. He was proud to wear those shoes. "How much do I owe you?"

"Five dollars a shine, sir."

Tyler reached into his pocket, but found nothing less than a ten-dollar bill. "Here's ten," he said, handing it over. Tyler glanced down at his watch again. Minutes left. "Keep the change," he added quickly.

"Thank you, sir," the man said happily. "That's very kind. Come back anytime!"

Tyler jogged toward the office building. He evaded hot, irritated pedestrians and ignored another do-not-cross sign. He went left and then right on the crowded sidewalk until he reached the doors. Finally, a dash through the lobby and back into a waiting elevator. Lucky again.

The elevator emitted a high electronic ring. It reached the ninth floor. The automatic doors opened to the long empty hallway. Blue tiles. Tyler marched down it quickly—his freshly shined shoes smacking the tiles. He glanced down anxiously at his watch, still catching his breath. Two minutes late. Damn.

Green tiles. Rebecca's door was open. She was inside working at her desk.

Tyler leaned his head inside and tapped the door twice to be polite.

"Tyler! Welcome back."

"Thanks. It's good to be back," he found himself saying. He noticed that Rebecca was smiling. She removed her glasses and seemed genuinely happy.

"Have a seat," she said. "How was the drive?"

"Fine. It's beautiful out there," he said as he sat down in front of her desk.

"Yes, I bet. So, let me get right to it. I read your piece."

Tyler nodded and prepared to listen to her thoughts.

Rebecca put her hand up as if holding back the excitement from erupting from her mouth. "I think it's the best thing you've ever written for us."

"Really?"

"I read it three times."

"Wow," he said, smiling. "Thanks so much."

"But the ending! It broke my heart," she said, frowning with dismay.

"Oh, the ending," he said. "We need to talk about that."

"Did you want to change it? Because I think it's perfect. Heartbreaking, but perfect."

"No, it's—something happened. I'm not sure how to explain it."

Rebecca waited for him to try. She leaned forward awaiting the true ending to the story. What could he add? It was already so wonderful.

Tyler's eyes scanned the ground, as if looking for words. There was carpeting in Rebecca's office. No tiles. He had not yet tried to put what he experienced that morning into words. It would sound crazy. He was looking desperately for the right way, but nothing that came out of his mouth was quite right. He tried though. There was a pause. The two looked at each other. Rebecca put her glasses back on.

"I'm not exactly sure what you mean," she said, trying her best to understand.

"It was like new again. The entire thing."

"But he had it painted over."

"Yes."

They looked into each other's eyes, and for a moment, no one spoke.

"If I drove out there right now I would see it?"

"Yes," Tyler said, sitting up straight in his chair. "I recommend it, in fact."

"I'm confused," she said.

"I think maybe I can explain it better in writing."

"Of course. I look forward to reading it. It is strange, I have to say."

"It's the truth."

"People won't believe what they're reading."

"Maybe, but they can see it for themselves if they're willing to look."

"Well, the new ending is okay with me."

"I'll finish it today." Tyler stayed in his chair. "There's something else too."

"That sounds ominous," she said, warily. "Do you want to do it in writing?"

"No," Tyler said, smiling.

"Okay. Well, let's hear it." Rebecca feared for a moment that Tyler may quit.

"I've been thinking—I think I want to turn this into a book."

"A book?"

"A novel, actually."

Rebecca was suddenly adrift, as if listening to something no one else could hear but her. She smiled.

"What is it?" he said.

"It's nothing. I think it's a really great idea."

"Really? You know, my Dad was a writer—a novelist."

"Must run in the family."

Tyler nodded. "He always wanted me to do this."

In the warm office space across the hall, where the rows of identical cubicles awaited his overdue return to the city, Tyler sat down by the window. He opened his laptop on the desk in front of him. There he began to write. His hands moved freely across the keyboard. He did not pause or retreat from his words by hitting the delete button again and again, as he had sometimes done. Words flowed. He was alone in the room too. He preferred it that way. There was no Harry Gleason or anyone else there to discourage him with cynical words. Nor was there a friendly coworker lingering nearby to chat and waste precious minutes with inane conversations about sports or politics. There was only the constant tapping of computer keys. And the sun was lowering slowly outside his ninth floor window, giving birth to an aura of pink and orange light and disappearing behind the buildings of the city.

It took three hours for Tyler to rewrite the ending to his story. The words had come easily. The prose was clean and rich. He smiled and turned to the other cubicles to share the good news. They were empty though. No one was left in the office. Even Rebecca had gone home. Tyler couldn't remember ever being in the office when she was not. Someone had turned on the lights. Perhaps when the sun went down. Or maybe they were on the entire time. He wasn't sure. Tyler's stomach was gurgling with hunger now too, demanding his immediate attention. He'd completely ignored it since he left Ketchum. He would just send the new version of the article to Rebecca. Then he could go home.

XL

That evening Tyler Anderson returned to his small apartment for the first time in days. It was dark, and the smell of dusty and stale air assaulted him as he stepped inside. Redd was sitting patiently on the kitchen counter, meowing as soon as Tyler closed the door behind him. "Did you miss me, Redd?" Tyler scratched behind the cat's ears. Redd purred loudly. Tyler set his travel bag down and took his laptop to his writing desk. Then he adjusted the A/C control panel on the wall. A sudden influx of cool air poured into the apartment. It felt wonderful.

Hungry, Tyler turned to his refrigerator and fished out something to eat. As he chewed, he glanced over at the small television in the corner. There was silence in the room. Outside, there was a police siren and a faint bass drum thumping in rhythm. There was also a loud argument somewhere. Ordinarily he would turn on the television and add to the noise. Tonight, he had no urge to do so. In fact, he cringed at the sight of it. "That's it," he said. Pulling out the plug, he tucked it up under his arm. "You're going away." Glancing around the room, television under his arm, he pondered the costs of hurling it through the window but finally headed for the closet. He made quick room for it next to a laundry basket full of dirty clothes. "There," he said. "That's better." And he closed the closet door firmly, as if he feared it might escape.

Laptop open at his desk, Tyler sat, fishing his bothersome car keys out of his pocket. A scrap of paper came with it. He placed the keys and the scrap of paper—Audrey Betz's phone number—down on the desk. Then he took a tack from his desk drawer and pinned the scrap of paper to the wall in front of him. He felt his feet planted firmly on the floor (confirmed by the wiggle of his toes). A hundred thousand memories were at his disposal—if needed. The moment—long delayed—had come. He looked at his father's photograph on the wall. It would start from here.

He turned inward and began to type: "The front side of the white SUV was thoroughly smashed. It had spun over 180 degrees and now sat still, pointed due east. The driver had tried to make an ill-advised—and illegal—turn over the light-rail tracks, swerving around the crossing barrier..."